THE TOWN IN BLOOM

As Mouse bluffs and charms her way into the engrossing affairs of the Crossway Theatre she meets handsome actor-manager Rex and young stage director Brice. When, with her close friends Molly and Lilian, she shelters from a storm, the three girls meet rich, enigmatic Zelle, and this leads to a momentous outing to a Suffolk village pageant. While dealing with the effects of her first love, illicit relationships, and uncertain friendships, Mouse makes a series of difficult choices. Only when a reunion makes her reflect on these does she realise how powerfully that shared summer affected them all.

THE TOWN IN BLOOM

THE TOWN IN BLOOM

by

Dodie Smith

Magna Large Print Books
Long Preston, North Yorkshire,
BD23 4ND, England.

ISBN   978-0-7505-3725-4

This edition published by Corsair,
an imprint of Constable & Robinson Ltd., 2012

Copyright © Dodie Smith 1965

Cover illustration © Sara Mulvanny by arrangement with
Constable & Robinson Ltd.

The moral right of the author has been asserted

Published in Large Print 2013 by arrangement with
Constable & Robinson Ltd.

Magna Large Print is an imprint of Library Magna Books Ltd.

Printed and bound in Great Britain by
T.J. (International) Ltd., Cornwall, PL28 8RW

BOOK ONE

A Trap to Catch a Gazelle

1

It was near the top of *The Times* Personal column:

Calling Moll Byblow, the Mouse and the Gazelle. Madam Lily de Luxe reminds you of a long-standing luncheon engagement, at one p.m. next Thursday. The window table is reserved. Do not fail. This may be the last reunion.

I read it on Saturday morning, Lilian having sent me a cutting from Friday's *Times*. (She'd repeat the advertisement up to the morning of the lunch party.) I felt sure that Molly, too, would have received one. I rang her up and found she had.

I said, 'What did you think of it?'

'Darling Lilian being a wee bit hot-making, perhaps?'

Lilian would never have permitted herself such a dated expression. Molly would barely know it was dated – and certainly would not mind.

'More than a wee bit, surely.'

'Still, I couldn't care less. Hardly anyone but ourselves will remember the old names now. And they just might fetch Zelle. None of Lilian's dignified reminders ever have.'

'Probably Zelle never saw them, though she did sometimes read *The Times;* also *Dracula* and the Bible.'

'That's more than I have. Of course you're coming on Thursday?'

'I suppose so, or Lilian will never forgive me. But it's a bit of an effort.'

'Quite time you made one,' said Molly. 'We haven't met for ages. If you drive, be sure to park the car outside the West End. We always do now.'

'Me, too – not that I've been up this year. Molly, how long is it since you saw Lilian? Is she all right?'

'Of course she is. I had tea with her the week before last, when I went up to the dentist, and she looked blooming. Why wouldn't she be all right?'

'I just thought – well, it worried me that she put in "This may be the last reunion."'

'Oh, that's just an extra effort to attract Zelle,' said Molly. 'Lilian couldn't be better – anyway, physically; mentally she's a bit peculiar and one can't altogether blame her, the life she leads now. And all this nostalgia for the past...'

I said I sometimes suffered from that myself.

'But you, dear child, have so many pasts and anyway you seldom talk about them. Lilian focuses on that one little period when we knew Zelle, and this last year she's never *stopped* talking about it, sort of putting it through a fine sieve.'

'Have you ever discovered why?'

'Well, she did once try to explain but I can't go into that now. This call's costing you money.'

'I don't mind. What did she say?'

Molly, addressing shouting children and barking dogs, all of whom I could hear, said: 'Quiet, fiends!' in a tone which neither expected nor got results. Then she told me she couldn't remember what Lilian had said – 'Probably because it didn't make sense. Anyway, don't worry. She'll be all right once the reunion lunch is over.'

'Thank God she only holds them every five years.'

'Oh, I quite enjoy them. Now will you excuse me? There's a dogfight starting *and* childfight. They'll probably end in a foursome. I must *dash.*'

Never had I seen Molly so much as hurry, let alone dash.

I considered telephoning Lilian to let her know she could count on me, then decided a postcard would do. Telephone calls to Lilian were apt to prove ruinous. And I'd some more telephoning to do. If I had to go to London I must make good use of the trip.

On Thursday I woke to find a perfect September morning, summer with the first gentle hint of autumn, exactly the wrong day to be away from the country. I would have gone for an enormous walk – except that, while in the bath, I saw exactly how to finish the book I was writing, after being stuck for weeks; though as things turned out, I doubt if I should have walked or written, because during breakfast I suddenly *knew* how to paint the view framed by my open window. I had been threatening to paint for months, sometimes seeing myself as a primitive, sometimes as an abstractionist. Today the primitive mood was in the ascendant. I saw the white fence, with flat flowers against it, and the grey lane on top of the fence, with a flat child cycling along it, and the green field on top of the grey lane, with flat cows

13

against it, and a blue sky on top of the green field, with flat white clouds. I knew not only the whole of the composition but the actual brush strokes I would use. So eager and confident was I that, on my way to London, I stopped at the first little town and laid in a stock of paints – oils; I had once tried water colours and they ran about too much.

Regret at leaving the country lasted as long as the country lasted. Then, as usual with me, the pull of London began, growing stronger whenever I drove through places where there were fairly large shops. It would be pleasant to do some shopping in the afternoon if Lilian would permit it. Not that I hankered to buy anything in the shops I was passing. I just wanted to paint them, particularly the gaudiest clothes shops; I got the chance to study one while I was held up by traffic lights. But could paint simulate the astonishingly vivid dyes now popular? Perhaps I could achieve a kaleidoscopic effect with dots, dashes, triangles of colour; a little Klee-like? I had stopped being a primitive. Then, in the outer suburbs, I gave up my mental painting, needing to concentrate completely on my driving; it was nearly a year since I had coped with so much traffic.

As always I had allowed myself two hours to reach St John's Wood, where I usually left my little car. Today the drive had taken longer. And it was some time before I could find anywhere to park. Then I took a taxi to the hotel.

Molly and Lilian were there ahead of me, talking to the head porter. I saw them before they saw me and, as so often before, felt a pang

14

because they looked older than my mind's-eye picture of them. Then they became the no-age, or all ages, of friends one has known from their youth. Now, as then, Molly looked large, beautiful and placid. Now, as then, Lilian looked slight, beautiful and anything but placid. When alone with Lilian I thought of her as tall; next to Molly she seemed barely of medium height.

'Dear child, you get smaller and smaller,' said Molly, turning to envelop me in an embrace.

'You're late,' said Lilian, before offering her cheek to be kissed. I was one of the few people she kissed in return.

'No luck with Zelle, I suppose?'

'Oh, there's time yet.' Lilian's tone sounded defensive. 'Actually, I've one of my "feelings" that she'll come today.'

'And we all know dear Lilian's "feelings",' said Molly. 'Count on them and they let you down. Jeer at them and they come true. Could we eat? I'm ravenous.'

Lilian had a last word with the head porter. 'You'll be on the look-out for our friend? She's very fair.'

'How do you know she's still fair?' I asked as we walked towards the restaurant.

'Oh, that colour of hair looks fair even when it's turning grey. She'd only need a fair rinse.'

If there is any grey amidst the night-black of Lilian's hair only she and her hairdresser know about it. There really is no grey amidst my unspectacular mouse-brown. I often remind myself that does not *prove* I am young for my age.

Lilian, her mind like mine still on hair, went on,

15

'Isn't that the perfect hat for Molly? Exactly the right shade.'

It was a close-fitting cap of russet velvet leaves.

'Well, I like to pretend I'm still a red-head,' said Molly. 'But the tide of white flows in.'

'You're a fool to let it,' said Lilian.

The restaurant always looked to me just as on our first visit; beautiful, formal, dignified yet light-hearted, gleaming with silver, damask and glass, and flooded with light from its tall windows. Beyond them stretched the park, where the grass was still dried by summer, the trees still in full leaf, though the autumn seemed just a little nearer here than it had seemed in the country.

We were shown to our usual window table. Our reception conveyed that we were honoured guests of many years' standing and that this was an important occasion. The table was laid for four and our waiter made no attempt to remove the setting we did not need. Five years before he had been prevented from doing so by the head waiter, who had told him another lady was expected. As I sat down I mentally counted up how many times Zelle's place had remained unoccupied.

It was no use hoping for a menu. Lilian would have ordered the lunch in advance and it would be an exact replica of our first lunch. Smoked salmon would be followed by chicken and chicken by a pudding of extreme richness which Lilian – though often slimming sternly and unnecessarily – would finish to the last mouthful. It was as well she did not know what vintage of champagne we had originally drunk as she could hardly have gone on repeating it throughout the years. She settled for

16

the same name.

I began a normal conversation with Molly but was cut short by Lilian.

'You're not to talk about the present. You're to think yourselves into the past – so that the past becomes the present. I'm twenty-three, Molly's twenty-one. And you, Mouse, are eighteen.'

'Must you call me Mouse?'

'I must for today. And I always think of you as Mouse. What have you against it?'

'I never felt it particularly suited me. And as one grows older, comic nicknames seem a bit ridiculous. Anyway, they're dead out of fashion now.'

'Since when have you cared what was in fashion or out?'

Come to think of it, what name did I most recognise as mine? Certainly not my real, much too long Christian name; though for years now I had nagged Molly and Lilian to use it, or corruptions of it. And I could remember at least half dozen nicknames, acquired at different periods of my life. But was there any name more 'me' than any other? I found myself accepting 'Mouse' – for today, anyway. Lilian's mood was catching.

She was determinedly recreating the past. Unable to remember much that had been said at the first lunch, she was inventing what might have been said. This presented difficulties, seeing that she and I had then been keeping our innermost thoughts to ourselves. So had Zelle. Only Molly had been hiding nothing, and she'd been too happy to feel the need to talk of her happiness.

I have a better memory than Lilian has (though

17

hers is no slouch, nostalgia and memory being blood brothers) so I helped her out. I was beginning to feel very sorry for her; there could be little doubt that Zelle was not going to turn up. Again and again poor Lilian looked at her watch and then, entreatingly, at the door. Already we were finishing the smoked salmon.

Molly, eating her last slice of brown bread and butter, said, 'Whatever happened to Veda bread? Do either of you remember it?'

What joy for Lilian, a new-minted bit of nostalgia! The three of us at once pooled our memories of Veda bread. I said, 'You two fed it to me the first night I spent at the Club. Wonderful! But even better when we could toast it.'

'How did we toast it?' said Lilian. 'There were no gas fires in our cubicles.'

'It was later, after Zelle came. There was a gas fire in her room. Oh, Molly, I have such a vivid mental picture of you kneeling in front of it.'

'So have I, now,' said Lilian.

'I wonder why they stopped making Veda,' said Molly, 'and when they stopped. Funny, I can't remember when it vanished from my life.'

Lilian's dark eyes, so often restless, had a visionary stillness. I guessed she was seeing Zelle's attic at the Club. After a moment she said, 'That was our last meeting with Zelle, at one of those Veda toast sessions. Oh, dear!' She looked at her watch again, then shook her head sadly. After that she obviously accepted the fact that Zelle was not coming and the conversation was allowed to drift from the past into the present.

For a while we chatted casually. This was plea-

18

sant enough but not particularly interesting as none of us had any important news to tell. Half my mind was occupied in wondering why, among the many women I had met, they had remained my closest friends. It was not merely a matter of affection; I had felt affection for many friends, both men and women, and yet let them drift out of my life. Was it Lilian's tenacity that held us together? It seemed to me that the tenacity was the result, not the cause, of the mysterious fixative in our friendship. And there was no doubt that the little period of summer months which so obsessed her had been of the utmost importance to our lives; to Zelle's too, surely, yet for her the fixative had not worked.

I was thinking of this, gazing across the park and giving little attention to Molly and Lilian, who were now exploring one of my least favourite subjects: their recent minor ailments. They then drifted into a discussion of the blatant sexual laxity of present-day youth. I was about to join in by reminding them there had been as much laxity in our own youth, if rather less blatancy – and blatancy *could* be equated with honesty – when I noticed an odd-looking woman seated on one of the park chairs some thirty yards away. Her crouched figure suggested old age; and her clothes, of extreme shabbiness, were at least two decades out of date. One could see little of her face as a battered hat came down to her ears, a mangy-looking bit of fur rose up to them, and in between fur and hat was a large pair of steel-rimmed spectacles. She was knitting something only recognizable as grey. I found myself reminded of the crones said to have sat knitting round the guillotine during the Reign of Terror.

She looked up – straight at me, it seemed – then quickly looked back at her knitting. I felt ashamed to be finishing an enormous lunch when there were still women as poor as that around. Should one go out and present her with a few bob? But perhaps she was merely eccentric; would a real down-and-out be knitting? I had another look at her, rather a longer one. It would have been even longer if Lilian had not asked what I was staring at.

I said – absurdly keeping my voice low, 'Now listen carefully and, whatever I say, don't look out of the window. There's a woman in the park who just might be Zelle. Lilian! I told you *not* to look!'

'Well, she couldn't possibly have seen a flicker of a glance like that,' said Lilian. 'Anyway, I only saw an old woman.'

'She's not a normal old woman. She's an absolute crone – and surely there aren't any real crones nowadays. I just thought Zelle might have dressed up. You'd better have a real look now but be prepared to look away if she looks up.'

Lilian did it very cleverly. She got a hand-kerchief out of her bag and dabbed her nose, while taking a number of swift looks rather than a long one. Then she said: 'Zelle couldn't be as awful as that, however hard she tried. And there *are* still crones. I saw one the other night, after coming out of a theatre. She was huddled in a doorway, asleep. I put some money beside her without waking the poor old girl.'

I said, 'Well, this woman can't be quite broke or

she wouldn't have chosen a chair she'll have to pay for sitting on. There are plenty of free benches. And why is she sitting facing us? There aren't any other chairs facing this way.'

Molly was delving in her outsize handbag. She said she had exactly what was needed– 'My tiny pair of opera glasses.'

I stopped her hastily. 'If you look at her through those you'll scare her even if she isn't Zelle. Just take a casual glance.'

'Without some kind of glasses I'd barely see the park, let alone anyone in it,' said Molly. 'But I'll be crafty.' She took a shopping list from her bag. 'Now, I'll pretend I'm reading this but I'll use my long distance lenses and really look over the top of it.'

This complicated operation took some minutes. Then Molly reported she was on my side. 'That crone's too croney to be true. And she's taking a suspicious interest in us. I saw her look up – twice.'

Lilian said, 'Wouldn't it be ghastly if it's Zelle and she's not in disguise – if those clothes are the best she's got? That coat, with those square shoulders, has been a good one. She might have saved it from her better days. Suppose she's sunk to the depths? She'd never let us know, not after the way things ended.'

'Well, anyway, I don't see what we can do,' said Molly. 'Either it isn't Zelle, or it is and she doesn't want to meet us – in which case we can hardly rush out and force ourselves on her.'

I suggested one of us should walk past the woman quite casually.

'You do it,' said Lilian. 'Zelle would be more willing to meet you than us. It was you she left the note for. Oh, God, she's moving. We're too late.'

I sprang up. 'Perhaps I can overtake her.'

'You'll have to run,' said Lilian. 'She's walking fast.'

It is not the kind of hotel one runs in, but I ran – along the corridor, across the hall and out into the street, then back along the front of the hotel until I could turn into the park. The woman was a considerable way ahead of me but I thought I could catch her if I ran full tilt. The distance between us was narrowing when she looked over her shoulder at me and then herself began to run. That settled it for me: she must be Zelle. I tried to increase my speed – how many years was it since I had run like that? Zelle's legs were longer than mine but she wasn't running as fast as I was. I should catch her–

Then she reached an exit from the park. I followed her through it only in time to see her getting on a bus.

A cruising taxi slowed up beside me. As I opened its door the driver said, 'Thought you might need me. Saw you sprinting.'

I jumped in and said, 'Follow that bus!' It sounded so melodramatic that I felt I'd better explain. 'There's someone on it I want to catch, a friend I've lost touch with.'

The driver said the bus would probably get held up at the next traffic lights and so should we. 'Do you want to get out then and jump on it?'

Did I? No, I couldn't talk to Zelle amidst other people. I said I wanted to follow the bus until my friend got off it. 'And then we'll follow her and I'll make up my mind what to do. What I want most is to find out where she lives. I'm not really sure I ought to rush at her. You see, she was running away from me.'

He was a kind man and quick on the uptake; I always seem to get nice taxi-drivers. He asked if my friend was the old girl he'd seen hop on the bus – 'Looked as if she'd come down in the world, and that can make people touchy.'

'Exactly. So it might be wiser to write to her rather than force her to talk to me now.'

'Hope the bus doesn't get through traffic lights where I get held up.'

By good luck that never happened; and in not much more than five minutes Zelle got off the bus and turned into a street lined with expensive flats.

'Now we've got to be clever,' said the driver. 'If she knows we're following her she might give us the slip. Lucky there are no shops round here where she can go in at one door and out at another. That's the way you lose them.'

I asked if he often had to follow people and he said quite a lot of it had come his way. 'Usually detectives following husbands or wives – though sometimes wives do their own sleuthing. Needs a bit of knack when you're following someone who's walking or they spot you. I don't think your friend has yet, still we'd better pull up and let her get ahead.'

He waited until she turned the next corner, then drove on quickly. When next we caught sight of Zelle she was crossing a well-kept old square.

I said, 'Surely she can't be as poor as she looks if she lives near here? Not, of course, that I can be sure she's going home.' I'd only just thought of that.

'Anyway, there's a street of tenement flats behind this square,' said the driver. 'She might be making for that. Yes, I bet you she is.' Zelle had left the square and turned a corner. 'Not sure she didn't catch sight of us then – see her look over her shoulder? We'll have to hurry now or we may lose her.'

When we followed her round the corner I saw that, as so often in London, a shabby district was embedded in the heart of an expensive one. The tenement flats occupied land which must by now be fabulously valuable. We were just in time to see Zelle go in at a doorway.

'Now we'll go past and you can get the number,' said the driver. 'And then I'll take you into the next street and you can make up your mind what you want to do.'

The block of flats Zelle had entered was of red brick with yellow facings, dark now with London soot. I looked at the windows, hoping to spot some touch of individuality which might indicate where Zelle lived but the curtains were of an almost uniform drabness. This was no slum but, to me, it was more depressing than one. There is often a touch of drama, even gaiety, in the life of a teeming slum; here there was only a grim, grubby respectability.

I noted the doorway Zelle had entered, and saw that it served eight flats. If I wrote to her it might not matter that I did not know the number of her flat. But it now struck me that I did not even know her present name – most likely she had married. And even if my letter reached her she might ignore it. The only certain way of getting in touch with her was to enquire at each of the flats until I found her. Was I going to?

The taxi-driver, having turned the next corner, had pulled up and sat patiently waiting. I tried to think things out. Zelle had not wanted to meet us. She had run away from me. But might she not feel differently after even a few minutes' conversation? And surely we ought to help her? I still had a hope that she might be in disguise – that mangy-looking fur was a bit too fantastic – but she could hardly be well off if she lived in this dreary place. I could only do a little for her myself but Molly and Lilian could afford to do plenty. And Lilian desperately longed to see her. Yet somehow...

One thing I was sure of: I must not let Lilian know where Zelle could be found without Zelle's permission. But suppose she would not give it? Could I face telling that to Lilian – and withstand her demands? Or could I, having talked to Zelle, lie and say she had escaped me? My thoughts went on and on, considering possibilities. And always I was conscious that the girls were waiting at the hotel. 'The girls' – absurd phrase for us now but it still came naturally to me. And for an instant I saw us as we had been when we first lunched at that window table, with Zelle as hostess. So soon after that the break with her had come. Had she felt bitter? Perhaps she still did. But she had come to have a look at us.

It was no use. I should never make up my mind

while the driver sat waiting, tactfully silent though he was. Besides, the steadily ticking-up meter was unnerving. Just across the road was a café, a poor little place but it would do to think in, over a cup of coffee. I paid off my kind driver.

'Bet you look her up in the end,' he said. 'After all, she can only show you the door. Still, if the old girl ran away from you...' He shook his head. 'Pride can mean a lot to people, all the more when they're poor. Did you know her well?'

'Very well, but not for long and it's a long time ago.'

And had I really known her well? I found myself wondering, while I waited for my coffee. Certainly not in the way I had known Molly and Lilian. Of course I had known them earlier, months before that July day when we all, so unexpectedly, met Zelle... Retrospection beckoned but was rebuffed; no doubt my problem was rooted in the past but it would have to be decided in the present – and quickly. And anyway, I didn't approve of retrospection; hadn't for years. Why exactly? Because it led to nostalgia? Or was my disapproval really funk? Some day I must find out.

BOOK TWO

The Town in Bloom

1

On my first night at the Club I sat up in bed and wrote in my journal:

I am here at last! I arrived this afternoon, at Marylebone Station so I only had a short taxi drive – I wished it could have been longer as it was thrilling to be driving through London all on my own. And it was such a lovely day. The trees here are further out than they are at home. Home! I haven't one any more. That thought doesn't make me feel sad. It makes me feel wonderfully free.

This morning, because of my trunk, I had to take a taxi all the way to Manchester and we went past the house that was my home for fifteen years. I really think I should have been happier there these last months than at a dreary boarding house, but everyone said I must not stay on there alone. Already the new tenants are in, and someone was standing by the French window where Aunt Marion so often sat. There were still some late daffodils on the lawn. I always loved the garden – and the house, too. I used to think it an old, romantic house though it is really only Victorian. As we left it behind this morning I felt a pang for the past, but long before we got to the station I was again looking forward to the future.

This Club– But before I describe it I want to pay a sort of goodbye tribute to Aunt Marion, to record my loving thanks for all she did. Looking after me ever since my parents died must have meant sacrifices, especially as she kept trying to save money out of her annuity so that she could leave me some. (Since I last wrote here I have heard I shall have about forty pounds a year.) I particularly want to thank her for taking me to so many theatres – in Manchester and on our wonderful trip to London when I was twelve – and for never discouraging me from going on the stage. Of course, she loved acting herself and only gave up her amateur work because of her heart, which was weak long before she let me know about it. I suppose I ought also to thank her for paying for the secretarial course she persuaded me to take as an insurance against failure. (I WILL NOT FAIL.) I hope she never knew how much I disliked the training and I wish she could know that I loyally stayed on for three whole months to finish it. Well, thank you and good night, dear Aunt Marion, and when I make a success it will be in your honour as well as for my own.

Now about this Club. It is rather a handsome building with a lot of heavy stonework; large and square, at a corner – quite an old house, I think. I had booked a room but there was some muddle and I had to sit in the hall while the receptionist tried to telephone the housekeeper, who couldn't be found. Two girls came downstairs and the taller – she must be quite six foot – looked at me through a lorgnette (I never saw a young girl use one before) and said, 'Do I understand that this small creature is bedless? If so, there is an empty cubicle in our village.' (I found that by 'village' she meant one of the groups of cubicles into which some of the big rooms are divided.) The receptionist, who was very busy because she had to cope with all the incoming telephone calls, asked if I would take the

30

cubicle just for one night, so I said I would. But I think I shall stay on in it because I like it very much and it is cheaper than a room.

It is almost private as the partitions are solid and go up to within a foot or so of the ceiling. And I have a good big cupboard, a washstand combined with a dressing-table which has long drawers, a folding table and a chair. There is a large window (some of the cubicles don't have windows) and from my bed I can see tall trees in the quite large Club garden. You would hardly know you were in London except when you see the tops of buses above the high garden wall.

I am alone in this 'village' at the moment as I have come to bed early. Molly Lorimer, the tall girl I met in the hall, told me that this is mainly a theatrical village and I must not mind if people come to bed late and talk into the small hours. I shall quite like that, if they talk about the theatre. Molly and the girl who was with her, Lilian Denison, are in musical comedy. Glorified chorus, Molly said, but Lilian said they had small parts. They were very fashionably dressed, in shapeless clothes that barely covered their knees. I think this is an ugly fashion. Anyway, Aunt Marion said I ought to have a style of my own and I shall always strive for one.

Though Molly and Lilian were extremely kind – they gave me tea in the Club lounge and I had dinner with them – I doubt if they will become real friends of mine as they are not interested in serious acting. After they had gone to their theatre I met someone who will be more important to me. She spoke to me when I was sitting alone in the lounge. Her name is Evangeline Esmond and she has played leading parts – I can't think why I have never heard of her. She was sur-

31

prised that I wasn't going to train at some school, and when I told her I couldn't spare the time or the money, she offered to coach me and said she would only charge me half price as she was sure I had talent. I explained that my aunt had taught me voice production but Miss Esmond still thought I needed tuition – she said she could give me introductions but only if she had trained me. I told her about the introduction I had brought with me and she said, 'Oh, my dear child, you'll never get work at the Crossway Theatre without training. I happen to know Rex Crossway very well indeed.' Perhaps I will afford myself a few lessons with her but I shall try on my own first.

Now I am going to put the light out and think. Someday this journal entry will bring back how it felt to be me, at eighteen, on my first night alone in London.

But does it? Yes, perhaps the scribbled words do make me feel a little nearer to the girl who wrote them. But as regards actual facts, the entry mentions only a fraction of what I remember. How could I have dealt so cursorily with that first entrance of Molly and Lilian?

They stood on the stairs looking down on me, two streaks of beige from the crowns of their felt hats to the toes of their glacé kid shoes. The hats were cloches which came down so low that it was only later I learned that Lilian was dark, with a sleek shingle, and Molly a redhead, who wore her hair in a plaited coronet. (She thought, rightly, that a shingle would make her head seem too small for her height; and apart from that, few women would have cared to sacrifice such magnificent hair.) Both girls were strikingly pretty, Lilian with a gardenia-like sophistication and Molly with a milkmaid freshness.

Why were they so kind to me? Later, I asked them and Molly said: 'You looked so funny and pathetic – a sort of Little Black Riding Hood.'

I wore a circular black cape and a black straw hat that resembled a coal-scuttle bonnet – placed well back on my head to show the thick brown fringe of my childish, straight, bobbed hair. My dress was pale grey, tight-bodiced and full-skirted. Not for me nude-looking stockings. Mine were grey and my black shoes had cut-steel buckles. I was, I believe, quite nice looking, though slightly too strongly featured for a girl of my tiny physique – not that this worried me. When I studied my face in a dressing-table glass I knew I could play Lady Macbeth; when I pranced in front of a long glass I felt I should make an ideal Puck. I was thankful for such versatility, both of talent and appearance.

After it had been decided I should take the vacant cubicle Molly said: 'Lilian, I think we should now give this little person tea. Come, child.'

I never found Molly's manner of speech patronising or affected. It seemed somehow suitable for her height and the superb way she carried herself. And I was, from the first, conscious of her kindness of heart.

She put one finger on my shoulder and piloted me into the lounge. It was a long, cream-painted room with tall, window-seated windows looking onto the garden. The curtains were broadly striped in violet and magenta. Cream cane chairs were grouped around red lacquer tables. There was a grey carpet. I was used to old-fashioned furnishings, my aunt having made few changes in those she had inherited from her parents, and it was some little while before I realised what a beautiful room the Club lounge was.

Tea was brought by a maid wearing a rose-pink uniform and mobcap. There were watercress sandwiches. 'Watercress is *stimulating*,' Molly pronounced, and I have felt well disposed to watercress ever since. Why do I only remember things that were said by Molly? I can't believe that Lilian wasn't holding her own in the conversation. Ah, now it comes back to me: Lilian asked questions. No doubt she was placing me, and also noting Molly's reactions to me. Lilian was always something of a suit-follower; or rather, a suit-improver, clever at building up on other people's ideas.

I can see her clearly as she was that day in the lounge, with her eyes, too dark to be called blue, flickering backwards and forwards between Molly and me. Lilian's eyes were astonishing. They were rather small but she habitually kept them so wide open that they seemed enormous. And they shone; they were the only eyes I ever saw that really deserved to be called starry. Her features were all charming but it was those shining, wide-open eyes that *were* Lilian.

Molly's grey-blue eyes really were large but she seldom troubled to open them fully. And her short-sightedness gave them a vague look. She used a lorgnette because spectacles both spoilt her appearance and hurt her babyish nose. Her whole face suggested that of a particularly beautiful baby – increased to a size suitable for a six-foot woman. I once told her I could imagine her being pushed along in a giant perambulator, benignly cooing at admiring passers-by. She said, 'Oh, lovely – but I couldn't be bothered to coo. I'd just drift into a lovely sleep.'

Did we find out much about each other at the first meeting or only by degrees? Like myself, they were orphans. Molly's mother had been a Gaiety Girl, her father an officer in the regular army whose family had always ignored Molly and her mother; though they did now give Molly a small allowance. Lilian's father had been a bank manager in a London suburb. Molly had been on the stage for two years, Lilian for nearly four. They had always played in West End musical comedy.

After tea we went to my cubicle and I unpacked my trunk, which was then taken to a box-room. Molly and Lilian left me on my own until they took me down for an early dinner. The dining-room, under the lounge, looked out onto a flagged area with the garden above it and only the tables near the windows were still in full daylight. We sat at the longest of these and at first had it to ourselves. Then an elderly woman joined us, looked at me, sniffed and said: 'Foreign bodies around this evening.' Lilian remarked coolly, 'This is a friend of ours who will be sitting here.' The elderly woman then gave me a cheerful grin and chatted pleasantly. Only when I had been at the Club some days did I fully realise how lucky I was to be sponsored in the dining-room. New members were usually scared away from favourite tables, to sit humbly at a draughty table near the door, known as the Lost Dogs' Home.

I doubt if dinner was really good; Club meals were apt to be a bit meagre. But it was pleasantly served on brightly decorated earthenware, and our nice, pink-uniformed waitress was said to get specially good helpings for her tables. I enjoyed everything and had become quite friendly with the elderly woman before we finished eating.

Molly and Lilian then hurried off to their theatre. I had coffee in the lounge, studied the *Stage,* and was firmly talked to by Evangeline Esmond – who turned out to be one of the Club bores; her triumphs, when not fictitious, had all been in long ago No. 3 touring companies and she now eked out a small income by giving lessons. With me, first impressions have so often been wrong ones.

I then went to bed, wrote in my journal, and slept until nearly midnight. I woke to see light above the partition between my cubicle and Molly's and to hear her say: 'Do you think that small mouse will be asleep?' Then there was a thump, as if someone had dropped something heavy, and a voice I did not know said, 'Blast!' after which Lilian said: 'Well, she'll be awake now, all right.' A moment later there was a tap on my door.

'Pray, Mistress Mouse, are you within?' said Molly, thus presenting me with my nickname – perhaps suggested by my smallness; no one could have thought me timid. I leaned from my bed and undid the catch of my door. Then Molly came in and switched the light on.

'Ah, good child, you sleep with your blind up and your window open. That's a great help to those of us who don't have windows. Are you hungry?'

'*I* am,' said the voice that had said 'Blast'.

'You shall have something in a minute, Frobisher,' said Molly. 'Do you like Veda bread, Mouse? It's the mainstay of village life as it keeps fresh so long.'

I had never tasted Veda bread. I said I would like to.

'Cut some, will you, Lilian?' called Molly, sitting down on my bed. 'And don't overdo the butter as it's a trifle high.'

I said I'd understood from the Club prospectus that one must not bring food into cubicles.

'Oh, *that!*' said Molly scornfully. 'Though they do get slightly peeved if one cooks cabbage on the landing gas-rings. Well, child, did you have a pleasant evening?'

During the next few minutes she undeceived me about Evangeline Esmond, concluding, 'Sorry as I am for the poor old thing, we can't have you wasting your money, can we?'

Lilian was heard calling, 'Coming over, Frobisher!' before throwing nourishment over a cubicle partition. Then she came in with some thick slices of brown bread and butter. The bread was malty, almost sticky, and seemed to me marvellous. And the occasion had charm for me, suggesting 'tuck in the dorm'. Happy though I had been with my aunt and at my high school, I had sometimes hankered to go to a boarding school.

'How's that bed?' asked Lilian. 'Some of them

are terrible.'

I said mine seemed all right. I had not yet begun to mind what beds were like.

'My friend Madam Lily de Luxe is a trifle fussy,' said Molly. (So Lilian must already have had her occasionally used nickname. Molly's came later, on a never-to-be-forgotten occasion.)

'You must be thinking we look ghastly,' said Lilian and explained that they seldom bothered to put their full offstage make-ups on after taking their stage make-ups off. 'It's such a waste of time when we're coming home on a dull bus.'

I asked if they ever went out to supper with admirers who waited at the stage door.

'You've been reading about the days of the Stage Door Johnnies,' said Molly. 'Nobody waits outside our stage door but sentimental girls and kids wanting autographs.'

From the landing came a shout of 'Kettle boiling!'

'That could be ours,' Lilian said, and went to investigate. I learned that kettles queued up for gas-rings; an owner, removing a boiling one, would replace it with the next in the queue. Lilian returned to say their kettle had just been put on, so they went to undress while it boiled.

Shortly after that, a deep voice said: 'My God, Frobisher, how that man kissed me in the taxi!'

Molly shouted: 'Kindly moderate your language, Macgregor. We have an innocent young mouse in our midst.'

'Oh, sorry, infant,' called Macgregor. 'But anyway, you won't stay innocent long, not in *this* village.'

I said, 'Oh, don't worry about me. I'm quite unshockable.' And I believed it to be true. Aunt Marion, a great admirer of Shaw – many of her triumphs in amateur theatricals had been as Shavian heroines – had brought me up on what she considered emancipated lines. Had I presented her with an illegitimate baby she would have uttered no word of reproach. But flippancy about sex had never come my way and when it did – there was a good deal of it at the Club – perhaps I was, at first, a little shocked; or to say the least of it, astonished, particularly by the fact that girls I took to be living perfectly respectable lives could regale each other with highly indecent stories. Macgregor, a dab-hand at these, was said to have a private line to the Stock Exchange.

The sixth occupant of our village soon arrived and joined the Frobisher-Macgregor conversation. She was addressed as Lofty, short for Loftus. I was to find that most Club members were called by their surnames, or abbreviations of them. But Molly and Lilian were called by their Christian names and I, from the first, was 'Mouse'.

Molly soon came in for my tooth mug and brought it back filled with tea. She then went to drink her own tea in bed. Conversation continued until she called: 'It's time we all went to sleep. Mouse, you should brush your teeth after that bread and butter. You have good teeth and should take care of them.'

I got up and did as I was told, and heard Molly and Lilian also busily brushing. Then Molly called: 'And in case you have need, there is a lav, just across the landing. In this village we only use our pots in emergencies.'

When I came back, Molly and Lilian had put their lights out but the others were still talking loudly.

'Friends, I should appreciate silence,' called Molly.

There were groans from Frobisher, Macgregor and Lofty but they did slightly lower their voices; and before long, they too put their lights out. I remember thinking it was strange to be sleeping so close to other people. Except during a few of our holidays I had never shared a room even with my aunt. I also remember thinking that I would describe the recent conversation in my journal. But I never did; the journal was in for a period of neglect. Had I written in it the next day, should I have recorded that I now thought Molly and Lilian would become real friends of mine? I doubt it. I think we slid into close friendship so easily that I never noticed it was happening.

No one in the village snored. It seems to me that no one so much as turned over in bed. Perhaps the six of us slept the profound sleep of youth; or perhaps it was just that the depth of my own youthful sleep blanketed out all sound.

2

I was awakened at nine-thirty by the clatter of crockery in the next cubicle: a maid was bringing Molly her breakfast in bed. Remembering, from the Club prospectus, that breakfast in the dining-room was served only until nine-forty-five, I sat up and wailed that I should never get down in time.

'Of course you won't,' said Molly cheerfully. 'Darling Charlotte will bring you something.'

Darling Charlotte was heard saying she would do no such thing. She then informed me that breakfast in bed had to be ordered the night before. 'You need to write your name in a book, miss.'

'But she didn't know that,' Molly explained. 'And you'll *want* to help her, because she's a poor small mouse in mourning for her aunt.'

I wasn't. Aunt Marion had disapproved of mourning.

Charlotte then told me she would see what she could do. 'But it'll only be toast and marmalade – it's too late for a fried egg. Tea or coffee, miss?'

I chose coffee and thanked her profusely. While she was gone I went along to the lavatory and saw, as I passed between the two rows of cubicles, that Frobisher, Macgregor and Lofty were already out of the village. (Frobisher was a music student, the other two were out-of-work actresses. Of course I

41

eventually met them face to face but I always knew them better by their voices than their faces.) Lilian, seeing me through her open door and across her breakfast tray, asked me to notice if there were any finished-with trays already put out on the landing from which I could glean any unwanted pieces of toast. She said hers were unusually thin. I found three pieces and brought them back to her. She was looking very decorative in a blue chiffon bed-jacket.

'One piece for me, one for Molly and one for you,' she said, giving me her sudden, wide smile that was almost a grin. That smile did a lot for Lilian.

When I took Molly her piece I found her wrapped in a fleecy white shawl. That was when I first saw her as an enormous baby.

Soon after I got back to bed Charlotte brought my breakfast. She was a tall, boney Cockney to whose angular features the Club mobcap was most unbecoming. Though always very kind to me, her real devotion was reserved for Molly, who treated her with bullying affection and usually called her either 'my faithful serf' or 'darling Charlotte the Harlot', both of which names appeared to give great pleasure.

Breakfast trays came up on a service lift but had to be carried some distance. I don't recall feeling guilty that mine was carried by a woman about three times my age. And I feel sure Charlotte did not mind, though she didn't get the sixpence charged by the Club for the service. Neither did she get tips; giving them was against Club rules. I fear most of us took the almost invariable kindness of Club servants completely for granted.

After breakfast I was initiated into the never-ending Battle of the Bathroom Door. There were plenty of 'cold bathrooms' where there was hot and cold water in the wash basin but only a cold tap for the bath. Access to cold bathrooms was free, but one could only get into a 'hot bathroom' by putting tuppence into a slot-machine on the door. Molly believed cleanliness should be free, always left bathroom doors open, and took advantage of any she found open. Lilian, while admitting the Club's right to charge, objected to paying for baths which often turned out to be tepid. She went in for complicated mental book-keeping and could be heard saying, 'The bathroom door owes me three tuppences from last week,' and so on. This might have indicated acute honesty on her part had she ever failed to take a free bath if she could get one. I adopted Molly's system and never closed a bathroom door behind me – any more than, throughout my life, I have ever deliberately closed the door on leaving a pay-lavatory.

My bath that day was certainly tepid, but even had it been hot I should have spent little time in it as I had plans for the morning. While reading the *Stage,* the previous evening, I had discovered that a new play was being cast at the Crossway Theatre. I intended to hurry there and present my introduction.

It had been given to me by my aunt not long before her death. Some five years earlier, when Rex Crossway had brought his company to Manchester, she had met him at a lunch given in aid of some charity and made such an impression that he had driven out to our suburb to have tea with her. (She was an unusually pretty woman.) When I got back from school – late, after a music lesson – he had just left, and I well remember taking deep sniffs of the air he had so recently breathed and patting the back of the chair where, my aunt assured me, his head had rested. She looked very bright eyed when she told me how interested he had been in her amateur acting; he had said she must come and see him if ever she went on the professional stage. I think she might have been tempted to, had not her heart trouble already begun though I did not know this until much later.

When she handed me the letter of introduction she said, 'I think I can, without flattering myself, feel sure he will remember me.' Although she smiled, as if with pleased reminiscence, it was a deeply sad moment, for we both knew the letter would only be presented after her death.

Before going to my bath I had told Molly and Lilian about the introduction and my determination to deliver it that morning. Lilian at once said, 'Wait! Couldn't you afford yourself one smart outfit before you try to see Rex Crossway?'

Molly squashed this. 'Smart clothes wouldn't suit her as well as her own do. She needs to be original.'

Lilian considered this idea, then made it her own and began improving on it. 'Then she should be even more original. Let me see all your clothes, Mouse.' She opened my cupboard door.

My aunt, too, had favoured originality for me,

though, paradoxically, the word had often meant for her that my clothes should be like somebody else's. I had a taffeta dress with a fichu said to be 'like' Marie Antoinette, and a high-waisted chintz dress 'like' Kate Greenaway girls. My black cloak worn without a hat (over party dresses) was 'like' a conspirator; worn with my straw bonnet it was 'like' Jane Eyre; accompanied by a small black tricorne hat it became 'like' Dick Turpin. Then there were my 'Studio' frocks. (Neither my aunt nor I had ever set foot in anyone's studio.) These were of excessively bright colours. Everything was well made; my aunt had employed a good dressmaker. But nothing bore any resemblance to what was being worn in the middle nineteen-twenties. Lilian, inspecting an orange wool dress intended to be worn with an emerald shawl, had remarked, 'Seriously, Molly, if she goes out in that she'll get mobbed.'

By the time I got back from my bath the girls had decided that the black cloak and grey dress in which they had first seen me would be best for my onslaught on Mr Crossway. 'But I've cheered things up a bit,' said Lilian. She had taken a small pink feather from one of her own hats and pinned it on to my coal-scuttle bonnet. It looked like a pink question mark.

I wore my best pale grey suede gloves and carried a handbag made of black velvet trimmed with cut steel. This had a draw-string like a work-bag and could, if swung when it contained a good supply of coppers, have proved a formidable weapon. I also had a grey umbrella which had been my aunt's. She had been a tall woman and it was a tall umbrella – unusually so, with its length increased by the ivory shepherd's crook which formed its handle. I thought highly of this umbrella. Molly admired the handle through her lorgnette and then we all went downstairs and out to the bus stop.

As the bus approached Molly wished me luck and said: 'I shan't be at all surprised if Miss Mouse comes back with a job.'

'Neither shall I,' said Lilian, flashing her wide smile. 'In fact, I have one of my feelings about it.'

Molly instructed the bus conductor to put me down as near as possible to the Crossway Theatre. He eyed my umbrella handle with interest and said he would take good care of Little Bo-Peep.

My visit to London six years earlier had only lasted a week, and though I vividly remembered all the theatres I had been taken to, I had no idea where they were. Looking out of the bus window I could not believe I should ever learn my way about. And when I got off I lost myself almost at once, in spite of the conductor's careful directions. But at last, after several enquiries, I reached the theatre.

It was at the juncture of four narrow old streets – I remembered my aunt saying it was named with double aptness as it was both at a crossway and the property of the Crossway family. One of London's oldest theatres, it still retained its late Regency façade, now freshly painted cream. Baskets of dwarf tulips swung between the slender pillars of its portico. On my earlier visit the baskets had been filled with pink geraniums. At twelve, I had gazed at that theatre with far more reverence than I had felt at Westminster Abbey. This had been a year before Rex Crossway had so miraculously come to tea with my aunt, but I had already seen him at Manchester's Theatre Royal and installed him as my favourite actor.

The first time we came to the Crossway it was to book our seats for *The School for Scandal,* in which Rex Crossway's more famous father, old Sir Roy Crossway, was giving his farewell performance. (He died soon after retiring.) While my aunt stood at the box-office I discovered that the stairs to the dress circle also led to the offices of the Crossway Company. I now planned to find these offices and present my letter; it seemed likely that, as a play was being cast, Rex Crossway might be there. But first I looked at the playbills and the framed photographs of the play that was still running. Some of these were on the long side wall of the theatre and beyond them was a sign saying STAGE DOOR – the very words excited me. It then occurred to me that Mr Crossway might be in the theatre itself, rather than in the offices. I would ask at the stage door.

As I approached it, a girl overtook me and went in. I heard her say, 'Good morning. I have an appointment.' I reached the door in time to hear the stage door keeper say, 'Right, miss. The audition's down on the stage.'

I instantly felt I must get into that audition. So I followed the girl, said what she had said (wasn't my letter as good as an appointment?) and barely waited for the stage door keeper's instructions before pushing through the swing doors. Then I went down stone steps until I reached a heavy

47

iron door. I opened it and, a moment later, stood for the first time in my life on the stage of a professional theatre.

I could see very little, because the stage set cut off most of the light that was illuminating it. But there was a bright patch from a window in the set, and near this the girl who had come down ahead of me was standing with a slight, dark young man. Presumably she was telling him who she was – I saw him pencil a tick on the notepad he was holding. Then he waved her aside and she joined some other girls, who were seated in a row.

I went towards the young man. He said, 'Yes? What's your name and what time's your appointment?' Though he spoke only in a whisper he managed to make it a very brusque whisper and he was most noticeably unsmiling. I had been feeling excited, adventurous; suddenly I felt nervous.

I said, 'I haven't exactly got an appointment but I've brought a letter of introduction to Mr Crossway and–'

The young man interrupted me. 'Well, you can't give it to him now. You'd better post it. Excuse me.' He turned away.

'But, please,' I begged, 'as there's an audition on now, couldn't I get into it?'

He turned back to me. 'Certainly not. We're running late as it is. And anyway, you'd be all wrong. We need a tall girl – a Society type.'

A voice I recognised as Rex Crossway's called loudly, 'Brice! What's happening? Why this hold-up?'

The young man called back, 'Sorry, Mr Crossway,' then turned to the waiting girls. 'Who's next?'

A girl stood up and he took her out to the front of the stage. I heard him introduce her to Mr Crossway, who asked what work she had done. When she answered I thought she spoke very sloppily; she didn't sound to me like a Society girl. I could well imagine myself playing one – and surely they weren't *all* tall? I heard Mr Crossway say, 'Well, now, just read me a little of the part. You've had the chance to look at it, haven't you? Mr Marton will read with you – just imagine he's me. And this time, Brice, cut my long speech and only give her the cue. Now off you go.'

The girl began to read deplorably and was not helped by Brice Marton, who read in a curt monotone, a louder version of his brusque whisper to me. Very soon Mr Crossway stopped them, thanked the girl and told her he didn't think she'd had quite enough experience. 'But write to me again later,' he added kindly. The girl returned to the wings and Brice Marton came with her and took another girl back with him.

I decided to go on listening but I wanted to hear better than I could from where I was. So I walked down into the prompt corner. (I knew all about such things as prompt corners, having twice played children's parts in amateur theatricals before my aunt gave up acting.) It did not strike me that I was doing anything outrageous and I had stopped feeling nervous of Brice Marton. A man who read as badly as that couldn't be of the least importance; still, I was glad to find he had

49

his back to me.

This girl read better and was allowed to go on to the end of the scene, thus giving me a clear idea of the part. I felt I could play it admirably and I was sorry to hear Mr Crossway, say to the girl, 'Come down and have a word with me. Brice, show her the pass door.' It sounded as if she might get the job before I'd had a chance to win it.

I hastily got out of the prompt corner and was careful to keep out of Brice Marton's sight when he brought the girl back to the wings, took her down some stone steps, and opened a narrow iron door for her. He then went back to the stage, taking another girl with him. I went closer to the open pass door and could see the rose-red carpet and the brocaded walls of the theatre. A moment later, I heard Rex Crossway's voice, and though I could not see him I felt sure he had come to the side of the stalls to talk to the girl. He was speaking too quietly for me to make out the words so I went right down the steps to the pass door, determined to find out if the girl really had got the job. I was in time to hear him say, 'Well, I mustn't decide for a few days but you can count on hearing from me one way or the other. Now perhaps you'd like to go out of the front of the theatre.' Then he held open one of the swing doors of the stalls – I could see him now. The girl went out and he turned to go back to the middle of the stalls.

I flung myself towards him saying, 'Please, please! Just a minute! Will you *please* read this?'

He swung round, looking startled; then said,

'Good gracious, what is it? A reprieve?'

I suspect my explanation was far from coherent but he got the hang of it quickly and said he remembered my aunt very well and was indeed sorry to hear of her death. He then accepted my letter, saying he would read it later and arrange to see me.

I said, 'But then it may be too late for this part. Won't you please let me read it to you now?'

He said that would be unfair to me as I'd had no chance to study the part. I assured him I'd listened to two girls and knew what kind of a part it was. He still shook his head so I added, 'Then let me do something on my own. Shakespeare, Sheridan – I've an enormous repertoire.'

He capitulated. 'All right. Do anything you like, but keep it short. I'd better hear you at once.' He went to the front of the stalls and said: 'I want to slip someone in here, Brice. She's coming up now. Sorry, my dear' – he turned to the girl who was waiting to read – 'I'll hear you in a moment.'

I rushed through the pass door and up to the stage. Brice Marton was just coming into the wings. He stared at me and gave a disgusted snort, then said, 'Someone will have to lend you a script.'

The girl who had come off the stage with, him offered hers. I thanked her politely but said I shouldn't need it. 'And I shan't need you, either,' I said to Brice Marton, not at all politely, and sailed out to the front of the stage.

Feeling that I could not be at my best if trammelled by hat, cloak, handbag, gloves and umbrella, I flung them from me. Then, having decided how I could best show my talent for Society comedy, I smiled into the dark auditorium and announced: '*The School for Scandal* by Richard Brinsley Sheridan.' (Aunt Marion had trained me to let people know what they were in for.) After which, I launched into the first quarrel scene between the Teazles.

I played both of them. First, as Sir Peter, I looked to my right and used a deep, rich voice. Then, looking left, I became Lady Teazle and used a lighter voice than was natural to me. Backwards and forwards from right to left I went, speaking fast because I feared Mr Crossway would stop me. I particularly wanted to reach what was, for me, the high moment of the scene, when Sir Peter tells Lady Teazle she had no taste when she married him. Lady T. then goes off into fits of laughter – that is, she did in my interpretation. And never had I laughed better, louder or longer than I did for Mr Crossway. I checked my laughter with some very amusing gasps and continued the scene. Still Mr Crossway did not interrupt me. So I went on until Lady Teazle's exit when I sketched a pert curtsy to Sir Peter – and then made a very deep one to Mr Crossway.

From the dark auditorium came his voice and he certainly sounded impressed. 'Thank you, thank you. Come down and see me again.'

I dashed off the stage, forgetting all my belongings, and ran down the steps to the pass door. Brice Marton called after me, 'Come back for your clothes!' but I took no notice. When I reached the stalls Mr Crossway was coming to meet me.

'That was really remarkable,' he said, smiling

broadly. 'And you were especially good as Sir Peter. When I play that part – and I'm nearly old enough – I shall come to you for hints.' Then he probably guessed from my expression that I thought he was making fun of me, because he went on, 'Seriously, I was impressed by your diction, and you know how to project your voice. And you use your hands prettily, though rather too much even for period comedy. Yes, yes, you undoubtedly have, er...' He paused to choose the word.

'Yes, individuality. And I wish with all my heart I had work to offer you–'

I interrupted him. 'But you have. That part the girls have been reading–'

'You're out of the question for it. You'd have to play a scene with me – and you'd make me look a giant. I simply must have a tall girl.'

Just then there was a slight thud: my belongings had been thrown through the pass door.

'Dear me, that was very rude of my stage manager,' said Mr Crossway. 'We're in disgrace for interrupting the audition. Now I really must send you away.'

He picked up my cloak and put it round me, then handed me the rest of my things, remarking, 'What a very tall umbrella!' I told him it had been Aunt Marion's. His smile faded and he said, 'That dear, pretty woman. I *am* so sorry she's dead. Now go up to my offices – you can reach them through the foyer – and give your name and address to my secretary, Miss Lester. And tell her from me that she's to be very nice to you.'

As he turned to open the swing door for me a

young man came hurrying through it. Mr Crossway spoke to him. 'Everything all right, Tom?' The young man said, 'Yes, sir. I chose lilac. They'll deliver it this afternoon.' Mr Crossway said, 'Good. Now get back to Brice. I'm in his bad books for borrowing you.' Then, turning to me, he said, 'Goodbye, my dear,' very kindly, and held the door open. My spirits sank as it swung to behind me. I had been elated at getting into the audition, and by his praise ... but I hadn't got the job.

And there was something else troubling me, something I only realised fully when I got to the foyer. Here, amidst the mirrors, rose-red brocade and cream and gold paint, was an oil painting of Rex Crossway as Charles Surface. *That* was the man with whom, for years, I had been in love. True, the words meant no more to me than when I used them about a character in history or fiction, and I knew one did not really fall in love with men one had not met. But I had never fallen in love with any man I *had met* and Rex Crossway had at least been the most exciting man I had ever seen. The man in the stalls had been kind but scarcely exciting. There had not been enough time, or light, for me to study his face carefully but my impression had been that, though pleasantly humorous, it was almost ordinary, a shade plump and surmounted by hair barely bright enough to be called fair (a poor substitute for Charles Surface's gleaming white wig). And whereas I had thought of him as a tall man with a magnificent figure, he was – if certainly tall – a trifle heavy. Worst of all, he seemed to be definitely middle-aged. Well, I knew from reference books that he was forty and, come to think of it, that *was* middle-aged. But I never *had* thought of it before.

I stood in front of the oil painting trying to believe that Rex Crossway in the stalls had at least borne some slight resemblance to Rex Crossway as Charles Surface. It couldn't be done. So, one way and another, I was depressed as I started to walk up the stairs from the foyer.

At the back of the dress circle was a door marked: 'To the Crossway Company offices only'. I opened it and found a much narrower staircase and went up and up. It ended at last at a landing, where a door stood open. I could see no bell so I knocked on the door.

A woman's voice told me to come in and I went into an entrance hall dimly lit by a dirty glass roof. I saw several closed doors and one open onto an office from which the woman's voice called again: 'Come in here.'

I went into a long, low room which had four not very large round windows. The parapet of the roof hung out over these a little, cutting off some of the bright morning sunshine. The effect was curiously pleasant, the parapet somehow suggesting sun-blinds protecting the room from high summer heat.

Close to one of the windows a woman was seated in front of a typewriter. I took in that she had light brown hair and was pretty but no longer young; probably in her late thirties. She said, 'Yes?' rather vaguely and did not return my smile. I explained how I came to be there, concluding by saying, 'And Mr Crossway said – he really did, I'm not making it up – he said I was to tell you from him to be nice to me.'

She was smiling by now. 'Well, I hope I would have been, anyway – though it *is* a busy morning. Now sit down and give me your particulars. And tell me some more about yourself.'

She listened with apparent interest, asking questions until she must have had a pretty clear picture of my background. Then she said, 'And now I'd like to hear just how you crashed into that audition.' When I'd told her all I could remember she said, 'Well, bravo, you! But don't ever again watch another girl from the prompt corner; that's against all stage etiquette. Not that I want to inhibit you. Oh, dear, how annoyed Brice Marton must have been with you!'

'He was indeed. I hated him.'

'Well, you shouldn't. A stage manager has to be boss of his stage and Brice has to be a bit extra bossy because he's so young for the job – only twenty-five. He started here as a call boy. By the way, he comes from your part of the world, but from right in Manchester, not a suburb.'

I said I didn't know that anyone lived right in Manchester.

'They do when their mothers are theatrical landladies, as Brice's was,' said Miss Lester. 'Listen, that secretarial course you took: how did you get on?'

I told her I had done fairly well.

She got up and went to a smaller desk than her own, where there was a second typewriter. I noticed that she was tall, and well-dressed in a casual way that came near to being untidy. Putting some paper in the machine she said, 'Let me see what you can do.'

'But why? I don't mean to be a secretary.'

'I know that. Still – come on.'

I sat down at the typewriter. She dictated a letter addressed to me, regretting that Mr Crossway had no work to offer me. I made no mistakes.

'And you've set it out nicely,' she said, 'Now we'll try some shorthand.'

She dictated again, so slowly that I had no difficulty in keeping pace with her. When I read the words back to her she said. 'Now don't jump down my throat. I'm badly in need of help here. I've been keeping the job open for a girl who's been ill and has now decided she doesn't want to come back. Why don't you join me, while you're looking for stage work?'

I stared at her. 'But how could I look for it if I was working here?'

'Quite easily. I want someone who'll come in the afternoons and evenings. You could have the mornings off – well, most of them. And if you'd any special afternoon appointment I'd let you off for that, too.'

She went on talking persuasively, pointing out that the money she could pay me would help me to keep going until I got a job on the stage. I could see that, but I had an almost superstitious fear that if I once became a secretary I should go on being a secretary. Then she said something which completely changed my feelings– 'And perhaps Mr Crossway would let you understudy something in the new play; from what you've told

57

me, he must think you're promising. Or he might – not that you must count on it – give you some introductions.'

I said, 'Oh, goodness, do you think he would? In that case, of course I'll take the job.'

'Splendid. And I think you'll enjoy it. This is a fascinating theatre, for anyone who's really interested in the stage. But I daresay you're only interested in your own career.' She said it quite nicely.

I assured her I was particularly interested in the Crossway Theatre and its history and had once seen Sir Roy Crossway act. She told me she had worked as his secretary for many years and had thought the world of him– 'Of course his temper could be frightening but he seldom lost it with me. And he was a wonderful man – the last of the great actor-managers.'

'But surely Mr Crossway's an actor-manager?'

'Oh, yes, but he's not interested in the managerial side. Acting has always come first with him. Now you'd better leave me to get on with my work. Could you start this afternoon? No, I shall be too busy with Mr Crossway to show you the ropes. How about this evening at six-thirty? We'll have a meal together. That is, if you really want to join me here. I don't want to over-persuade you.'

'Oh, I'll come. And it's kind of you to want me.' I added with belated modesty, 'I can't think why you should. I'm not really efficient.'

She smiled. 'The truth is that I rather like you. And I can't work with people I don't like, however efficient they are. Now off you go.'

I went down the stairs feeling cheerful; with the prospect of understudying I could think of myself as an actress, not a secretary. Perhaps I could understudy the part I had heard read at the audition. I opened one of the doors into the dress circle hoping to do some more listening, then decided this might be against stage etiquette like watching from the prompt corner. Just before I reluctantly withdrew, a cleaner who was quietly polishing brass whispered, 'If you're looking for Miss Lester, she's up the stairs, right at the top.'

'Yes, I know, thanks,' I said nonchalantly. 'I work here.'

3

Back at the Club, I found Molly and Lilian in the lounge and told them about my morning.

'It's simply staggering,' said Lilian. 'Getting a job the first day you've looked for one! I can't believe it.'

'But you told me you had a feeling I would.'

'Oh, that was just to encourage you – or did I really know?'

This was my introduction to those 'feelings' of Lilian's which it was never safe to count on or discount.

Molly said, 'Personally, I'm not one bit surprised, Mouse.'

'Fancy him remembering your aunt,' said Lilian. 'Do you think he had an affair with her?'

I said he only came to tea.

Lilian giggled. 'Well, he's said to be a fast worker.'

'But he's married, Lilian.' I had noted it, with regret, in a reference book.

'Oh, that doesn't stand in his way,' said Lilian.

'Well, it would have stood in Aunt Marion's. And I'm sure she wouldn't have had an affair with anyone. She went on caring for her fiancé, who was killed in the war.' The very thought of an affair for my aunt seemed shocking, so I dropped the subject by saying, 'Of course, I haven't got a job on the stage.'

Molly said it was sure to lead to one.

'And think what fun you'll have, being in the know,' said Lilian. 'Perhaps you can get *us* jobs – our show may not run through the summer and I'd quite like to be in a straight play.'

'I wouldn't,' said Molly. 'All I want is to find a marvellous man, so that I can marry him and have dozens of children. Until then, the chorus will do nicely.'

Lilian glared at her. 'Don't keep saying we're in the chorus.'

We went down to an early lunch; it was Wednesday and the girls had a matinée. Lilian pointed out that the Crossway midweek matinées were on Thursdays, so they could go to one if I could get some complimentary seats. She said it was usual to paper the house when a show was coming off.

'The child probably thinks you mean they get the decorators in,' said Molly. 'Paper means free seats, Mouse.'

Later I got quite a number to scatter around the Club – or, rather, for Lilian to scatter; she enjoyed doling them out.

After lunch I wrote to Aunt Marion's solicitor. He was legally my guardian but my aunt had told him I was to be free to try for work on the stage. He had done what he could to help me, finding out about the Club (which was for actresses, musicians and artists) and arranging for my membership; but he took a poor view of the stage as a career for me and would be relieved to know I had a secretarial job. I also wrote to several friends, taking pleasure in describing my adventures and saying I should be sending further instalments – which never got written; from that day on I lost interest in everyone connected with my old life, because my new life was so all-absorbing.

When I had finished my letters I went up to my cubicle and studied my dresses. I had already decided they must be shortened; I doubt if many young women can be happy in dresses longer than other women are wearing. But I still did not hanker for shapeless tubes; I much preferred my tight bodices and full skirts. Lilian had told me the attendant in the Ladies' Room would do alterations for me so I took down an armful of dresses. An American girl who came in said they were the cutest things she'd ever seen.

After tea, with stimulating watercress sandwiches, I started for the theatre in time to get off the bus at Piccadilly Circus and walk up Shaftesbury Avenue, looking at playbills and photographs. Then I got lost in the small streets surrounding the Crossway, but I still got there well before six-thirty.

Miss Lester looked pleased to see me. 'Good child. I've lots for you to do. But first we're going out to dinner. There's a pub round the corner where they do quite good meals.'

She put on a small felt hat and slung a fox fur over her shoulder. I always remember Eve Lester's clothes as elegant, rather than smart or fashionable. She usually wore plain, dark suits which, while conforming to fashion, seemed somehow dateless. And she wore them, and all her clothes, as if she never gave them a thought; she seldom looked in a glass when putting on her hat. She used little make-up. On first sight she had seemed to me pretty but what she really had was a faded beauty; or perhaps only a dimmed beauty which might have shone had she helped it to.

I had never been in a pub and did not much fancy a meal there. But I found there was a pleasant old upstairs dining-room, where outsize cruets stood on white tablecloths. As we sat down Miss Lester said, 'By the way, we charge our dinners here to the theatre. That's been a rule ever since Sir Roy's day – when the office staff works on in the evenings.'

I mentioned that I hadn't worked during the day.

'Doesn't matter. When you work at night, you get fed.'

I asked if she worked mornings, afternoons and evenings. She said, 'Usually, and sometimes even on Sunday. Thank God I don't have far to come. I've a barely sanitary old maisonette just along in

Covent Garden. My work at the theatre's my whole life – has been almost since I first came to it, twenty years ago. I was just your age then. Do you smoke?' She offered me a cigarette. 'And how about a drink?'

I said I didn't drink or smoke. 'But perhaps I should. Most people on the stage do, don't they?'

She laughed. 'Well, you'll get no encouragement from me. I withdraw both offers. Incidentally, if you take to swigging double whiskies here, don't charge those to the management – not that Mr Crossway would mind, really; he's as generous as his father was. I have a drink if I'm dead tired but it doesn't help me much, which is just as well; if I depended on drink as I do on cigarettes I'd be dead by now. Where's that waitress? I haven't too much time.'

We had a good, solid meal of steak-and-kidney pie and apple tart. 'No coffee, unless you pine for it,' said Miss Lester. 'It's poor stuff here, and I always make some during the evening. Now we ought to hurry.'

When we got back to the theatre there were quite long queues waiting for the pit and gallery. This surprised me, as the play was coming off.

'Oh, we shall fill our cheap seats until the end of the run,' said Miss Lester, 'but the stalls and circles have dropped off badly. And now it's going to rain – that's bad for the doors.' Seeing my puzzled expression she added, 'That means people who haven't booked seats but decide to come at the last minute. Not that we get much passing trade here, as they do in Shaftesbury Avenue and the Strand. There's hardly anyone

63

about here after the shops close; one might be in some little country town.'

The Crossway, with its four narrow streets, certainly looked unlike my idea of London. Some of the shops still had their old wooden shutters, and the street lamps gave only a dim light. But the theatre was brilliantly lit and there was an electric sign giving the name of the play, with 'Rex Crossway in' above it. As I looked upwards, Miss Lester said, 'Sir Roy wouldn't like that sign and it does rather spoil the facade, but one must move with the times; not that we do in all ways and I can't say I'm sorry, but we probably need to if the Crossway's to go on paying.'

'Surely it does very well?'

'Well, we haven't done too badly with this last show, though it's a pretty weak play. You must see it before it comes off. Now I'm going my rounds. You can tag along with me and learn your way about the theatre; it's a rabbit warren of passages and staircases.'

First we went to the box-office and one of the two elderly men inside unlocked the door for her. She went in and closed it after her. When she came out she said there would be a better house than she had expected. 'And it's going to *look* nice, anyway. I hate seeing empty seats.'

'I suppose it'll be papered?' I said knowledgeably.

'And with good-looking paper. It's quite a job to paper houses tactfully. I'll let you have some seats for your Club if you'll give them to people who'll dress.'

An old, white-haired man came through a door

64

marked 'Private'. She introduced him. 'This is Mr Fortescue, our front of the house manager. Someday you must get him to tell you about the old days here.'

He said he would be delighted to, then asked her to spare him a few minutes. She went into his office with him; and when she came out she looked back to say, 'Now don't you worry. I can easily sort that out for you.' As we started towards the stalls she said, 'He's such a darling but he's always forgetting things. Well, what can you expect? He's nearly eighty.'

'Oughtn't he to retire?'

'People here never retire of their own accord. And Mr Crossway never has the heart to ask them to. Many of them date from his father's early days.'

We went down to the stalls bar, which looked rather like a rose and gold drawing-room. The two barmaids seemed little younger than Mr Fortescue. They were eager to see Miss Lester and indignant about some supplies which they said had been deflected to the dress-circle bar. She promised to do something about it and eventually we went off to the pit bar, then to the dress-circle bar – where there was counter indignation to the stalls bar indignation – and then to the bars at the back of the upper circle and the gallery. Almost always there was some problem to iron out.

I said I'd never realised a theatre had so many bars.

'God bless them all,' said Miss Lester. 'We've always kept control of them and their takings often mean the difference between profit and loss on a week. Now I'll show you how to get from the gallery to the offices; it's complicated.'

I had found the geography of the whole theatre complicated. There were wide public staircases and narrow private ones – or semi-private ones; the public could use them if it could find them, which seemed unlikely in most cases. Their decor corresponded to the part of the house they served: rose carpet and brocaded walls for the stalls and dress circle; linoleum and wallpaper for the upper circle; stone steps and drably painted walls for the gallery. It was that tour of the theatre which first made me notice the deliberate impoverishing of surroundings in proportion to the decrease in the price of seats. As we walked along the back of the gallery I looked down and said, 'Couldn't there be backs to the seats – even a railing? Surely that wouldn't cost much?'

'But if we make the gallery seats more comfortable, people won't pay for the pit. And if we make the pit more comfortable then heaven help the upper circle. Still, I do feel sorry for galleryites. But at least this gallery has a good sight line.'

She took a key out of her handbag, unlocked a door, led the way along a narrow passage and up a few steps, then through another door into the entrance hall of the offices.

She now had to dole out programmes and chocolates to the waiting programme girls – not that they could, with truth, be described as 'girls'. One of them was complaining bitterly about her feet. 'You girls from the cheap seats don't know how lucky you are, walking on nice lino. Carpets are hell.'

I was so astonished at this that I butted in and said I'd have thought carpets would be soft to walk on.

'Oh, they're soft all right, but they burn the soles off your shoes.'

(Years later I noticed that chambermaids, walking the long passages of hotels, avoid the strips of carpets and walk on the lino.)

Soon after the 'girls' went down, I heard a rumbling noise.

'That's the gallery coming in,' said Miss Lester. 'One wall of the Throne Room backs on to it.'

'The Throne Room?'

'Mr Crossway once called it that, satirically, and the name stuck. I want you to work in there tonight.'

She took me into a room which, like the office, had four round windows; but it was larger than the office, L-shaped, with the short part of the L jutting out towards the back of the gallery. On the long wall facing the windows were three oil paintings. Switching on the lights over them, she said: 'Behold the Crossway dynasty.'

The largest painting was of an actor playing Hamlet. Miss Lester told me it was Mr Crossway's grandfather, King Crossway. I asked if that had been his real name.

'King was, believe it or not, but his surname was really Crossthwaite. He changed it when he managed to get hold of the Crossway Theatre. It's a shocking painting – and one gathers he was a shocking actor; just a barnstormer with a flair for business.' Her eyes travelled to another of the paintings. 'That's Sir Roy, much as he was when I first knew him.'

I asked if Rex Crossway had children to carry on the dynasty. She said, 'No, unfortunately. That portrait of him was done when he was a young man, by a very mediocre painter. The one of Sir Roy is a Sargent.'

I could find no resemblance between the painting and the old man I had seen playing Sir Peter Teazle. In middle age, Sir Roy had been darkly handsome, with a slightly satanic expression which I thought attractive. Mr Crossway was nothing like as interesting, either in the painting here or as his present-day self seen by me that morning – though in the painting he certainly had brighter hair and more of it.

Miss Lester was now pointing out a genealogical tree of the Crossway family. 'It takes them back to an actor of Shakespeare's time. Sir Roy was very proud of it, but Mr Crossway says nothing further back than the early eighteen hundreds is authentic. There are all sorts of things in here that will interest you. Letters, souvenirs...'

I was looking at an old print of the Crossway. 'How marvellous it must be to own a theatre and to hand it on from generation to generation!'

'I regret to say the Crossway family have never actually owned the theatre,' said Miss Lester. 'The barnstormer just had a very long lease at a fantastically low rent. Since then the lease has had to be renewed four times and the rent has soared higher and higher. But at least Mr Crossway's still the direct lessee. So often managements have to rent from a sub-lessee and then rents really do go sky-high. Well, now: tonight I want you to work on press-cuttings; they're terribly in arrears. Just sort them into date order and paste them in.'

She had set everything out for me on the very long table in the front part of the room. I said, 'I suppose I mustn't take time to read the cuttings?'

'Oh yes, within reason. There's no desperate hurry and they'll help you to get the feel of the theatre. But I should think you'll soon find them boring. And it's messy work, I'm afraid. The job somehow has to go on, year after year, though we hardly ever need to look back at cuttings. I'll be in my office if anything puzzles you.'

I did not find the cuttings boring; nothing connected with a theatre could have bored me then. But I did find the work tricky as the cuttings were so mixed up. And I soon realised I should never get finished if I read many of them, so I rationed myself to the letter-press under photographs. After a while I heard music and guessed that the theatre orchestra was playing. A few minutes later, Miss Lester came back.

Saying she was going to give me a little treat she switched off the lights, leaving the room lit only by a glow from the electric sign below the round windows. Then she told me to come and look through the spy-hole. We went into the short part of the room's L and she slid open a very small, oblong section of the panelling.

I looked down over the people sitting in the gallery, down, down through the dark theatre, and was just in time to see the curtain rise to reveal a drawing-room. The orchestra was still playing but very softly. Miss Lester whispered, 'You can stay here until I come back. But be sure to keep quiet; and if you leave the spy-hole, close the panel.'

The music dwindled into silence. The play began.

An elderly lady was talking to a butler – the little figures were so far away that I was surprised how well I could hear them. The elderly lady chatted pleasantly, treating the butler as a human being. The audience obviously thought this unusually kind, also funny; there were ripples of pleased laughter. Then a door was flung open by a pretty woman, laden with parcels, who said: 'Mother, darling, I've kept you waiting!' The butler went. Mother and daughter proceeded to talk about daughter's husband's infidelities. Mother wanted something done about them. Daughter pretended to be more interested in the contents of her parcels. But her frivolous behaviour was just a ruse to hide her deep feelings; and though Mother was fooled, the audience wasn't – because Daughter (by now I had realised she was the leading lady) gave it a few hints Mother wasn't in on.

Soon Mr Crossway came on, looking rather less ordinary than at the audition but by no means glamorous; and his acting was so quiet that it barely seemed like acting. Mother departed and he and his leading lady played a scene I found unexciting as they were supposed to have been married for ten years. However, I cheered up when the leading lady was replaced by a young actress who made overtures to Mr Crossway. Knowing that 'daring' plays were fashionable, I thought (and hoped) she might have some luck, but before she'd made much progress Miss Lester returned and asked me to close the panel.

'Sorry to tear you away,' she said, 'but I want you to sit in my office while I go down to Mr Fortescue – in case the telephone rings.'

'If it does, shall I take a message or come and find you?'

'A message, unless it's something important. I'm expecting a trunk call from an actor Mr Crossway wants in the new play but that shouldn't come through till later.'

I asked if there was anything I could be doing for her and she said I could grind some coffee beans. She measured them out.

I had never ground coffee beans before and rather enjoyed it. Then I sat at the desk I knew would be mine and watched. the heavy rain now beating on the round windows. After a while it seemed extraordinary that I should be alone here at the top of a theatre. Since early childhood I had occasionally had a strange feeling that I was not who I was or where I was, and what was happening wasn't real. I had this feeling now and, as usual, found it more interesting than frightening, though I always suspected that if it went on long one might go mad. But it never did go on long; one failed to concentrate or got interrupted. Tonight the telephone rang.

I planned to answer, 'Crossway Theatre. Miss Lester's assistant speaking.' But somehow this came out as, 'Hello.'

A woman's voice, high and confident, said, 'Miss Lester? This is Nancy Warden, back from

Paris. I bet *you* chose that lovely lilac.'

I said I wasn't Miss Lester and asked if I could take a message. Then, feeling the recipient of the lilac must rank as important, I added, 'or I could go down and find her for you?'

After a second's silence the voice said, 'Oh, just give her a message. Ask her to let Mr Crossway know I'm expecting him for supper tonight. Did you get my name? Lady Warden.'

She had only just rung off when Miss Lester returned. I reported the whole conversation. She looked puzzled and said she'd chosen no lilac.

'Someone called Tom did,' I informed her and told what I had heard in the stalls that morning.

'You do take things in, don't you?' she said amusedly. 'Well, I must let Mr Crossway know about supper but I can't go round yet; my trunk call may come through any minute now.'

'Can't you telephone Mr Crossway in an interval?'

She said he refused to have a telephone in his dressing-room and objected to taking calls at the stage door. 'You'd better go round for me.' She scribbled a note and put it in an envelope. 'Take this to his dressing-room and wait for him; he'll soon be off-stage for nearly ten minutes. Just explain that I sent you. And, er, don't mention that you took the telephone call or know what's in the note.'

She gave no reason for this and I needed none. Lilian's views on Mr Crossway, the ominous word 'supper', and the sophistication of the play I had just been watching, all combined to make me think the worst – and I enjoyed thinking it;

this was life in the London theatre world. Also, it did something for Mr Crossway. Who was I to find him unglamorous if Lady Warden didn't?

I went to get my cloak.

'And take your umbrella,' said Miss Lester.

But I had not brought my umbrella. It had, that morning, provoked more comment than I cared for.

The rain was heavier than ever. I asked if I couldn't go through the pass door instead of out to the stage door. Miss Lester said that would be all right if I tiptoed through the wings– 'And be sure to lock the door after you.' She gave me the key.

'Will Brice Marton be in the prompt corner?'

'No, Tom – he's the assistant stage manager – will be on the book. Brice will be on the other side of the stage, coping with some off-stage noises; I shouldn't think you'll see him. Hurry up. Mr Crossway will be coming off in a few minutes.'

When I got down to the back of the dress circle I allowed myself a glance at the second act of the play. The young actress now appeared to be making good headway with Mr Crossway; she'd got her arms round his neck. I was sorry to see him detach himself. Tearing myself away I hurried down to the stalls and the pass door. I unlocked it, went through, locked it behind me and went up the steps. From the top I could see into the prompt corner, where Tom stood in readiness to prompt. ('On the book' – I had stored up that phrase.) There was no one else to be seen and I was instantly conscious of an almost undescribable atmosphere. It was something like that of a cathedral when one wanders around while a service is taking place at the far end. But here in the wings I should have felt it blasphemous to wander around. The very air seemed quietly attentive, as if fully aware that everything here must be utterly subservient to what was happening in front of the audience.

I heard Mr Crossway addressing the young actress. 'And now, my dear child, I shall beat a hasty retreat, still in good – well, fairly good – order.' I took this to be his exit line so I made a dash for the door which led from the stage.

His dressing-room was so close that I found it at once. His dresser was standing by the open door. I had just started to explain what I'd come for when Mr Crossway arrived.

He gave one look at me and exclaimed, '"Lady Teazle, by all that's wonderful!"'

I told him I was glad he hadn't quoted, "Lady Teazle, by all that's damnable!" He laughed and said that would have been most ungallant, and that he'd been delighted to hear I was joining Miss Lester. 'Don't let her overwork you, as she does herself. Has she sent you with some message?'

I handed the note and he asked me to wait in case it needed an answer; then read it, looked pleased and said 'Tell her I shan't be coming up to the office after the show tonight. But don't run away yet. Sit down and talk to me – and rather less fast than you did this morning. I couldn't take everything in.'

I doubt if I slowed up much; I was too eager to tell him my entire past history and all my ambitions for the future. Again and again he smiled or laughed outright at what I said, and though I was talking with the utmost seriousness I couldn't feel offended, because it was so obvious that he liked me. I liked him, too, and I decided that he had a particularly charming smile, and that he looked rather younger than I had thought. Suddenly he said, 'What are you staring at? Is my toupee adrift?'

I stared harder. 'Is it a toupee?'

'It is indeed. But only my number one. You should see me in my number two – it brings my hair line so low that I look positively simian.' He turned to the glass. 'No, it seems to be all right.'

I said, 'How fascinating everything to do with make-up is! And greasepaint has such a lovely smell. Could I sniff a bit, just to keep me going?'

He handed me a stick and said what a happy life I must have lived with my dear aunt, to be so blessedly un-shy. This had the effect of making me *feel* shy – I had never before considered the subject of shyness. But the moment passed and I was soon eagerly asking what I could understudy in the next play. He looked dubious, then said there was a maid's part– 'Though parlour maids need to be tall. Oh, well, we must manage something.'

Then the call boy tapped on the open door. Mr Crossway, giving me a last smile, said, 'Good night, my child,' and returned to the stage.

I waited a few minutes to let him make his entrance before I went back through the wings, so that I could listen to him then. I was extremely happy. Already I as good as had an understudy, though I wasn't going to be content with understudying a maid; I would end by understudying the part I had fancied in the morning. And Mr Crossway was very, very nice. It scarcely mattered that he wasn't romantic. (That toupee had been a bit of a shock, though.)

When at last I began my return journey I found the wings much darker than they had been before. A dimly lit scene must be in progress – yes, there was a lamp flooding moonlight through a window. Quietly I moved in the direction of the pass door. Mr Crossway, now back on stage, was again resisting the young actress. I heard him say: 'You naughty girl! How could I know you'd be waiting for me here?' Then there was a tap on a door and the leading lady's voice said: 'Who's in there? Why is this door locked?' Mr Crossway whispered: 'Keep dead quiet!' And at that perfectly chosen moment I tripped painfully over something hard and fell forward onto the lamp that was flooding the stage with moonlight. There was a very loud crash, and the moon went out.

I had barely picked myself up before Tom reached me from the prompt corner. Then Brice Marton came racing round from the far side of the stage. He positively dragged me to the iron door leading to the passage, flung me through, told me to wait, and then went back to the wings – presumably to see what could be done about the moon.

I waited in a state of dazed fury, with myself more than with Brice Marton. The minute he returned I said, 'I'm terribly, terribly sorry.'

'What the hell were you doing there? How did

you get past the stage door keeper?'

I realised he did not know I was working in the office so I explained. He barely heard me out before saying, 'Well, you can go back to Miss Lester and tell her– No, I'll tell her myself. Now get out.'

I stopped feeling apologetic and said furiously, 'Anyway, you've no right to have obstructions in the wings. What was that iron bar doing there?'

'It was a brace holding up the scenery, though God knows it'll take more than iron bars to do that if you're around. Now I've told you: get out!'

I said I should be only too happy to. 'But you'll have to unlock the pass door for me. I dropped Miss Lester's key when I fell.'

'You're not going through the pass door.'

He grabbed my arm and hurried me up the stairs to the stage door. As we reached it I freed myself from his grasp and said, 'But it's pouring. I shall get wet.'

'I don't care if you drown,' said Brice Marton, and went back into the theatre.

I made a dash for it, keeping close to the wall, and didn't get too badly soaked. The minute I was back with Miss Lester I burst into my story, finishing by asking if we could look through the spy-hole and see what had happened about the moon.

She said we should be too late. 'That moonlit scene only lasts a few minutes, even without your intervention. I'm entirely to blame, of course. There's a sort of unwritten law that one doesn't use the pass door during a performance, and though Brice doesn't mind when I do it I oughtn't to have sent you. He was quite justified in being angry.'

'But not in being so rude, surely? And he was so rough.'

'He has a violent temper. Well, I must patch things up between you. Not that you'll see much of him – unless you understudy; he rehearses the understudies.'

'How ghastly for them. And I *am* going to understudy. I've just asked Mr Crossway.'

She looked amused. 'Not bashful, are you?'

A sudden fear came to me. 'Oh, goodness, will Mr Crossway be angry about my accident?'

'Not with you. An accident's an accident. He might be annoyed with me, for sending you; but he's never annoyed with anyone for very long. What's the matter?' She had noticed I was rubbing one of my ankles. 'Did you twist it when you fell?'

'Only bruised it a bit. It's not at all bad.'

'Still, you must have been jarred. It was a horrid thing to happen on your first night here. I'm going to send you home in a taxi – you can charge it to petty cash as you got injured in the line of duty.' She rang up for a taxi, then said I must have coffee while I waited. A percolator was bubbling on a gas-ring.

The coffee smelt marvellous but didn't taste as it smelt; even with three lumps of sugar I found it bitter. She said that in future, I could have mine with milk. 'They've got milk in the bars, for the coffee trays. But believe me, strong black coffee does more to get one through the evening.'

I asked if she would be working late – and

remembered to tell her Mr Crossway wouldn't be coming up. She said in that case she'd clear out quite soon– 'Unless I wait till the curtain's down and then make our peace with Brice. Poor Brice, he really suffers when anything goes wrong on his precious stage.'

'I should have thought it was Mr Crossway's stage.'

'Do you know, in an odd way it isn't? Not as much as it's Brice's, when a performance is taking place. Brice is like the captain of a ship and Mr Crossway's merely the ship's owner. Your taxi will be here now. See you tomorrow at two-thirty. And don't worry about Brice Marton.'

I did worry a little – or rather, I still felt indignant. But soon I was enjoying the ride through the shining, rain-wet streets. We passed a coffee stall, the first I had ever seen, and in spite of my solid dinner I at once felt hungry. I asked the taxi-driver if coffee-stall food was good and he said he'd take me to a stall where I could get first-rate ham sandwiches – it turned out to be quite near the Club. I bought four sandwiches, one for me, one for Molly, one for Lilian and one for the taxi-driver. He said none of his fares had ever treated him to one before.

4

I can't believe my first spring and summer in London were as sunny as my mind's eye remembers them; one is apt to surround memories in weather that suits their mood. But apart from specific occasions – such as my first, torrentially wet evening at the Crossway, and an afternoon of downpour in July which had dramatic results – I can only visualise myself as walking through, or looking out on, sunlight; and in the evenings watching clear skies turn to a deeper blue when lights were first switched on. As for the nights, there were always very large stars – if not a new or a full moon, my two favourite kinds.

All this indicates that I was happy; and for much of the time I knew I was. In the early days I was a little troubled because I had not yet made a start as an actress, but even then I could pass what must surely be one valid test of happiness: I was reluctant to let each day come to an end. Back in the village, after the theatre, I would willingly have talked all night.

What did Molly, Lilian and I talk about? Their theatre, my theatre, their men friends (I had none), the Club, clothes ... never the state of the world. And why did we laugh so much? I fancy they laughed more than I did and very often *at* me, but it was affectionate laughter and it encouraged me to talk more and more. I feel sure they didn't think me witty; just funny. My schooldays and my amateur theatricals were funny. The fact that I had read many books was funny and my occasional use of unusual words was a positive scream – though Lilian would often add the word to her vocabulary. (Not so Molly, who almost invariably remarked, 'Our Mouse has swallowed the dictionary.') I was always telling them of things I had done which seemed to me quite normal but which doubled them up with laughter. Even my having come from Manchester was funny, though I could never discover why.

Frobisher, Macgregor and Lofty combined wistfulness at not quite being able to hear what we were laughing at with wistfulness for peace and quiet. We sometimes obliged by speaking louder; never by shutting up. But sooner or later Molly drove herself and us to silence and sleep by some such remark as, 'We shall all look *hags* tomorrow.'

In the mornings I was far more tired than I ever felt at night. Darling Charlotte the Harlot, after waking us by the delivery of breakfast trays, would go backwards and forwards between Molly's cubicle and mine making sure we did not go to sleep again. Lilian always woke at once; she thought it idiotic to pay for breakfast in bed and then let it go cold. Sleep seemed to me more desirable than food – until I was persuaded to sit up. Then the day took over and I was eager to breakfast, talk, wage the Battle of the Bathroom Door and get downstairs.

During my first couple of weeks I spent my mornings in the Club and got to know many members. Students and girls in jobs were mostly out, elderly members often came down late, so the company in the lounge seemed mainly composed of out-of-work actresses waiting for telephone calls from agents and managers, which seldom came. Some of these girls were doubly out of luck as they also awaited calls from elusive men friends. (So many members were in the midst of unhappy love affairs, so few in the midst of happy ones – and even the fortunate few put in a good deal of time waiting for telephone calls.) Every time the lounge door opened girls raised their heads hoping to hear their names called; then, when disappointed, sank back into apathy.

Molly would go round rather as if visiting the sick, enquiring about jobs and men. Lilian told the girls they should be more strong-minded. Molly once said to her, 'It's all very well for us, we're in work and not in love.' Then she added reflectively, 'Not that I wouldn't like to be in love, if I could find someone really suitable. He must be a tall man but not a *spindly* tall man. I want a *massive* tall man – and men of that type seem to prefer cossetting some tiny girl like you, Mouse. And I can't have any complications; so many of the girls here are in love with married men. I want someone who will call for me openly at the Club, and wait unashamedly in the hall.'

'Carrying a large bunch of roses,' said Lilian.

After that, 'Roses in the hall' became a Club expression, denoting the kind of love affair perpetually longed for but rarely achieved. As many of the girls were attractive one would have expected them to have shoals of admirers, but even Molly and Lilian, who were outstandingly pretty, could only boast of three– 'One each and one who doesn't know the difference between us,' said Lilian. 'And they're all dull and not even rich. It's my belief that all the best men are now snapped up by Society women. Actresses don't stand a chance; anyway, not if they're respectable – because Society women are so *willingly* immoral.' Lilian had a love-hate for Society women and would spend hours studying them in glossy magazines.

One morning in my third week she took me for a walk in Regent's Park. (Molly hated walking.) We went round the Outer Circle, where Lilian particularly longed to live, and amused ourselves by choosing houses for her. That afternoon I happened to learn from Miss Lester that Mr Crossway lived on the Outer Circle and, as it turned out, in Lilian's favourite terrace. The next morning we again went to Regent's Park and she decided his was her very favourite house. She insisted on walking past it so often that I was glad to feel sure he wouldn't be there to see us, rehearsals for the new play having started.

'I can't think why you don't find him exciting,' said Lilian. She had now been to one of our matinées. 'It's a pity he has a wife – she's tall, dark, and *very* Society. When men have wives it interferes with my thoughts.' She gave a last look at the house. 'I'd love to see inside it. Perhaps you'll get the chance to. I do think you're lucky, seeing so much of Rex Crossway.'

Actually, I had seen very little of him. At first he had been in and out of the office, but I had often been working in the Throne Room; and when rehearsals began, while the old play was still running, he saw Miss Lester in the mornings or she went to his dressing-room during the performance. As nothing more had happened about my understudying I asked her about it, but she said we must not worry Mr Crossway yet. 'He's got so much on his mind while he's playing and rehearsing – and directing. Just wait till the theatre goes dark.'

It went dark – a new expression to me – a few days later. Miss Lester and I went to the last night of the play, sitting at the back of the dress circle. I felt pleasantly in the know because I was aware that parts of the magnificent house were 'papered' – with very good-looking paper. Some of the best-looking was in a box, where Lady Warden sat; I had heard Miss Lester arranging this. She told me Lady Warden was about to go abroad– 'Her husband's going to govern some place.' I studied handsome Lady Warden with interest; no doubt she was one of Lilian's immoral Society women. Mr Crossway's 'tall, dark, *very* Society' wife was not there. According to Miss Lester, she seldom came to the Crossway except on first nights.

The play closed on a Saturday. When I got to the office on Monday I reminded Miss Lester that it was time to ask what part I was understudying. She looked distressed and said she had that morning talked to both Mr Crossway and Brice Marton about it. 'And there really is no part you could cover. You see, understudies need to be the same *type* as principals. And the girls in

84

this play are Society types.'

'Well, there's such a thing as acting, isn't there?' I said indignantly. 'And surely the maid doesn't have to be a Society type? Mr Crossway told me–'

'I reminded him of that. But he now agrees with Brice that you wouldn't be right. Parlour maids should be tall – and quite conventional.'

'Well, I could *act* conventionally.'

She smiled. 'One doubts that. Anyway, understudying's a soul-destroying job and you'd loathe rehearsals, with Brice drilling you into an imitation of whoever you were understudying.'

'I wouldn't let him.'

Again she smiled. 'So he suspected.'

'He's my enemy. Mr Crossway would have given me something.'

She did not deny this, merely said, 'Well, Brice has to take the responsibility for understudies and he's right in saying they mainly need to be just solidly reliable.'

'How dare he imply I'm not reliable – just because I fell over his blasted brace?'

She tried different tactics. 'Is it really so bad, working with me?'

I said of course it wasn't. 'I'm enjoying it. But I can't go on and on, wasting my youth.'

'Damn it, you've barely been here three weeks! Now cheer up. I'll tell you something that'll help. I asked Mr Crossway to give you some introductions and he says that, once the new play's launched, he'll think about it. And he said how much he liked you.'

I then had the grace to thank her for doing her best, but I doubt if I fully appreciated her invariable kindness to me. I was apt to take kindness for granted. This was mainly due to the confidence which was the outcome of my upbringing. I was like a much-loved dog that counts on affection from everyone. (Hence my astonished resentment of Brice Marton.)

It was true that I enjoyed working with Miss Lester. She preferred to cope with most letters herself so I did little typing and even less shorthand, though she sometimes dictated to me, simply so that I should not forget all I had learnt. As a rule I did quite interesting and varied jobs, answered the telephone, and occasionally went shopping for her in the small streets around the theatre. And if I had any time to spare I read plays; there were always piles of scripts on the old leather office sofa. They had already been turned down by Mr Crossway's play-reader but Miss Lester always feared he might have missed something good.

I tried not to sulk about not understudying but my depression must have been obvious. Miss Lester coaxed me into eating a specially good dinner at the pub that night. (I remember those pub dinners as richly brown, whereas Club lunches were likely to be pale beige or dim pink.) And she kept me amused by telling me about her early days at the Crossway. She seemed so modern that I was surprised she could remember Edwardian London. She said the atmosphere was very gay then and there were more flowers about.

I said, 'But there are lots now, surely? I'm always seeing them – in shops and on barrows and in flower women's baskets; and of course in

Regent's Park. Window boxes, too.'

'Are there? I don't seem to notice them now. Remind me to have those tulips in the hanging baskets replaced by geraniums.'

'Even though the theatre's dark?'

'Yes, indeed. One must always give a particularly good impression when a new play's in production. It encourages the advance booking.'

The theatre *felt* dark when we went back to the office. I asked if we were the only people working in it. She said Brice Marton would be back-stage somewhere – 'He spends as much time here as I do. We'll knock off early tonight.'

But we didn't. When we had finished work we sat talking over our coffee. I now drank it black – having got bored with carrying up milk – and was becoming an addict.

'Are you still miserable about not understudying?' she asked, pouring me a third cup.

'A bit. You see, while I thought I'd get an understudy, I could tell myself I'd made a start on the stage.'

'Shall I send you home in a petty-cash taxi?'

'No, thanks. I'm not eager to get back. I shall have to break my bad news to Molly and Lilian.'

'Poor Mouse.' I had told her the girls called me that and she now did, too. 'But we really should go. It's nearly eleven.'

On my way to the bus I decided to walk part of the way home; walking had often helped me during my aunt's long illness. I went now along Shaftesbury Avenue and saw the audiences coming out of several theatres. Not one theatre had I been to since arriving in London. I had been too absorbed to worry about this, still ... ought I to let myself settle down as a secretary? Those introductions from Mr Crossway might never materialise.

I intended to take a bus at Piccadilly Circus but they were so crowded that I went on walking. I was half-way up Regent Street when a large chauffeur-driven car stopped beside me. One of its rear doors opened and Mr Crossway leaned out and told me to get in. As I sat down beside him he said I ought not to be walking alone at this time of night.

I assured him I hadn't minded at all.

'Well, I mind for you. You're too young – and you look even younger than you are. Someone might kidnap you. What's the address of this Club you live at? I'll drive you home.'

He relayed the address to the chauffeur, then told me he had been to a first night. 'My wife went on to the management's party but I said I had work to do. There's nothing, nothing, worse than a first-night party after a doomed play.'

'Is this one doomed?'

'I fear so. And I keep thinking, "But for the grace of God there go I" – in three weeks. Oh, I've just remembered: you're probably out of friends with me. I take it Miss Lester's told you I can't let you understudy?'

I nodded. 'It was a bitter blow.'

'You're well out of it, really.' He then said everything Miss Lester had, about the dreariness of understudying.

'But even so, I'd have had all the interests of rehearsals – of seeing you bring the play to life.'

'You flatter me – and the play, judging by this

morning's rehearsal. But I'm always pessimistic at this stage of things.'

'I suppose I couldn't slip in sometimes, when Miss Lester could spare me?'

He said he was afraid not. 'No one unconnected with the play is supposed to be there. It makes the company jumpy if there are strangers around, not to mention what it does to me when I'm directing.'

'Would I count as "strangers"?'

He laughed. 'Well, not to me. But I couldn't break the rule for you.'

'Suppose I sat with the understudies? Then the company wouldn't notice me.'

'*No,* young woman. Not that you've yet learned to take no for an answer, for which I admire you. I wonder...'

As he didn't go on, I said after a few seconds, 'Did you have some idea?'

'Not a good one, I'm afraid – probably quite impracticable. Still, I'll talk to Miss Lester about it. Now don't ask questions, and don't count on anything. Tell me about this Club of yours. Have you made some pleasant friends?'

He firmly kept the conversation on the Club until we reached it. Then the chauffeur came round to help me out. I thanked Mr Crossway for bringing me home and begged him not to forget the idea he'd had, whatever it was. He said he wished he hadn't raised my hopes as there was only the barest chance... But he smiled very kindly as he said it.

When I talked to Molly and Lilian, up in the village, they thought my having been driven home by Mr Crossway quite outweighed the sad news that I wasn't understudying.

'Our Mouse is in with the Management,' said Molly.

'That usually means a girl is sleeping with the Management,' said Lilian.

'But our innocent Mouse has achieved it through charm and personality. Give her a slice of Veda bread.'

None of us could think what Mr Crossway's idea could be. My best guess was that he would let me sneak in at the back of the gallery sometimes. It would be better than nothing, I supposed; but it would hardly compensate for not being in the company. In spite of being 'in with the Management' – if I really was – I felt pretty depressed when I finally settled down to sleep.

5

The next morning, when I was in the lounge with the woeful waiters for the telephone, I was surprised to be called to the telephone myself.

It was Miss Lester, asking me to come to the office. She said she had news for me. 'Oh, don't get too excited – it's not an understudy. But I think you'll be pleased. Can you come now?'

'This minute. Can I take a petty-cash taxi – the one I didn't have last night?'

She laughed and said I could.

When I got to the office she told me Mr Crossway had suggested I might act as his secretary during rehearsals, sitting beside him and taking notes. 'He always needs someone in the last weeks of rehearsals and I usually have to do the job myself. It's agony being tied up when all my own work's waiting, but when I got him to try my assistant he hated her. I wonder if you realise what a compliment he's paying you.'

I said he was doing it out of kindness.

'A bit, perhaps. But he wouldn't do it if he didn't like you. I must give you some hints before you join him this afternoon. He doesn't really need you yet but he thought you might as well get started.'

I asked if it would be difficult for her to spare me. She said it would be easier than sparing herself to do the job. 'And there's not so much work here when the theatre's dark. Besides, I'm hoping you'll come back to me for the evenings, though it'll mean a long day. Of course you must have extra money. I'll arrange for it.'

I said that would be marvellous and I didn't mind how long I worked. Then she settled down to give me advice.

I gathered it was particularly important to hear what Mr Crossway said the first time he said it. 'He dislikes being asked to repeat anything but dislikes it even worse if one gets the notes wrong. Lean towards him the minute he starts to speak. If he's in a note-giving mood, use shorthand – and memory. Then write the whole note out in long-hand, very clearly, when you get the chance. Use two pads, one for your jottings, and one for the written-out note, which he'll take with him

91

when he talks to the cast after the rehearsal. He may want you with him then, to remind him what he *meant* by the note. Of course you may not know, but I usually do. If you concentrate on every line of the play you can generally follow what he means, and remember.'

'How can I concentrate on the play *and* write out my notes?'

'Sometimes there are breaks, when he discusses things with the cast or talks to Brice Marton, or something. And while I think of it, keep your notes short. He hates it if you sit beside him scribbling madly. And use your torch as little as possible; I mustn't forget to give you one. Oh, you'll just have to feel your way into the job.'

'I'm beginning to doubt if I can do it. No, I'm not. I shall manage.'

'For one startled second I thought you were losing your supreme self-confidence. We'd better have lunch now and I don't want to leave the office, so cut out and get us sandwiches.'

A little before two-thirty I went down to the stalls carrying two large note-pads, a tiny torch, and a supply of fiercely sharp pencils. Mr Crossway was not yet back from lunch but I could tell where he would be sitting by a rack, fixed to the back of a stall, with a script on it. I settled myself near this and watched the company assemble on the stage. I felt a pang when the understudies came through the pass door and sat at the back of the stalls. Taking notes might be interesting but it wasn't being an actress.

Then Mr Crossway came in, sat beside me and said, 'Well, are you pleased?' I said, 'Terribly.' He said, 'Good,' turned towards the stage, and the rehearsal began.

As he was still at a period when he interrupted the cast to say what he wanted, I guessed that the few notes he gave were just practice for me. After about twenty minutes he had to go on stage to play his own part. He told me to come with him and sit in the wings. When I got there I saw Brice Marton at a table in the prompt corner, with a script and various notepads in front of him. He gave me a civil but unsmiling 'hello' and got me a chair. It was the first time we had met since the night when he pushed me out of the stage door.

Every now and then Mr Crossway came over and gave me a note – as they were all unimportant I suspected he was merely establishing me in the eyes of the company. I wasn't introduced to anyone but several people smiled at me pleasantly. When the rehearsal ended I handed my notes to Mr Crossway, who said they were beautifully legible, and I could now rejoin Miss Lester and assure her I had managed very nicely. 'I believe she calls you Mouse, doesn't she? Well, you may tell her you've lived up to the name and been delightfully quiet and unobtrusive. I'm so thankful you're a silent breather. She once wished a girl on me who breathed like a steam engine.'

When I reported this to Miss Lester she said she was relieved– 'Oh, not about the breathing but as regards the unobtrusiveness. I forgot to warn you not to offer advice. Most girls would be too overawed to need such a warning, but you're not exactly backward in coming forward.'

I said I'd try to restrain myself.

'Yes, do. But it's a queer thing, though Mr Crossway loathes anyone to volunteer advice when he's directing, he'll sometimes ask for it from anyone who happens to be around: me, the understudies, cleaners, even the stage cat – yes, honestly; once when it got into the stalls and rubbed against his legs he was heard saying, "Oh, pussy, pussy, *what* can I do with the end of that act?" If ever he asks your opinion, answer quickly and decidedly – and stop the minute he's had enough. Never argue, and if he does take a hint from you, never remind him that he did. That's where authors make their mistake. They need to slide their ideas in and then praise the director for inventing them. We've got one thing to be thankful for with this play: the author's in America.'

'I should have thought authors could be a help at rehearsals.'

'So they can, sometimes. But I doubt if they make for any net gain when Mr Crossway's directing, because they paralyse his inventiveness. He says handling a play with an author watching is like teaching a child in front of its fond parents. Still, he'll soon be raging because the author isn't here to do bits of re-writing and agree to cuts.'

This proved true and in a few days Miss Lester was coping with mammoth cables to and from New York.

Mr Crossway gave me very few notes during the rest of the week so I was able to watch, listen and get to know the play thoroughly. It seemed remarkably like the one that had just come off. That had been about a faithless husband and a patient wife. The new play was about a faithless wife and a patient husband. In both plays a young girl made a dead set at Mr Crossway. But in the previous play the girl, though 'daring', had been childish enough to arouse Mr Crossway's nobler instincts. In the new play all his instincts were noble; and the girl, rather a dark horse until Act III, seriously menaced them, in a well-written scene in which she told him what a much better wife she would make than his present one. The errant wife, overhearing this scene, decided to reform. The girl's part was the one I had heard read at the audition. It had finally gone, not to the girl whose reading had impressed me but to a very tall young actress who seemed to me dull. Mr Crossway, however, appeared pleased with her.

Late one afternoon he dismissed the company except the girl and his own understudy, and said he would watch the last-act scene from the front, with the understudy playing his part. When they finished he praised the girl, said a few kind words to his understudy (who seemed to me awful) and told them they could go. Then, while picking up his script and notes, he said to me, 'Now you see why you couldn't have played that part.'

I said, 'I see why you think I couldn't, but I could really. And I'd make it funny.'

He laughed and said he was sure I would. 'But it isn't meant to be funny. She has to be a girl without a sense of humour.'

'But shouldn't that be made funny?'

He considered this seriously, then said, 'No, not in this case. Audiences often like characters who make them laugh, and they mustn't like this girl or it will be bad for the wife, who has to win sympathy at the end of the play. Still, it's an interesting idea. Have you any more you'd like to wish on me – especially about my own performance? The director gets no direction.'

Miss Lester had advised me to answer any request for an opinion quickly and decidedly. I practically shot my answer at him. 'I think you should be more dramatic.'

'Good gracious! And I always feel I'm overacting – as I was made to, in my early days, when my father directed me. *Where* should I be more dramatic? No, don't tell me yet.'

He looked up at the stage, where Brice Marton and Tom Morison were waiting for him, called to them that he would be up in a moment, and then steered me out of the stalls and up a narrow staircase, into the little sitting-room behind the royal box. Here he sat on the edge of a gilt table and said: 'Now, shoot!'

I plunged into one of his most important scenes; I already knew much of the play off by heart through repeatedly hearing it. But I had to pull up at last and say, 'I don't quite know that speech yet.'

'You know it better than I do. How I envy such a memory.'

Anxious not to waste this God-given opportunity both to help him and demonstrate my talent, I pressed on. 'Then there's a bit in Act II...'

He made no effort to stop me. I finally broke off because I saw he was shaking with suppressed laughter.

'Of course I'm deliberately exaggerating a little,' I said deflatedly.

'You're exaggerating gloriously. My dear, delightful child, you want to turn me into my barnstorming grandfather.'

'Of course I don't! But I do hanker for a touch of you as Charles Surface.'

He sighed. 'You and all the nice old ladies who come to matinées. I keep that portrait in the foyer to make them happy. My dear, those days are over. And perhaps I do fall backwards a bit to *show* they're over for me. Bravura's so against the trend of modern acting.'

About to argue, I remembered Miss Lester had warned me not to. So I checked myself – it was an effort – and apologised for ranting. (Not that *I* thought I'd ranted.)

He said soothingly, 'Oh, you had to, in order to convey your meaning. Now I must go and confer with my stage staff. You wouldn't believe the time we spend finding chairs with legs the right height to suit my leading lady's legs, clocks with the right kind of chime, off-stage effects that make the right kind of noise.' He held the door of the little room open for me, then concluded, 'Thank you for an honest opinion, which I may have taken to heart more than you think.'

The next day I eagerly watched for a change in his performance but I could see none, then or ever.

We had now reached a time when the company had to do without scripts. I had been getting more and more interested in the play. Miss Lester had told me this would happen– 'Unless a play's absolutely awful, you like it better and better. But then it gets set-backs.' It certainly got one now, as people floundered for words and kept beginning speeches with 'Well', to give themselves an extra second to think. Some of them also held things up while they made excuses and swore they had known every word last night. There was one man who usually shouted: 'Don't tell me! Don't tell me! I've got it – no, I haven't. Tom, what *is* the blasted line?' Poor Tom, on the book, was highly unpopular for prompting too soon or too late. Mr Crossway was particularly indignant if prompted while making a deliberate pause. Once, when Tom was called to the telephone, I did the prompting myself, from memory. I prided myself on knowing Mr Crossway's pauses; but he put in new ones, so I came to grief.

He knew very little of his part. Miss Lester said he always had difficulty in memorising – 'He won't concentrate; too many things on his mind. I suppose he's showering notes on you now?'

He was indeed, and he had taken to having me with him when he talked to the company; sometimes he referred to me as his little shadow. Once, when we had a discussion about what he had meant by a note and he decided I was right, he said he would bow to his co-director. The company must have seen that he treated me with kindness and amusement; perhaps for that reason, they did too.

As people got steadier with their lines the play came to life again, especially when Mr Crossway, desperate at his lack of memory, seized a script and read his part. Then we suffered a worse set-back: the scenery arrived.

I had been looking forward to this. But nothing was what I had expected or – more importantly – what the company had expected. They complained that distances seemed different (though they had been clearly marked out on the stage floor). Stairs now had to be climbed instead of floated up mentally; doors had to be *used* – and so on. As for me, the whole play seemed unreal because my imagination was no longer giving it an extra dimension.

The worst set-back of all came near the end of rehearsals, when Mr Crossway told the company to take a whole day off to study lines and cope with final fittings of clothes, while he worked on lighting the play. I thought it insane to waste so much time when rehearsals were desperately needed, but Miss Lester said the lighting could barely be done in one day.

She did not think Mr Crossway would need me, and hoped he wouldn't as she felt sure I should be bored. He decided I might as well be around, and I certainly was bored. It took hours to set the most ordinary lighting effects, and anything out of the ordinary led to arguments between Mr Crossway and Brice Marton, arguments between Brice Marton and the electrician, dreary hold-ups – and a result I barely noticed.

I was given no notes and sent on no errands and Mr Crossway talked to me very little. Sometimes he asked my opinion but rarely took any notice of it; effects I hankered for were usually said to be impossible because they would 'upset the balance', or some such – to me – meaningless phrase. So I did wonder why he wanted me there. The nearest I got to understanding was at the end of the very long day, when he thanked the understudies for so patiently standing-in for the principals, to be carefully lit. He then gave me a smile and said, 'And thank you for your comfortable presence.'

The next day rehearsals were resumed and everything was chaotic as Mr Crossway was now without both his script and most of his lines. After the rehearsal he came up to the office and told Miss Lester to get him out of a party he'd said he would go to. 'I must get these lines into my head if I have to sit up all night.'

Miss Lester asked if he would like either of us to work with him, giving him his cues, but he said he'd rather fight it out alone, just staring at the script, as what memory he still had was photographic.

'Do you think you really can be word-perfect by the first night?' I asked, dubiously and not exactly tactfully.

He laughed. 'I'd better be – otherwise you will prompt me in ringing tones from whatever part of the house you're in.'

'Do I come to the first night?'

'Of course. Miss Lester will arrange it.'

But after he had gone, she advised against it. 'I never go myself – I mean, I never have a seat. One gets claustrophobia, especially if anything goes wrong. I always roam about, to get the feeling of the house. There's usually something one can perch on or lean on. You could be with me, if you like.'

I said I would. 'Anyway, I couldn't go in a grand seat as I haven't a really grown-up evening dress.'

'We must find you something in our wardrobe, and have it altered when the wardrobe mistress isn't so busy. By the way, Mr Crossway wondered if you'd like to go to the first-night party at his house. But I don't think you'd enjoy it; there'll be so many people you don't know. And the atmosphere will be ghastly if the first night hasn't gone well. Nothing would get me there. I always sit up here until the small hours and then go out and get the early editions of the papers. Keep me company if you fancy it – though do go to the party if you want to.'

I should have been glad to see inside that Regent's Park house but I couldn't go without a real evening dress. So I said waiting up for the notices would be more exciting.

Mr Crossway knew more about his lines the next morning and the rehearsal went well. But in the afternoon there was a dress parade which upset most of the actresses; the leading lady actually wept. The famous dressmaker who had designed the clothes was calm; I gathered such scenes were usual. The wigmaker was disappointed that Mr Crossway wouldn't wear a number three toupee, with a beautiful deep wave. 'Makes you look ten years younger,' said the wigmaker. 'I don't want to look ten years younger,' said Mr Crossway. 'I just want to look better-looking. My God, man, you've given me a kiss-curl.'

After the dress parade we rehearsed until late in the evening. Mr Crossway's lines again forsook him – but came back on duty next morning when we had an almost uninterrupted run-through. Then the company were dismissed until the dress rehearsal, due to start at six-thirty. The minute they were off the stage Mr Crossway decided to make some changes in the lighting. So the dress rehearsal didn't start till eight.

It ended at two in the morning, by which time I didn't see how the play could open the next night. Everything conceivable went wrong and not one person gave a good performance. Miss Lester, who sat with me, said she had seen worse dress rehearsals – 'But not *much* worse, I admit. Still, if things had gone well one would be just as worried, because that's unlucky. A good dress rehearsal's supposed to mean a bad first night.'

'Well, if that works in reverse we should have a marvellous night tomorrow.'

There was no rehearsal the next day but Mr Crossway never left the theatre. He was still changing lighting and even having bits of scenery altered. I was on duty, running messages and bringing him cups of tea. Late in the afternoon I asked if it would help if I sat on the opposite side of the stage from Tom, ready to prompt. He considered this, then said he must leave it to Tom. 'I did have an extra prompter once, who spoke through the fireplace. But it was confusing – and I kept looking up the chimney. Don't worry too much. I *have* weathered other first nights.'

But I did worry. By the time the audience was coming in I felt quite sick with nervousness. I told Miss Lester, adding, 'I suppose it's silly of me.'

'Silly or not, I'm just the same – after all the

first nights I've been at. It's so awful being afraid there'll be catastrophes and knowing one can't possibly help.'

She suggested I should go down to the street to see some of the fashionable first nighters – I could not stand in the foyer as I was not in evening dress. 'But come back when the bells begin ringing to get people to their seats. Then you'll be in time to see the curtain go up.'

Outside I found quite a crowd of onlookers but I managed to get a good view. It was a fine June evening, not yet dark. Most of the women arriving were luxuriously dressed in short, shapeless frocks of pastel shades. Almost every head was shingled. There were choker pearls round almost every neck and flowers on almost every shoulder, with fur wraps dropped low enough to show them. I did not particularly admire any of the clothes but I did feel wistful for a really beautiful evening dress.

Bells rang. I hurried up to Miss Lester and we slipped into the back of the dress circle just as the house lights went out. The curtain rose.

It still staggers me to remember how smoothly that performance went and how swiftly I stopped feeling nervous; my heart ceased pounding soon after Mr Crossway came on. He gave the impression of being completely at ease, and before long I felt sure he would go on giving it – which he did, even when inventing lines instead of remembering them. Act I went unbelievably fast, as did the whole play, really, now there were no interruptions. The leading lady had to be prompted once in Act II, but otherwise I cannot remember any hitches throughout the evening. The third act went best of all and when the curtain finally fell the applause was terrific. I asked Miss Lester if all Crossway first-night receptions were warm. She said they were apt to *sound* warm– 'But don't worry. This is genuine warmth.'

Mr Crossway made a speech, finishing by telling the audience he was its humble and obedient servant. To me, that speech was the high moment of the evening. I fully realised he had played most skilfully but I still thought he under-acted and lacked some quality of magnetism he'd once had. And there, suddenly, it was, in his speech of thanks. Miss Lester told me it was one of his few gestures of respect for the past to make the same kind of speech his father had always made.

Back in the office, I said: 'What do we do now?'

'We just wait. I'll make some coffee.'

Soon the audience was out of the theatre and the last car door was slammed. Then Mr Fortescue came up and said the Press seemed pleased– 'Though that doesn't mean they won't go back to Fleet Street and write a stinker of a notice.' Not long after that, Mr Crossway dashed in, dropped a sheaf of first-night telegrams on Miss Lester's desk and asked us how we thought things had gone. We both said wonderfully well and I said he hadn't dried up once.

'Some of my inventions were a bit startling, though. Thank God the author wasn't there. You girls ought to be drinking champagne, not coffee. I shall bring you some tomorrow as you won't come to my party. Bless you both. Good night.'

We heard voices, and cars driving away as the

company left for the party. Then everything became as quiet as it always was at the Crossway very late at night. I was quite startled when I heard footsteps.

'That'll be Brice Marton,' said Miss Lester. 'He always waits with me until we go out for the papers.'

'Does he know I'll be here?'

'I didn't mention it but he probably takes it for granted. Why? Have you two had any more rows?'

'We haven't had *anything*. He's rarely said a word to me beyond "hello" and when he managed that he didn't manage a smile.'

'I doubt if he deliberately didn't smile. He probably had something on his mind.'

He came in then and did not smile at either of us but I hardly blamed him; he looked absolutely exhausted.

'Give me some of that horrible black brew of yours,' he said to Miss Lester.

'Wouldn't you rather have whisky?'

'If I drink whisky now, I shall go to sleep. Just let me have some coffee.'

While he was drinking it she asked him how much sleep he'd had the previous night. He said two hours – 'And three, the night before. And there won't be much of tonight left after I've taken the papers to Mr C. Oh, well, one survives.'

'But surely things aren't always as bad as they've been this time?' I spoke to Miss Lester, rather than to him. 'I mean, the scenery having to be altered and the lighting reset or whatever they call it. And – oh, everything.'

'Things are often much worse,' said Miss Lester.

'And you can't really blame Mr C.,' said Brice Marton. 'He has the sets up earlier than most managements. But something always goes wrong. If the scenery's perfect there's a last-minute cast change or trouble with the stage hands. I only remember one play when everything went smoothly and that came off in a week.'

He and Miss Lester began chatting about past productions, and I just listened. I noticed that he always referred to Mr Crossway as 'Mr C.' and with a satirical edge to his voice. I began to think he didn't like Mr Crossway; and once I got the idea, it fitted with his behaviour at rehearsals. His manner had always been civil but he had never responded to the warmth and humour in Mr Crossway's. Sometimes Mr Crossway had lost his temper but never for long. Brice Marton had never lost his, but he had often stone-walled Mr Crossway in the most uncompromising way. And when Brice Marton had said something was impossible, Mr Crossway had accepted this. I wondered if it was usual for an important manager to be on such terms with his quite young stage manager.

Now, as I sat drinking cup after cup of black coffee, I took a good look at Brice Marton – something I had never troubled to do before. I had thought of him as dark, slight, not very tall and not in the least striking. I now realised he had unusually fine eyes, dark brown and very sombre, seeming almost too large for his small, neat features. His skin, like his eyes, was brown;

his hair black and smooth. Molly, Lilian and I had recently amused ourselves deciding what animals girls at the Club resembled, and I suddenly saw Brice Marton as a Manchester Terrier. My aunt had bought one, a slim black and brown dog, when I was five and it had nipped me quite painfully; and though we came to love each other, I remained a trifle wary. It died, of natural causes, when it was ten – to my sorrow but to the considerable relief of visiting tradesmen.

Well, Brice had certainly started by biting me but I couldn't see us coming to love each other. I couldn't even like him, though I did feel respect for the authority he had shown at rehearsals. As for his liking me, at the moment, as so often, he simply wasn't seeing me.

I think it was around two o'clock when we went out for the papers. The small streets round the theatre were utterly deserted. As we passed some shuttered shops I said, 'We might be back in the eighteenth century.'

'It's time some of these houses came down,' said Brice Marton. 'They're little better than slums.'

I said I'd hate to see them go. 'They're a real link with the past.'

'The one I have rooms in certainly is,' said Brice Marton. 'Not that slums are a novelty to me. I was brought up in one.'

'You should grow out of boasting about that, Brice,' said Miss Lester.

We went to some office where stacks of morning papers had already arrived. It astonished me that notices could be written, printed and distributed so quickly. We read them, standing under a lamp post. They were all good, though one critic said: 'Mr Crossway, having recently had a success with a pleasant play, has had it written again, by a different author.' However, the notice went on to say that, as the new play was rather better than its predecessor, all should be well. Mr Crossway's acting was praised by every critic, though one of them wrote: 'Of course, he no longer acts; he merely *behaves*. And in spite of all the ease and charm, and the skill that disguises skill, there are some of us who miss the dashing juvenile of his father's company.' I was glad to think it wasn't only the old ladies at matinées who felt as I did.

When we had finished reading, Miss Lester asked Brice Marton if he thought the new play was better than the last one. He said he found them equally bad. 'But I'm beginning to think I don't like any plays or any players.' She laughed and said he'd feel different after a good sleep; then added, 'Though you haven't too much talent for liking things or people.'

'None whatever,' said Brice Marton. 'I only like them in spite of myself.'

They were half joking; but only half.

After that, we managed to get two taxis. Miss Lester took one and asked Brice Marton to drop me at the Club on his way to Regent's Park. As we drove off I said, to make conversation, that the notices wouldn't spoil Mr Crossway's party. Brice Marton gave a grunt of agreement. Then we remained silent until, after a good five minutes, he said abruptly:

'I owe you an apology.'

'Goodness, what for?' I was utterly astonished.

'For losing my temper with you, that night you fell over the brace.'

'Heavens, that's ages ago. I'd forgotten it.' I hadn't, but it seemed the civil thing to say.

'Nonsense. Neither you nor I could possibly have forgotten it. You had Miss Lester's permission to come back-stage. You merely had an *accident,* for which you instantly apologised. It was unforgivable of me (a) not to accept your apology and (b) to lose my temper with you.'

'Well, I forgive it, anyway.'

'I don't. I never forgive myself for losing my temper – except when I lose it deliberately, as I have to sometimes in my job, and then it isn't really lost. When I lose *control* I chalk it up against myself – forever, really. But one can't go on brooding about it. Sooner or later I straighten the account as well as I can and try not to let it happen again.'

He seemed so seriously worried that I asked why he hadn't got it off his mind before. He said the opportunity hadn't arisen– 'Besides, I should have found it difficult to apologise to anyone these last weeks, when I needed all the authority I could muster.' I was surprised he should talk so freely, until I guessed it must be part of 'straightening the account' – and straightening it less with me than with himself.

'Well, you mustered plenty for rehearsals,' I told him. 'And you never lost your temper once.'

He said, 'Thank you for noticing that,' then relapsed into silence.

After a few minutes I felt him leaning on me

heavily. I instantly remembered hearing, on my first night at the Club, 'My God, Frobisher, how that man kissed me in the taxi!' and it flashed into my mind that Brice Marton might have been attracted to me on sight and been fighting not me but himself. I found this idea exciting. I also found that Brice Marton had merely gone to sleep.

When we got to the Club I woke him and warned him he would soon be at Mr Crossway's. He thanked me and said good-night, but without the nicker of a smile. In spite of the conversation we'd had I did not feel we were on fully friendly terms; just civil terms.

The elderly night porter let me in and said: 'What hours you young ladies do keep,' then reminded me to write my name in the breakfast-in-bed book. I thankfully remembered Miss Lester had said I need not come into the theatre in the morning. When I tiptoed into the sleeping village the dawn was breaking. I undressed without putting the light on.

6

When I got to the Crossway the next afternoon the whole theatre radiated success. Bill-posters were pasting up extracts from the favourable notices, there were rows of camp stools outside the pit and gallery doors, and a queue in the foyer waiting to book seats. Up in the office Miss Lester was typing 'thank you' letters for Mr Crossway's first-night telegrams. She used a formula for most of these (though he often added a personal post-script) so I was able to help with the typing.

'It's such bliss to feel we've a real hit,' she said. 'You can't imagine how the atmosphere would be today if we'd had a flop or even a very tentative success. Everyone would be so hypocritically cheerful. Now we're all genuinely glowing – except, of course, the men in the box-office.'

'Why, what's wrong with them?'

'Oh, nothing, inwardly. But outwardly they preserve the utmost grimness – I mean, to the public. They think that if they're even civil, people won't believe the play's a real success. Happy box-offices always behave as if they're repelling invaders.'

In the middle of the afternoon Mr Crossway breezed in with the champagne he had promised us. He dictated some of the more important 'thank you' letters, then said he must go and see Brice Marton about various small changes. He paused beside my desk to say, 'Well, you won't have to work such long hours now. But I shall miss my little co-director,' then went on his way while I was saying I should miss him, too. I stared after him.

'What's the matter?' said Miss Lester.

'It's just dawned on me that I *shall* miss him – that is, miss rehearsals and being in on the production.'

She said she'd thought I'd feel that. 'But you'll soon get over it. And Mr Crossway says I can send you to a theatre every week or so – which reminds me, I've looked out an evening dress in

111

the wardrobe; I'm almost sure you'll like it. The wardrobe mistress will alter it as soon as she's finished the dresses for the understudies.'

I thanked her and tried to settle down to typing. But I must have looked gloomy, because before long she said, 'Would you like to cheer yourself with the champagne?'

'What, in the middle of the afternoon?'

'Some people drink it at any time of day. Personally I rather dislike it; so unless you do want to tackle it now, why not take it to the Club and share it with Molly and Lilian?'

I said I'd be glad to, as they were in need of cheering, having recently heard that their show would soon be coming off.

When I displayed the champagne in the village that night Lilian said she was more and more sure Mr Crossway was in love with me. This had been a favourite joke of hers for weeks. She and Molly were already full of tea so they did not fancy champagne just then. 'We'll keep it until we've something to celebrate,' said Lilian. 'And that bottle looks good for a wish.' There was a vogue in the Club for wishing on almost anything. She patted the bottle and said: 'Champagne, champagne, bring us something to celebrate with you soon.' As things turned out we felt the need of it soon but not on an occasion of celebration.

The very next morning, just after Charlotte had brought my breakfast tray, I heard a loud moan from Molly's cubicle followed by a wail of, 'Oh, no! Oh, God, how awful!'

Both Lilian and I yelled, 'What is it?' We got no answer; Molly just went on wailing, 'Oh, no!' I hastily moved my breakfast tray and dashed in to her, colliding with Lilian at the cubicle door. Molly was sitting up in bed holding a letter. She looked at us and said in a tone of the utmost tragedy:

'Girls, I'm a bastard.'

Afterwards I thought it was funny but I didn't then. And I guessed what Molly meant even before Lilian had snatched the letter from her and begun to read it aloud. It was from a firm of solicitors who wrote on behalf of Molly's father's parents: her grandparents, but they were never referred to as that. They wished her to know that when she became twenty-one, in a few weeks, they proposed to stop the small allowance they had made her since her mother's death and, instead, pay her a lump sum of a thousand pounds. And buried in the legal phraseology of the letter was the fact – which the solicitors obviously thought Molly was aware of – that her father had never married her mother. The words 'natural daughter of' were used several times.

'But, Molly darling, why do you mind so much?' I asked when Lilian had finished reading aloud.

Molly glared through her tears. 'Can't you understand? I'm a *bastard*.'

'Nonsense,' said Lilian. 'You're just illegitimate.'

'They're the same thing,' said Molly.

'They're not,' said Lilian. 'Bastards are only in history or Shakespeare. And they're always men.'

I said I thought there could be female bastards. 'But that's a nicer name in the letter: "a natural daughter".'

'Let me read the letter again,' said Molly.

We waited while she read it. I felt it must be an unusual letter to be read through a lorgnette.

'It serves me right for being a snob,' said Molly. 'I was proud because my father came of a good family, and proud of his D.S.O. Wouldn't you two mind if you were in my position?'

'Of course not,' said Lilian heartily; then added, 'Well, a bit, perhaps – but not the way you do.'

I said, quite truthfully, that I'd find it romantic. 'And it's more exciting to have an unmarried D.S.O. for a father than a married chartered accountant, as I had.'

'Chartered accountants can make a lot of money,' said Lilian, with interest.

'Well, my father doesn't seem to have. Did you never suspect, Molly?'

'Never. Of course he spent very little time with us – he was so often away with his regiment. We just stayed in our little house near Ranelagh. Now I see why Mother asked me to use her maiden name when I went on the stage. I thought it was because she'd acted under it herself and wanted it carried on. But it's really the only name I'm entitled to.' Again the tears flowed.

Charlotte came in. She had been doing Frobisher's cubicle and made no bones about having heard everything. Kneeling by the bed, she took Molly in her arms and assured her there was nothing to be ashamed of 'You're just a love-child, Miss Molly. We ought to have guessed it from your looks. All the most beautiful babies are love-children.' Molly wept more and more.

'Oh, stop it, Charlotte, you're making her worse,'

said Lilian; then threw me a harassed look. 'I must pull her together somehow. We've a matinée this afternoon.'

'How about the champagne?' I suggested.

'Wonderful! And it's terribly smart to drink it in the morning. But it ought to be iced.'

'I could get bits of ice from the kitchen,' said Charlotte.

'One's supposed to put the champagne in the ice, not the ice in the champagne,' said Lilian. 'Still – yes, see what you can do. And borrow some wire cutters in case we need them and some champagne glasses; tooth mugs aren't quite the thing.'

'And bring a glass for yourself,' Molly called after Charlotte, showing signs of recovery.

Charlotte came back with glasses and wire cutters but only a meagre supply of ice; still, it tinkled cheerfully and helped to make what I thought a very pleasant drink. Lilian praised the champagne knowledgeably, adding that of course it would be good, coming from Rex Crossway. She let us all have a glass and a half, then took a firm hand with Molly, refusing to give her any more. 'Enough's enough. You're looking positively blowsy.'

It was the right word. Molly's red hair was in disorder, her baby face was flushed with crying and champagne, and her shawl and nightgown had slipped off one shoulder. I suddenly thought of Moll Flanders and Moll Davis. Slightly flushed by champagne myself, I said: 'Here's to Moll Byblow,' then wondered if she would mind; but she didn't. A few minutes later, Lilian said,

'Now up you get, Moll Byblow,' and Molly had her nickname, as firmly as Lilian had Lily de Luxe and I had Mouse – though only rarely were Molly and Lilian addressed by their nicknames; these were mainly used when speaking *of* the girls, as: 'See if you can hurry Moll Byblow,' or 'Madam Lily de Luxe won't like that.'

Molly showed no signs of lasting distress about her illegitimacy but it had an effect on her manner. She discarded her half-playful and never offensive superiority and, though she still used her lorgnette – she had to – she no longer tilted her head back when she looked at people through it. I feel sure she was not conscious of any of this; it simply emanated from some inner loss of confidence. And from then onwards Lilian's behaviour to her was more dominating – Lilian got into her stride that very morning by taking her to the writing-room and making sure the thousand pounds was accepted. 'Just in case your illegitimate grandparents change their minds.'

Yes, Lilian was certainly in for a period of ascendancy. When I got back from the theatre that night she informed me that the three of us were going to leave the Club for a month and share a flat in a mews. A friend had called on her after the matinée to offer it.

'She's going to be away with a concert party and she says we can have the flat rent free if we'll water her window-boxes and forward letters and let her know if anyone important rings up. And it's a darling place – I went there to a party once – small, but terribly amusing. It's a *converted*

116

mews flat, of course – in Belgravia, couldn't be smarter.'

There would be room for us all as there were two beds in the bedroom and a divan in the sitting-room. 'It'll be fun cooking our meals,' Lilian went on. 'And think how we'll save with no rent to pay. That's important as our show will so soon be off.'

'I wonder when my thousand pounds will come,' said Molly.

'When it does you're going to invest it,' said Lilian. She then turned to me a trifle huffily. 'Of course you don't have to come, Mouse, but I thought you'd want to. It's bound to be terrifically exciting.'

I felt I could do with excitement. Life at the Crossway was now very flat, with a lot of work to be done and no time, even, to look at the play through the spy-hole. So I accepted Lilian's invitation enthusiastically.

Molly had already agreed, though she was troubled at the thought of losing our cubicles in this particular village and the services of Charlotte the Harlot. However, we didn't have to, as the Club secretary promised we could have them back in a month. We were, it seemed, in her good books because we paid our bills every week instead of waiting to be nagged.

So we had our trunks from the box-room and packed away everything but a suitcase of summer clothes each, as Lilian thought there might not be too much cupboard space. She said she wished she could remember the flat better – 'Though in a way it's more fun not to.'

We moved on the following Sunday afternoon, Lilian's friend having gone off that morning, after telephoning to say where we should find the key. As our taxi entered the mews Lilian cried: 'There! You can tell the flat by the window-boxes. Aren't they sweet?'

There were no other window-boxes and no other gaily painted front door. Probably all the other flats were occupied by chauffeurs or servants from the huge houses backing onto the mews.

We paid the taxi off and then Lilian got the key from the highly original hiding place of under the mat. When the door was opened we faced steep, narrow stairs so close that we could not shut the door until two of us were on our way up.

'Quaint, isn't it?' said Lilian.

'Smells of kippers,' said Molly as she mounted the stairs.

I followed her, with my suitcase bumping into the wall. It was almost dark, once Lilian got the door closed. She called up, 'I think the kitchen's ahead of you.'

'I'm in it,' called Molly. 'It's just a landing – not even that, really; just the top of the stairs. I'll move out so that Mouse can move in.'

She went through a door and I stepped up into the kitchen. It seemed that anyone using the gas-stove or sink would be in danger of falling downstairs backwards. I followed Molly into the sitting-room. It was quite pretty, with framed Underground posters on the walls. The afternoon sun was pouring in and the whole effect was cheerful, except for the remains of a kippery breakfast on the table. There was a note propped against the tea-pot saying: 'Sorry couldn't wash up or make the beds. Overslept and had to dash for train. I've left milk and bread and you can use any of my provisions if you'll replace them. Please pay laundryman tomorrow and I'll settle later.'

We went on into the bedroom, where there were two unmade beds. 'She must have had some girl friend here,' said Lilian.

'Not unless the girl friend used shaving soap,' said Molly.

'Nice to have a fitted washbasin,' said Lilian, ignoring the shaving soap. She opened a narrow door. 'This'll be the bathroom.'

But it was merely the smallest lavatory I ever saw. In order to close the door from the inside one had to edge past the seat, in danger of banging one's head against the cistern.

'Then where *is* the bathroom?' said Lilian.

'There isn't anywhere for it to be,' said Molly.

'But I'm sure she said there was a bath – and plenty of hot water.'

Just then I found the bath, under a bed. It was a round shallow rubber bath with a coil of piping curled up inside it.

'Oh, *I* see,' said Lilian brightly. 'One pipes the hot water from that dear little geyser over the washbasin. What bliss it'll be, not having to put pennies in the bathroom door. Which reminds me, there's a gas-meter somewhere that takes shillings.'

There was a fairly large cupboard only half full of its owner's clothes, and a half-emptied chest of drawers. We should have to keep most of our things in our cases.

'Before we unpack anything, we'll get the flat straight,' said Lilian. 'You do the washing up, Mouse, while we make the beds. I saw a pile of sheets on the divan.'

The washing up was not my idea of fun as the sink only had a cold tap; and when I put the kettle on, the gas ran out. But I found the meter, daintily be-frilled, put in a shilling and finished my job. Then I got tea ready. When I carried the tray into the sitting-room the windows were open and the smell of kippers had gone out. But a very peculiar smell was coming *in*.

I tried to analyse it while we had tea. I could detect petrol and a whiff of dustbins. But there was something else. At last I said, 'It's crazy, but there's a smell of horses.'

'Nonsense,' said Lilian. 'There can't have been horses here for years.'

'Our Mouse is psychic,' said Molly. 'She's smelling the ghosts of horses.'

'No, truly. There's a leathery smell and a smell of manure.'

Neither of them believed me but I was right. All the stables in that mews were now used as garages except the one under us. That housed some tradesman's horse. And either it was an insomniac horse or it was a confirmed sleep-stamper. Night after night I was fated to lie awake listening to it. And because I lay awake I learned, for the first time, how uncomfortable beds could be.

All the three beds were uncomfortable but they were uncomfortable in different ways. And Lilian decided it would only be fair if we each spent a week in each bed (and tossed up for the fourth week). So just when one had got the knack of avoiding the broken spring in the divan one had to learn how to dodge the lumps in one of the bedroom beds, and then cope with the uniform hardness of the other (here a cushion under the hip-bone helped). Lilian also insisted that we should each put in a week on kitchen work and then move on to other housework. Being small, I could fit into the kitchen fairly well, whereas poor large Molly invariably bumped herself. One day, glaring around the kitchen (or rather *at* it; 'around' was hardly a word one could apply to that tiny strip) she remarked, 'This place is supposed to have been converted. But if you ask me, it's still a heathen.' Ever afterwards, the mews flat was referred to as 'The Heathen'.

Lilian, to whom the past is always sacred but often amusing too, insists that a very funny book could be written about The Heathen. She is wrong. Our discomforts weren't particularly funny. One might work up something about Molly's attempt to empty the rubber bath single-handed. (The horse below must have thought it was out in the rain.) And there was a night when a drunk friend of The Heathen's owner, having had the front door shut on him, stood below our windows wailing, 'But I'm always *welcome* to a bed here.' And Molly and Lilian got a laugh when I fed the horse with sugar and it neatly removed my green hat. But for the most part we endured a month of bad nights, bad meals and sometimes very bad tempers.

I, at least, was at the theatre in the afternoons

and evenings, and I got a good brown dinner at the pub. Lilian and Molly spent far more time at The Heathen than I did, particularly after their show closed at the end of our first week; and there was no good cheap restaurant near. Sometimes they went all the way to the Club for dinner. And once, during very hot weather and a plague of flies in the mews, they tried to get our cubicles back. But the Club was full. We just had to stick our month out.

During the last few days of it, we worked hard getting The Heathen into perfect order; well, as perfect as The Heathen would permit. We cleaned and polished, refurbished the window boxes, bought flowers and provisions. The Heathen's owner had written to say she was bringing a new friend with her, ever such a nice boy. 'She hasn't had too much luck with her boy friends,' said Lilian, 'so we'll do our best to start her off well this time.'

At last it was Sunday morning. We put on clean sheets, washed up, packed, and all signed a glowing note of thanks to leave behind us. (After all, we hadn't paid any rent.) Then we bumped our cases down the narrow stairs, slammed the door, put the key under the mat and trudged along the mews. As the girls were now out of work we felt we must go by bus instead of taxi.

'God bless the old Club,' said Molly, as we entered the hall – only to learn we were not expected until next day and there was no room for us.

'But we left on a Sunday, for a month, so we come back on a Sunday,' said Lilian.

The secretary was off duty so the housekeeper was sent for. Her theory was that we must have left a day earlier than the secretary expected us to. Anyway, the booking sheet showed we were not due until Monday and our cubicles were occupied; so was every bed in the whole Club.

Molly suggested we should sleep on sofas. The housekeeper would not hear of it. She said, 'You'll just have to go to a hotel,' and left us flat.

We went down to lunch seething with indignation. None of us knew of a cheap hotel and none of us could afford an expensive one. Then Lilian remembered that, while looking for food shops near the mews, she had walked through a long drab street where dozens of windows displayed cards saying 'Apartments'. We could try there.

'Then we must have a taxi,' said Molly. 'I can't face another trek burdened with suitcase, coat, umbrella and handbag.'

Lilian pointed out it would cost a fortune to keep a taxi ticking while we went from house to house. She said that as it was a hot day, we could leave our coats and umbrellas in the Club cloakroom. 'And we can put our handbags in our suitcases – that'll mean we've only one thing each to carry. We'll just keep out enough money for bus fares. Mouse can put it in one of her Miss Muffets.' She referred to the smocked pockets on the full skirt of my chintz dress. This dress was considered very funny – possibly with justification, as it was patterned with elves sitting on toadstools.

The scheme worked well on the short way to

the bus stop; but once we were trailing up the long drab street even the suitcases alone became burdensome. And Lilian's dozens of 'Apartments' cards dwindled to four. The first three landladies would not take us for one night. The fourth would have, but had just let her last room; she apologised for not having taken her card down. As she was pleasant, we asked her advice and she told us of a cheap hotel only ten minutes walk away. She suggested we should leave our cases with her. If we got in, the hotel could send for them. And if we didn't, we were to come back and she'd try to think of somewhere else to send us.

So we thanked her and dumped our cases in her hall. It was bliss being without them. I swung my arms and said how free I felt. A few minutes later it dawned on me that I felt *too* free; our handbags were shut up in our suitcases. We thought of going back at once as there was quite a bit of money in our bags. But none of us distrusted the kind woman and we were already in the street where the hotel was said to be, so we just hurried on.

Again we were disappointed: the hotel was full. We went back towards our cases as fast as we could walk – indeed, I had to run to keep up with the girls. The sky had clouded over but it was very sultry, and we were all extremely hot by the time we got to the long drab street. And we then realised that we did not know which of the drab houses we had left our cases in. Why, oh why, had none of us noticed its number?

We went to what seemed the right part of the

street. There was no 'Apartments' card to be seen but by now, no doubt, the landlady would have taken it down. We asked at three houses and had no luck. Then Lilian said we must do the job systematically and try every house. This led to our trying the same three houses again and we got rude receptions.

After we'd tried a lot more houses I said: 'We're in the wrong street. The houses in the street we want had balconies.'

Molly and Lilian then remembered the balconies.

Lilian said, 'We must go to the main road and try to get our bearings. Oh, God, now it's starting to rain.'

We felt sure the street we wanted must run parallel to the one we were in; but when we reached the main road, we didn't know whether to go right or left. And it was now raining hard.

'We'll have to get a taxi,' said Molly.

'But we've no money with us,' said Lilian. 'And anyway, we wouldn't know where to drive to.'

'Let's find a café and have tea,' said Molly.

'Can't you take it in that we've *no money?*' said Lilian. 'And there *are* no cafés near here that are open on Sundays – if there was one, we might at least ask for shelter. I can't think, with this rain beating down on me.'

I pointed out that we were close to The Heathen and we might get Lilian's friend to take us in until the storm was over. 'Then we can comb these streets until we find our cases. And while we're at The Heathen we can use the telephone. I'll see if Miss Lester knows anywhere we can stay.'

'Or you could ring up Rex Crossway,' said Lilian, brightening. 'He won't want his Mouse to sleep on the Embankment.'

I said I thought he would be at his country house for Sunday. 'Anyway, the great thing is to get out of the rain and to a telephone. Let's run for it.'

We ran – through rain which now seemed a cloudburst. As we dashed into the mews a taxi went by us, spattering us with mud. We saw it pull up in front of The Heathen.

'Quick!' cried Lilian. 'They must be going out.'

Even as she spoke, the blue front door opened and a man and a woman hurried into the taxi. We yelled, and ran faster; but it was no use. The taxi drove out of the other end of the mews.

We stood in the doorway of one of the big houses that backed onto the mews. There wasn't much shelter as the rain was driving in. Our dresses were wet through and my elves had run into my toadstools.

'Never did I think I'd long to be back at The Heathen,' said Molly, staring at the closed blue door.

We couldn't even get in with the horse, as its owner always locked it up at weekends.

Molly then had a temporary return of grandeur. She said she was going to ring the bell at the doorway in which we were standing. 'And when someone comes I shall explain and ask to use the telephone. We are *not* going to stand here and drown.'

She rang the bell, keeping her finger on it a long time. Nobody came. She rang again and again, with no result.

'Oh, God, why is everything so hellish!' She turned in despair and leaned back on the door. It opened so suddenly that she nearly lost her footing.

'In we go,' said Lilian. 'And thank you, God, for a roof.'

It was a glass one, over a long flagged passage. Molly closed the door she had so nearly fallen through – the catch on the Yale lock had been left up – and said we would go boldly in and find a telephone. At the far end of the passage was a glass-panelled door through which we could see a kitchen.

'And it won't take much boldness,' said Lilian, 'as there's obviously no one in.'

All the same, I did not much like going into the kitchen. Suppose the servants came back? But we were barely through the glass-panelled door before I guessed that the kitchen was not at present being used. It was too scrupulously tidy and there were a lot of dead flies on the window ledges. And when I looked in the larder, to make sure I had guessed right, it was empty. I said: 'The servants must be away.'

'Then everyone in the house will be,' said Lilian. 'It's the kind of house where people don't stay without servants.'

She made for the stairs we could see through an open door.

'Oh, Lilian, don't!' I cried. 'It's bad enough, trespassing in the kitchen.'

A few seconds later she called down: 'It's just as I expected. There are masses of unopened circulars on the hall floor. And there's a telephone.'

So we followed her up, though I still felt scared. I considered myself reasonably brave but I had been brought up to have a horror of doing anything illegal. I longed to get the telephoning over and hurry out of the house.

I tried Miss Lester's number but got no answer. I tried the office in case she was working, but with no result. To Lilian's annoyance, I didn't know Mr Crossway's number, it wasn't in the telephone book and Enquiries refused to give it. The girls then tried to get their three men friends, but without success.

'Oh, come on,' I said at last. 'We shall soon find our cases if we search methodically.'

'But it's still pouring,' said Molly.

'And I'm going to look round,' said Lilian. 'I've always longed to see over a great London house.'

I remembered her interest in Regent's Park houses, and how she had sat at The Heathen's windows gazing up at the big houses backing onto the mews. 'Well, get it over quickly,' I told her.

'You're both coming with me. I dare you.'

As a child, I had often accepted dares to trespass in the grounds of large, empty houses – and quite enjoyed it. This present occasion was very different. Still, a dare was a dare.

'I think it's pretty safe, really,' said Molly. 'And we might find an electric fire and dry ourselves a bit.'

'But that would be stealing electricity,' I said, horrified.

'It doesn't *show* when you steal electricity,' said Molly. 'But if you like, you can soothe your conscience by sending an anonymous postal order. Personally, I can't believe anyone would grudge a little warmth to three shivering girls.'

Lilian led the way into the dining-room. I was glad to notice that the blinds – cream, with deep lace edging – were down; at least we should not be seen from outside.

'Fancy having blinds,' said Lilian. 'They're terribly out of date. And what a dull room! It's like a dentist's waiting-room. Still, this heavy furniture must have been expensive.'

There was a study at the back of the dining-room, with glass-fronted bookcases filled with uniform sets of books, and a colossal desk.

'Deadly!' said Lilian. 'Let's hope the drawing-room's better.' She raced upstairs.

It was a double drawing-room and the only nice thing about it was the parquet floor. Much of the furniture was dust-sheeted; and what with the dust-sheets and the blinds being down, the whole effect was funereal.

'Hideous curtains,' said Lilian. 'I should think the people who live here are elderly.'

'That's probably them,' said Molly, looking at an oil painting over the fireplace.

It was of a middle-aged couple, very stiffly posed, the man standing behind the seated woman. She was plain, with elaborately arranged fair hair. He was heavily dark, with a streak of white in his hair.

'She's dreary,' said Lilian. 'He's rather striking.' She lifted a dust-sheet. 'Goodness, what bad taste they have.'

'And no electric fires,' said Molly.

'They won't need them, with those huge, ugly radiators,' said Lilian. 'Well, let's look at the bedrooms.'

The front room had a massive white and gold bedroom suite.

'Ah, this will please Madam Lily de Luxe,' said Molly.

'Not really; it's old-fashioned. Still, it *is* luxurious.' Lilian sat down in front of the triple mirror.

I followed Molly through the large, tiled bathroom which led to the back bedroom – a man's room, furnished in mahogany.

'Need we go any further?' I asked.

But Lilian was determined to. On the next floor were two more bedrooms. The front one obviously belonged to two boys; there were school photographs and adventure books. Even Lilian doubted if the attics were worth exploring; she thought they would be servants' rooms. But we went up. And as it turned out, the servants' rooms must have been in the basement for the whole of the top floor was given up to a day nursery, a night nursery and a bathroom. And at last we found an electric fire. It was in the front room, the day nursery, behind a tall fireguard.

'Marvellous,' said Molly. 'We can drape our dresses over the fireguard. Now if only the electricity is on!'

It was, and the girls instantly took off their wet dresses and stockings, and practically forced me to take mine off too.

'You'll get a chill if you don't,' said Molly. 'And

even if anyone *should* come in downstairs, no one will come up here. This nursery hasn't been used for years.'

She was obviously right about the nursery. The pink wallpaper was faded and there was general slight dilapidation, whereas the rest of the house was in glossy repair. Presumably the children were now schoolboys. I relaxed a little. Perhaps we were fairly safe; and I was glad to get out of my wet dress.

Still, I wasn't happy. And I found it strange that the girls, who had told me they would never have had the courage to force their way into that audition at the Crossway, could now be so bravely unconcerned. I had *needed* no courage at the Crossway; I had just done what came naturally to me – and it hadn't been *illegal*. Perhaps my terror of the law was provincial? But I think the real truth was that I had a vivid imagination and, from the moment we entered the house, I had been creating mental pictures of our discovery and arrest. The girls simply did not visualise getting caught.

The nursery blinds were pink, and all the furniture was pink. With the electric fire on, the room was cosy. We wandered round looking at old toys and pictures. The girls, having found their *crêpe de chine* cami-knickers as wet as their dresses, had taken them off and were wearing only the tight silk brassieres that coerced their busts into fashionable flatness, and pink girdles from which suspenders dangled and jangled. My underwear was still childish and there was a good deal of it. Had I been as scantily clad as Molly

131

and Lilian were I could not have behaved with the complete unself-consciousness they had probably learned in theatre dressing-rooms. (Once, when I had undressed while they were in my cubicle, I had convulsed them with laughter because I put on my nightgown before removing my last layer of underwear. They called this 'The Modest Mouse's Tent Technique'.)

After a while, when Molly had settled in the Nanny's wicker chair and Lilian and I had managed to wedge ourselves into two tiny painted armchairs, we went back to talking about how we were to find our suitcases and where we were to sleep. Lilian suggested we should stay where we were. Molly said we should get hungry.

'Well, we might slip out for a meal,' said Lilian – and then remembered we hadn't a penny between us. We kept *on* forgetting about our handbags.

It was about then that I heard the telephone ringing below. All my terror rushed back.

'Now calm down,' said Molly. 'The fact that someone's ringing up doesn't mean a thing.'

I said it might mean someone was expected back.

'Anyway, it's stopped now,' said Lilian. 'So it must have been a mistake. It would have gone on ringing if someone was expected to be here.'

All the same, both the girls had been startled. 'Perhaps we *should* be moving on,' said Molly. She got up and peered round the blind to see if the rain had stopped, and said it hadn't. So we went on talking, getting nowhere. And after a few minutes I froze with horror because I thought I heard footsteps. The others froze too, when I told them, but not for long, because when we listened we couldn't hear a thing. Still, I now felt I simply must get out of the house so I said that, rain or no rain, we must find our suitcases.

'But when we do, we don't know where to go,' said Lilian.

Molly then suggested we should go to a police station.

'What, and sleep in the cells?' said Lilian. 'I don't think they'll let you if you want to.'

I said, 'We'll sleep in them without wanting to if someone finds us here. *I'm* going, anyway.'

I sprang up – and the child's little wooden armchair came with me. The girls exploded with laughter. Then Lilian tried to get out of her little armchair and found she, too, was stuck. She and I stood there with the chairs clinging to our behinds and we all laughed quite painfully.

And then the nursery door opened. I turned in horror and saw a figure in a hooded white rain-coat pointing what I took to be a revolver.

'Hands up or I fire!' said a falsely gruff voice.

That was Zelle's dramatic entrance into our lives.

7

We shot up our hands and Lilian cried, 'Don't, don't! We've only come in out of the rain.'

Zelle (I can think of her only by that name) said, 'It's all right – really!' and held out the 'revolver' to show us. It was a jewelled case to take powder and lipstick, made in the shape of a miniature pistol. As we leaned forward to look at it Lilian and I shed our armchairs. Zelle began to laugh. But she told us later that it wasn't the armchairs she found so funny; it was Molly's lorgnette dangling against her bare midriff.

We laughed, too; and through the laughter tried to explain. But we barely needed to, because Zelle had been sitting on the stairs listening to our conversation, which she had found fascinating. She had finally come in because she longed to know what we were laughing at. From the outset she made it plain that she was enchanted to know us.

She told us she had come to the house to meet its owner, her cousin, Bill, who was also her guardian; she said he was some kind of removed cousin, much older than she was. 'He'd like me to live here but his wife and I can't get on. They're away in the country but Bill comes up for a few days every week and stays at his club. I meet him here on Sundays and we go out to dinner. But he's rung to say he won't be coming up this week.'

She had reached the house just in time to answer the telephone; after which, feeling at a loose end, she had come up to the boys' bedroom to find something to read. 'Some of their books are quite exciting. And then I heard voices.'

I asked if she hadn't been frightened.

'Well, for a minute or two. But I soon thought you all sounded fun.'

By now she had taken her raincoat off and we were sitting around on the floor, each of us on one of the nursery rugs which lay like pink islands on the sea of blue linoleum. She had seemed tall in the long white coat but was really only a few inches taller than I was, and very slight. She was fair and pretty but not with the pink and white prettiness one associates with fair hair and skin. Her hair was a very dim gold and her skin nearer beige than pink and white. She wore scarcely any make-up. I doubt if 'under-stated' was then used to describe appearance but it would certainly have described both her prettiness and her always expensive clothes. She was now wearing a printed silk dress, pale fawn dappled with brown.

After she had told us a very little more about herself – we gathered she didn't *do* anything, just lived in a service flat and found life boring – she started to question us and at last got the complete hang of our difficulties. She then said we mustn't worry any more. She would ring up for a taxi and we would drive round until we found our cases, and then she would take us to dinner at a hotel where we could stay the night. We pointed out that we could not afford an expensive hotel. She waved this aside and said we must be her guests – 'I've masses of money with me – I went to the bank yesterday. And I'll stay at the hotel, too. It'll be fun. Put your clothes on while I go down and telephone the taxi rank.'

We dressed, switched the fire off, and trooped down to the hall; then Zelle took us down to the back door to wait for the taxi. She said she always came in and out the back way so that the front door could be left bolted. She had put the catch of the Yale lock up the previous Sunday, when going out into the mews to feed a cat.

'Then *anyone* could have got in,' said Lilian.

'Oh, well, they're insured,' said Zelle cheerfully. She looked up and down the mews. 'The cat's not here tonight – because of the rain, I suppose. So I'll leave her usual Sunday supper where she usually sits. Such a pathetic little alley cat.' She fished a paper bag from her raincoat pocket, took out a leg of chicken, and put it on a window sill.

When the taxi came we all made sure that this time the door was really locked. Zelle said thoughtfully, 'Perhaps I won't mention to Bill that his house was open for a week.'

Just as everything had gone wrong before, now everything went right. We soon found our cases; once we got the right street we recognised the house. The nice landlady offered to make us tea but Zelle said it would spoil our dinner. (I noticed she slipped a ten shilling note into the landlady's hand as we left.) Then we drove to a small but expensive-looking hotel where Molly, Lilian and I changed out of our spoilt dresses and hats in the Ladies' Room. After that, as it was still early for dinner, we sat in the lounge and had drinks. That was the first time I had a cocktail. I had decided that not drinking was dull.

It was while we were there that Zelle acquired her nickname. A man came in who was extremely like a pig and this started Molly, Lilian and me on our game of picking the animals people resembled. After we had done some of the people in the lounge, Zelle said: 'Now do me. Bill says I put my feet down like a pony.'

Her face could not have been less like any kind of horse but she did use her feet in a pony-like way, stepping both briskly and delicately; I had noticed it as she walked into the lounge. Thinking of this, and her colouring, and the way her eyes were set – and perhaps because of her dappled dress – I said: 'Could she be a gazelle?'

Molly and Lilian thought that was exactly right. It turned out that none of us quite knew what a gazelle was like but that didn't worry us. One of us then said that 'Zelle' would make a nice name for her. She had told us her name but I doubt if any of us had yet used it or if we ever did. From that moment, she was always Zelle.

We had a marvellous dinner with a vast number of courses. Zelle apologised for not ordering it *à la carte* – 'Bill says one always should but I'm not good at choosing.' We drank champagne and perhaps that reminded Molly of the morning she had learned she was illegitimate. Suddenly she told Zelle about it, finishing by saying, 'I thought you ought to know in case you mind.'

'Heavens, how could anyone?' said Zelle.

Molly said *she* did and would never get over it.

Then Lilian called her poor old Moll Byblow, which Zelle thought a lovely name, and soon we were all laughing again.

After dinner Zelle went to her flat to get clothes for the night. Lilian asked if we could come with her and see the flat but Zelle said she wanted just to dash in and out and the flat wasn't worth seeing– 'Bill rented it for me, furnished, before I came to London, and I've never let him know how dreary I think it is. But I shall furnish a flat for myself when the lease is up next year. By then I shall have control of my money.'

It seemed to me she was already in control of a good deal of money but we gathered that, until she was twenty-one, her guardian doled it out to her.

After she had gone, of course we discussed her, saying how miraculously kind and generous she was. We found that, in spite of having talked with her for hours, we knew hardly anything about her background. I said this probably meant we had talked too much about ourselves and there were three of us to one of her.

'It isn't only that,' said Lilian. 'Don't you find her a bit mysterious?'

I agreed. 'She has a *princesse lointaine* quality.'

'Now our gifted Mouse has swallowed a French dictionary,' said Molly. But when I managed to explain *lointaine* she saw what I meant. Lilian didn't – or rather, it wasn't what she meant by 'mysterious'. She said, 'I just mean puzzling. But anyway, I couldn't like her better.'

When Zelle came back we went on talking till midnight; the clock struck just as Lilian was asking where she had lived before coming to London.

'We'll postpone that dreary story,' said Zelle, getting up. 'Now we really should go to bed. I'm rather tired.'

She had taken two double rooms and asked me to share hers. I thought this part of the particular kindness she had shown me since I had mentioned how frightened I had been while trespassing in her cousin's house. Once we were on our own she showed no sign of tiredness and talked all the time we were undressing. (I noted that she practised my tent technique.) Her nightgown was heavy white silk, plain except for an embroidered monogram. I admired it much more than the rather fancy nightgowns worn by Molly and Lilian, usually pink or blue trimmed with *café au lait* lace.

Even after we put the light out she kept the conversation going, questioning me and seeming especially interested in my childhood. At last I pulled up and said, 'I've talked and talked and given you no chance to. And yet I long to hear about you.'

She said, 'Truly? Well, if you're sure it won't bore you.' Then she began speaking hurriedly leaving out details, as if she wanted just to state the bare facts. She told me our lives had been rather similar as she, like me, could barely remember her parents. But she had been brought up by a grandfather, not an aunt. They had lived in a remote Welsh mountain village, in an old house where everything was falling to pieces. She was supposed to go to the village school, but it was a long walk so she often stayed away and nobody bothered – 'You'll find me terribly uneducated.' She had always imagined they were poor– and then, when her grandfather died, it turned out he'd been a miser and there was plenty of money– 'Only it takes time to clear things up. Bill's doing that. Imagine the poor man's position, having it all wished on him, plus a girl of nineteen.'

She said he'd only known about it a few weeks before her grandfather died– 'He sent for Bill because he was our one relation. They hadn't met for thirty years and Bill didn't even know I existed, but he was wonderfully kind to me. At first he had me to live with him and his wife in their country house, but it was hopeless. So he took this dull flat. I've been there for a year – and never made any friends.'

'Well, you've made some now,' I assured her.

'Really? And you won't mind my horrid Welsh accent?'

I had noticed she spoke with a slight lilt but had not realised it was Welsh. Anyway, it was pretty. I told her so.

'Perhaps it's not as bad as it used to be. I've had elocution lessons. By the way, would you tell Molly and Lilian all I've told you, and ask them not to question me? I have a horror of talking about my life in Wales, but you're easy to talk to. Let's go to sleep now and then tomorrow will come quicker. It's so lovely to have something to look forward to.'

It was just what, as a child, I had often thought when I knew I was going to a theatre the next day.

I lay awake for awhile, thinking. Welsh mountains were a perfect background for a *princesse lointaine*. I tried to imagine the old house and the miserly grandfather and then Bill coming to the rescue. It seemed a pity he was elderly and married.

The next morning, while we were having breakfast in bed, I asked what had happened to the house. She said it had been sold– 'Sad, in a way, as the family had lived there for over two hundred years, but I couldn't stay on alone.' Then she talked about the house and gardens, speaking eagerly, not in the stilted way she had told me her history the night before. She described the panelling and wide staircase, and a rose garden, and lawns leading down to a lake. She made it all sound wonderful, though I thought that if her grandfather had been a miser the gardens must have been overgrown. I asked about this and she said, 'Oh, yes, of course they were. Let's not talk about it any more. And you *will* ask the others not to question me, won't you?'

I got the chance to, while Zelle was settling up with the hotel. I only had time, then, to give the girls a brief outline of what I'd been told, but they said they quite understood.

After that, Zelle came back to the Club with us; she wanted to join it. We made sure we now had our cubicles, and then showed her round and introduced her to various members. She was charming to them all, and one old lady notorious for snobbishness told her she was just the type of member the Club needed.

We were ashamed of the anaemic lunch we gave

141

her but she said she enjoyed it and would often come to lunch once she was a member, which would be in only a few days as there was a board meeting that week; Lilian and Molly would propose and second her. When I left for the Crossway she was planning to take them to a theatre that night. I was sorry to be out of it.

'Still, be thankful you've a job to go to,' Lilian called after me. She and Molly were gloomy about being out of work.

I got to the office full of our meeting with Zelle; Miss Lester was always interested in what happened to me. She knew I found life dull after my work at rehearsals and she had done what she could to cheer me up, sending me to matinées at several theatres. And as Mr Crossway still had not given me any introductions to managers, she had given me one herself, saying he was interested in my work. The manager had been charming but I did wonder if he might not be a little drunk. Everything I said made him laugh and I certainly wasn't trying to. At last he remarked blurrily, 'Yes, I see why Rex is interested. You're quite a little dear. But I do have some little dears of my own who need jobs. Rex must find you something himself.' When I told Miss Lester she laughed but said she mustn't expose me to anything like that again. I hadn't minded being exposed.

I had barely finished talking to her about Zelle when Lilian rang up to say they all wanted to come to the Crossway that night and could I help them to get seats? I hoped there might be some returned, also I knew some were withheld from sale until the late afternoon in case Mr Crossway needed them. So I asked Miss Lester and she coped with the box-office. There were four seats and she said she would give me one for myself and I could wear my new evening dress. I told Lilian I would meet them in the foyer.

From then onwards, much of the afternoon was devoted to getting me ready – luckily we weren't busy. My dress was still with the wardrobe mistress, the alterations only recently finished. It had been imported from Paris, a year or so earlier, for a temperamental leading lady who had refused to wear it. Miss Lester said it was a *robe de style*, independent of any prevailing fashion. At first I thought it was quite like my own tight-bodiced, full-skirted dresses, but I soon saw that the cut was very different and there were details which gave it the authority to defy fashion. The material was a corded silk in a deep shade of coral, and its little jacket was embroidered with white, gold and turquoise beads. It was not merely the most beautiful dress I had ever worn. It was the most beautiful dress I was ever fated to wear; a dress to be remembered for a lifetime.

Miss Lester sent me out to buy gold sandals and a small evening bag; there was a theatrical shoeshop quite near where I could get both and charge them to the management. She said they were a bonus for my work at rehearsals.

We went out to dinner early so that I should have time to dress. Walking back through the blue early evening I looked up at the brilliantly lit theatre and suddenly felt wildly excited. Later I told myself this had been a premonition that something was going to happen; but I was only being wise after the event. I needed no premonition to excite me. Even on an ordinary evening I found the lit-up theatre exciting – and tonight I should be showing that theatre, *my* theatre, to my friends. Also, up in the Throne Room waited that never-to-be-forgotten dress.

8

The girls arrived early and were in the foyer when I sailed downstairs, to be received by their admiring gasps. They all wore pretty dresses but I don't think I was flattering myself in believing mine was prettier; and I remained convinced that women's waists ought not to be round their behinds.

There was a very different atmosphere in the theatre from the one I had noticed on the first night. Then, even the audience had seemed overwrought. Now, one felt that everyone was confident the play would be good. Tension had been replaced by a sense of settled success.

We had the middle gangway seats in the fifth row and I was put on the outside as there was a low-sitter in front of that seat. Lilian was next to me and turned out to be a whisperer. Soon after the curtain rose she told me she thought the tall young girl who played the part I had hankered for was very dull. I more than agreed and it seemed to me that the girl was being even duller than I had remembered.

In the first interval we all went up to the office and had coffee with Miss Lester, who showed the girls round the Throne Room. Lilian gazed ecstatically at Mr Crossway's portrait and said, 'I can't think why our Mouse doesn't fall in love with him.'

'Our Mouse has too much good sense, I'm glad to say,' said Miss Lester, smiling at me.

I said, 'I think it's more that I'm too old to fall in love with actors. I was passionately in love with him when I was twelve. I mentioned it to his photograph every night, after my prayers.'

'You should tell him that,' said Miss Lester, laughing. 'He's rather vain about his schoolgirl admirers.'

Then we heard the bells ringing to call the audience in for the second act. As we went down, Lilian said, 'You didn't tell us Miss Lester was like that – terribly elegant in a don't-give-a-damn-about-it way. Not at all like most secretaries.'

In the second interval we walked about outside the theatre and were looked at a good deal, especially Molly, who put in heavy work with her lorgnette. When we went back for the last act I was sorry to feel the evening was so nearly over.

It must have been about five minutes later when I noticed that the tall, dull young actress was being worse than dull; she was being positively bad, saying her lines as if she didn't even know what they meant. This was during an ensemble scene so was not very noticeable at first. Then she failed to come in on a cue. I heard Tom prompt her but she just sat staring in front of her with a strained expression. Mr Crossway went on without the missing line, which meant skipping the line that should have answered it. For the next few minutes everyone acted with extra briskness, as if to distract attention from the girl; but they didn't distract mine and I saw she was sitting with her eyes closed and that her face looked drawn with pain. I knew she would soon need to rise and say, 'Come with me, Aunt Caroline,' and then go off, but when the cue came she neither spoke nor moved. The elderly actress who played Aunt Caroline was sitting, beside her and able to help her up, saying, 'Let's go together, dear.' They managed to get across the stage, the elderly actress practically holding the girl up, and off through an archway. Then, just as they were out of sight, there was a thud.

Lilian instantly whispered, 'Did you hear that? She's fainted.' And various people in the front stalls whispered to each other. Mr Crossway gave one quick look after the girl, then went on with his lines, and in a few seconds the leading lady came on from the opposite side of the stage and the play was continuing normally. I knew that the girl would not have to come on again for quite a while. Ten minutes? Perhaps a little longer. I imagined the scene in the wings, and Brice Marton or Tom dashing upstairs to warn the understudy–

And then I remembered. A couple of days earlier Brice Marton had been up in the office talking to Miss Lester about an understudy who was ill. He had grumbled because there weren't enough understudies– 'This girl's covering three parts. Even when she's not ill, it isn't safe.' Miss Lester had said Mr Crossway loathed paying understudies to sit around doing nothing, it was the only thing he was mean about. And the girl would be back on Monday, or Tuesday at the latest.

It was Monday now. *Was* the girl back?

I was hurrying out of the stalls less than a minute after that off-stage thud. If the understudy was not back this might be my great chance.

I rushed up to the foyer and round to the stage door. As I passed the stage door keeper he was telephoning for a doctor. I dashed downstairs hoping to find Brice Marton.

I saw him standing outside the iron door leading to the stage, talking to the leading lady's understudy, who held an open script of the play. As I raced towards them I heard her say, 'But I've never in my life been asked to do such a thing. I shall be ludicrous.' I guessed what was happening: she was being urged to go on and read the girl's last scene. And it certainly would be ludicrous as she was quite forty-five and wearing a most unbecoming tweed suit; also horn-rimmed spectacles through which she was worriedly looking at the script.

Brice Marton said, 'I've got to keep the curtain up.'

I reached him then and implored him to let me play, assuring him I knew every word, every movement. The leading lady's understudy received me as if I were an angel from heaven– 'But of course you must do it! Mr Marton, I simply won't go on now this child is available. Look at me – in these awful clothes; I'm just back from the country. Oh, you marvellous girl – and what an enchanting dress! Mr Marton, please!'

I thought he would argue but he only asked if I was sure I knew the lines– 'If not, you'd better read.'

'Absolutely sure. I swear it.'

'Anyway, we can prompt you. If you can even give a general idea of the scene–' He opened the iron door and listened. 'You've got nearly five minutes yet.'

'She ought to have some make-up,' said the leading lady's understudy. She scurried to the nearest dressing-room, which was the leading lady's. The dresser was at the open door.

'Do you want to look at the script?' asked Brice Marton.

I shook my head decidedly. 'I'm sure I still know every line. Have you cut anything since re-hearsals?'

'Not a thing. One move was changed, putting the girl more upstage for the long speech. But it doesn't matter.'

By then the leading lady's understudy was back with rouge, lipstick and a handglass.

'This is all there's time for. Thank goodness you've long, dark eyelashes.'

She put the rouge on for me, then held the glass while I did my lips. Brice Marton had the iron door open again, listening.

'Come on, now,' he said, and held the door for me.

'All the luck in the world,' said the leading lady's understudy.

There was still a minute or two before my entrance. Brice Marton stood with me, and to my surprise, put his arm round my shoulders. I said, 'Poor Mr Crossway, I suppose he doesn't know what's going to happen.'

'There's no way of letting him. But you can count on him. He's always wonderful in any emergency. If you forget your lines he'll cover up for you until you hear the prompt.'

'I'm not going to forget them. I've wanted to play this part ever since I came to that audition – remember? And I've played it in my mind dozens of times.'

'Concentrate, now. Your cue's coming. Good luck.'

I walked on through the arch. The lights were far more brilliant than at the audition or than any I had faced in amateur theatricals, and the auditorium was not merely dark; it seemed to me utterly black. And the blackness was alive with whispers. I knew that all over the theatre people must be saying to each other that I was a different girl, an understudy. The thought of the audience was so distracting that every word of the part vanished from my mind and I had a moment of absolute panic. Then Mr Crossway smiled at me and spoke. I answered – and instantly felt supremely confident. But confident is too calm a word. Standing in the wings I had felt excited (never nervous). Now the excitement had become elation. I was experiencing, for the first time in my life, something near to pure joy.

At the back of my mind I remembered Mr Crossway had said the part must not be funny, and I did not try to be funny. But soon the audience showed a tendency to laugh – and the laughs came in places where I thought they ought to come. I found this so intoxicating that I could not resist trying for any laugh I could get. And feeling a certain line warranted it, I put in a little pirouette which the audience loved – someone actually clapped. Then I got a laugh when I did *not* try for it. I had to say to Mr Crossway, 'But can't you see that we're perfectly matched?' As we were standing close together and the top of my head was barely level with his chest, we couldn't have been less well matched, and the audience certainly got the point.

However, I didn't think it mattered and it led to what I thought was a valuable idea. We were now nearing my big speech, in which I would implore Mr Crossway to leave his faithless wife for me. I had every intention of delivering this most seriously, and I could see I should be at a disadvantage if I had to look up at him – or, alternatively, talk to his chest. Brice Marton had said the speech was now spoken from further upstage, which might help me a bit, but surely it would be unprofessional to upstage Mr Crossway? I thought about this while he made a fairly long speech. How far up dare I go?

And then I noticed a conveniently placed footstool. If I stood on that, I thought, my head would be level with Mr Crossway's and I need not go upstage at all. And it seemed to me quite in character to use a footstool, if one was a small girl trying to make an impression on a tall man.

The first line of my long speech was: 'Now you

listen to me.' Should I say it before I got on the footstool or after? Before, I decided. My cue came. I said the line and jumped on the stool. Unfortunately I had miscalculated and it raised me some inches higher than Mr Crossway. The audience gave quite a howl of delight. I waited for the laugh to die and then held up my finger at Mr Crossway, as if lecturing a child – this winning idea just came to me. The audience gave another happy howl. I was afraid it would not fully quieten down for my speech so I said loudly, 'Please, please, listen!' – to Mr Crossway, of course, but it did quieten the audience. I then said the speech with intense feeling.

Its end was the leading lady's cue to come out on a staircase in time to see an embrace. Realising that embracing would be difficult while I was on the footstool I jumped down, which must have given the impression that I was pouncing on Mr Crossway. The happy audience laughed again, all the time the leading lady was coming downstairs. I then had to say to her: 'Oh, don't think I'm sorry! You should take better care of your property.' The tall girl always said this coldly and walked off with dignity. It seemed more in character, for me, to speak mischievously; so I did, and went off to an enthusiastic round of applause. To this day I remain convinced that the audience adored me.

I rather expected people would be in the wings, waiting to congratulate me, but nobody was. Then Brice Marton came from the prompt corner, where he had stood with Tom during my scene. He said, 'Bravo! Got to see if the doctor's come,' as he passed me. Well, at least he had said 'Bravo!'

Knowing I should have to go on for the curtain call I stayed, listening to the last scene of the play. The faithless wife had to show her intention of reforming; the husband pretended he had never known she was faithless, merely thought her indiscreet. She had to realise he was pretending but see she must accept the pretence. And she had to win back the sympathy she had lost earlier. The husband helped her by pointing out how happy she had made him in spite of her 'indiscretions'. Mr Crossway and his leading lady played the scene very quietly. On the first night, and whenever I had watched through the spy-hole, I had noticed how completely the audience was held.

Tonight, after only a few minutes, I knew something was wrong. There was a slight laugh on a line not meant to be funny. Soon after, the leading lady had to refer to me as 'that humourless beanpole of a girl'. This got a really loud laugh. Then things went on all right for a while, except that Mr Crossway played more forcefully than usual, which made the scene seem less real. Just before the end the leading lady had to refer to me again, by saying: 'She was something of a surprise.' The audience then laughed its head off.

By the time the curtain fell, the whole cast was waiting for the call. A nice old character-actor took me on with him and put me in the right place; then brought me off. While Mr Crossway and his leading lady went on taking calls, the actress who played Aunt Caroline whispered to me, 'I hear you got through splendidly, not a single prompt.' The old actor said, 'Most remarkable. And what a pretty dress!' Then they talked about the girl who had fainted; she was believed to have acute appendicitis and had been taken to a hospital. 'Dreadful, dreadful,' said the old actor. 'But you saw us through, my dear.' And other people came and congratulated me.

Then the curtain fell for the last time and I heard the leading lady shout 'Rex!' in a tone of outrage. Everyone near me moved quickly away except Aunt Caroline, who said, 'Come and sit in my dressing-room, dear,' and hastily steered me off the stage – but not before I had heard the leading lady say: 'How in God's name did it happen? Who let that little oddity loose on us?'

I knew it was no use trying to speak to Mr Crossway until the leading lady had finished complaining, so I went with Aunt Caroline, who told me, in considerable detail, about an occasion in her own youth when she played some large part at a moment's notice. I listened for about five minutes and then said I must go to the office. Actually, I went straight back to the stage.

Already most of the lights had been turned off. I wondered if Mr Crossway had gone back to his dressing-room. Then I heard him and also heard Brice Marton. They were quite close to me but hidden by the backing to the archway, and they were beginning a really furious row, using words I had never heard before. It took me several seconds to realise these must be bad language. I remember thinking they sounded idiotic.

The gist of the row was that Mr Crossway was angry because I had been allowed to play. Asked if he would have preferred to have the part read by a middle-aged woman in tweeds and spectacles, he said the occasion shouldn't have arisen. It was a stage manager's job to have a reliable understudy ready. Brice Marton pointed out that he had asked permission to engage an additional understudy, who would have 'double-covered' for the understudy who was away. He had not been allowed to. And by the grace of God there *had* been a reliable understudy ready, who was word perfect and beautifully dressed – and how was he to know the effect I would have on the audience? This conversation took some time, mainly because the bad language held things up so.

At last Brice Marton said: 'Well, what happens tomorrow?'

'The understudy plays, of course – you say you're sure she'll be back. And you find yourself a safe cover for her. Why consult me about understudies? You know I've got a kink about paying them. From now on, engage them on your own. And never again speak to me as you've spoken tonight.'

'I'm afraid I can't guarantee not to,' said Brice Marton. 'So I shall take it that you'll release me from my contract.'

'Don't be a bloody fool,' said Mr Crossway.

They came out from behind the backing – and saw me. Mr Crossway said, 'Oh, my God! What am I to say to this child?'

'You might start by thanking her for keeping your curtain up,' said Brice Marton. 'I'm going to.'

'No, leave it to me,' said Mr Crossway.

154

He put his arm round my shoulders and took me off the stage to his dressing-room. Here he pushed me into an armchair and told me to wait while his dresser helped him to change. They went into a part of the room that was curtained off; and in a few minutes came out again, Mr Crossway now in a dressing-gown. He told the dresser that would be all for tonight; and as soon as the door closed behind the man, turned a chair to face me and sat looking at me with a helpless kind of expression Then he smiled and said:

'Brice is right, of course. I should start by thanking you and I do. And I can honestly tell you that I admire your courage and your quite astounding confidence. Also, you look very nice; I'd no idea you could look so pretty. But – well, surely with your intelligence, you must know it was a dreadful thing to do?'

'You mean, to get laughs? I didn't try to. But once they started it seemed best to ... to develop the characterisation that suited my personality.'

'What a marvellous phrase! The truth is that you're still dead sure you're in the right, aren't you?'

'Not right for the play. I realise now that I spoilt the end of it. But I was right for *me*. I *felt* right. Though I can see I made mistakes. I shouldn't have jumped on that footstool. But if I could have a lower stool–'

'Good God, do you think I shall ever let you loose in that part again?'

I raised my voice protestingly. 'But you can't judge me by tonight. I haven't had one rehearsal.

155

I'll do exactly what you tell me.'

He said he doubted that. 'And even if you did, it would make no difference. You're incurably comic – it's partly due to your tinyness; tinyness combined with cock-sureness is always funny. Were you, as a child, taken to many music halls?'

'Certainly not. I don't *like* music halls.'

'All the same, you have a single-turn mentality. You might conceivably make a success in Variety.'

'Like Little Tich, no doubt,' I said indignantly.

He laughed. 'Exactly. I shall call you Tich from now on. No, you're not a grotesque. You're more like the first-turn soubrettes who come on swinging their stiff skirts. And in my grandfather's day you might have done well in melodrama what was called a singing chamber-maid.'

'Do you mean I'm old-fashioned?'

'It's not as simple as that.' He got up and mopped his forehead where the perspiration was coming through his greasepaint; then sat down facing me again. 'Now try to understand that I shouldn't say this to you if I didn't like you very much and want to help you. What you did tonight simply wasn't acting, in a professional sense of the word. It was ... charades, a child pretending to "be" someone, at best a kind of reciting. And don't imagine I'm judging you only by tonight. I could have told you all this after you crashed into that audition and gave me your one-woman performance of *The School for Scandal*. My dear, delightful, highly intelligent child, you cannot act and I don't believe you'll ever be able to – not in a way that's acceptable in a present-day West End production.'

Not one word of this was I going to accept. 'But the audience liked me,' I told him doggedly. 'I could feel they did.'

'They also like performing seals. Besides, audiences don't work things out. You were just a gallant little understudy in a pretty dress who was giving everyone a good laugh. And at what a cost! I seriously doubt if my leading lady will play tomorrow.'

For a moment I felt contrite. 'And I've lost you a good stage manager.'

'Brice? Oh, that will all blow over. I shall apologise.'

'*You* will?'

'Of course. I was in the wrong. And I'd grovel to Brice rather than lose him – for quite a number of reasons.'

It astonished me that he should feel like that about a mere stage manager, and such a young one. I said, 'You're a very un-grand man, aren't you – for such a great actor?'

'How nice of you to pay me such a double compliment, and when I've been so cruel to you. But I do sincerely want to save you from bitter disappointment, which I swear will come your way if you don't give up this idea of acting. Couldn't you settle down in the office? Eve Lester feels a real affection for you – just as I do. And you were a real help at rehearsals, not to mention a constant source of amusement, which is worth untold gold to me during a time of strain. I positively long for my next production with you sitting beside me.'

I said I couldn't think why he found me funny.

'Neither can I, really, which makes it all the

funnier. But I don't think you're funny now and I'm desperately sorry if I've hurt you. And remember, I could be wrong about your acting.'

'You *are* wrong,' I said fiercely.

He threw back his head and laughed. 'I adore you for saying that. Now come and sit beside me while I take my make-up off and then I'll drive you home.'

I moved to a chair by his dressing-table and watched him cover his face with thick white grease. I had, of course, been distressed by what he said about my acting but the distress had not lasted. I now felt cheerful; in fact, very much more than cheerful. I genuinely did not believe him; also I was still buoyed up by the exhilaration of facing an audience. But there was more to it than that. Ever since he had mentioned the rehearsals I had become conscious of a great contentment and a most pleasurable feeling of physical well-being. And as I sat watching him, I remembered that I had never felt ... somehow *right* since rehearsals ended. I had put this down to the loss of interest, the loss of being connected with the play. Now I knew that, far more, I had felt the loss of being with him.

He towelled his face; then, noticing he had not taken off his toupee, said he ought to have done that first. 'Now I've got grease on it. Well, here goes. You can watch me grow older.'

I said, 'Did you ever see a play called *Lady Frederick?*'

'Yes, I saw the original production, the year Maugham had three plays running together. But I doubt if you were born then. Surely you don't know the play?'

'I saw it done by amateurs. Watching you made me think of the scene where Lady Frederick gets her young admirer to watch her put her make-up on, to disillusion him.'

'And I'm taking my make-up off – that's the acme of disillusion.'

'Only it seems to work in reverse. I've just discovered how much I love you.'

He gave me a startled look; then laughed, but not quite naturally.

I said, 'That wasn't a joke.'

'I had a hideous suspicion it might not be. How exactly like you! Oh, not to fall in love with me – that's unlike your intelligent self – but to break the glad tidings to me without an instant's reflection.'

'I gather you don't find them glad tidings.'

'How can I, when they're liable to mean unhappiness for you? And do you think I want my valued little friend turned into a mooning schoolgirl?'

I said, 'I won't moon. And I won't even mention it again if you don't want me to. And I certainly won't be unhappy. I'm getting happier and happier every minute.'

'Good God! Come here.' He stretched out his hand and pulled me towards him. 'Now stand behind me and look in the glass. You're a child – and you look a real child, not a girl of eighteen. And I'm a middle-aged man. You *can't* be in love with a man who looks like I do at this moment.'

I said seriously, 'You do look your worst, don't

159

you? Your face is still so greasy. But it makes no difference to me, particularly as I've never admired your looks.'

'You haven't?' He sounded a trifle surprised.

'Oh, I did when you played Charles Surface. But I was horribly disillusioned when I met you in the flesh.'

We were still staring not at our real selves but at our reflections in the glass. I saw his lips twitch. Then he said, 'Don't make me laugh now. Just listen. I'm a hopelessly susceptible man, also very fond of you. If you persist in this foolishness, no doubt I shall succumb and make love to you – only very limited love, I trust, but even that will be enough to spoil our friendship when I come to my senses, as I quickly shall. Now will you make a real effort to cure yourself? And let's not see each other alone for at least a month.'

The only part of this speech that interested me was the bit that told me I could get him to make love to me. I went down on my knees beside his chair and butted my head against his chest. He said quietly, 'Well, I gather this is your answer. I might have known I was wasting my first effort to resist temptation. What thick soft hair you have! Most women's hair, nowadays, is as stiffly waved as corrugated iron. And I'm glad you don't shave your neck. The nape of a woman's neck is *not* a place one cares to find bristles.'

Then he got up, raising me with him and, looking down on me, said, 'In all my years both as an actor and a lover I've never kissed a woman of your height. Well, I trust my technique will be equal to it. No, don't stand on tiptoe; you'll totter.

160

Kindly remember, for once in your dynamic young life, that this is a time when you do *not* take the initiative. Relax, and leave things to me.'

9

Looking back, I find it astonishing that a girl of eighteen, respectably – if not conventionally – brought up, could so delightedly abandon herself to being in love with a married man. I did not find it astonishing then and I was, from the first, determined to get all the love I could in return. If my partner stuck to his noble intentions of making only 'very limited love' it wouldn't be my fault.

After he had kissed me half-a-dozen times (I proudly counted; quite a feat considering my daze of bliss) he steadied me and said firmly, 'That will definitely be all for tonight. Now wait here while I finish dressing. You'd better rub that rouge off your cheeks. And try – we must both try – to look less affectionate before we face my stage door keeper and my chauffeur.'

He went into the curtained-off part of the room, and I went to the glass, rubbed my cheeks with one of his towels, and tidied up my mouth; I had forgotten I still had some make-up on. When he came back I ran to him eagerly. He said, 'No, no, child. I am not going to kiss you again.' But he did, for some minutes, then remarked 'Well, thank God my stage door keeper's an old, dim-sighted man. Still, we'd better hurry past him.'

But we weren't able to, as he stopped me to say that three ladies had been waiting for me but had now gone, and Miss Lester had telephoned to know where I was. Mr Crossway told me to go out to the car while he rang her up. When he joined me he said one of the programme girls had let her know I was 'on' and she had seen most of my performance. 'She sent you her proud congratulations for getting through so well.'

'Did she think I was as bad as you do?'

'Not quite. She believes you suffer from an excess of individualism – whatever that may mean – and she feels sure something can be done about it. She'll tell you tomorrow.'

I did not see how one could have too much individualism and, anyway, I was more interested in being beside him in the nice dark car, which seemed to me perfectly private as he had made sure the glass division between us and the chauffeur was closed. I rubbed the top of my head against his face.

He slipped his arm round me but said, 'I never kiss women in cars. It's unsubtle – and dangerous; chauffeurs seem to have eyes in the backs of their heads. How nice your hair tastes.'

'Perhaps I didn't quite get the soap out.'

'Good God, you'll have me frothing at the mouth. Now could we be serious for a moment? Are you planning to tell all your little friends about your latest conquest?'

I said I'd never made a conquest before. 'Have I really made one now?'

'Well, enough of one to scare the wits out of

162

me. None of this ought to be happening. Is it any use asking you to be discreet? Few women are, of course – even when their own interest calls for discretion – which has made my life difficult. I don't think my wife would mind anything as innocuous as this little interlude must remain. Still, if you gossip–'

'She might get to hear, and think it *wasn't* innocuous. Don't worry. I shan't gossip. And I've no wish to take you away from your wife. That would be against my principles.'

He chuckled. 'I'm glad your aunt inculcated *some* standards. How would she have felt about your goings on tonight?'

'She'd have been sad that you didn't like my acting.'

'I was referring to your highly immoral behaviour.'

I considered this, then said, 'It can't be immoral to love anyone – as long as one doesn't hurt anyone by it.'

'But suppose you hurt yourself?'

I said, 'Oh, cheer up! Perhaps I'll tire of you before you tire of me,' which pleased him so much that he said, 'To hell with my chauffeur,' and gave me a quick kiss.

Just before we reached the Club he asked me to be especially discreet with Miss Lester. 'She'd think it very wrong indeed. Of course she'd blame me far more than she'd blame you.'

'How can you be to blame when I've thrown myself at you? Do you mind that? I've read that men don't like it.'

He said that, with me, it was part of my fatal

163

attraction; then added hastily, 'My God, that was a dangerous thing to say! Now behave, and be ready to say a conventional good night to me.'

The car drew up. I whispered urgently, 'Shall I see you tomorrow? Please!'

'Yes, I'll manage something.'

The chauffeur opened the door and helped me out. I called back, 'Good night, Mr Crossway,' and wondered, as I ran up the Club steps, when I should first call him 'Rex'. But perhaps it would never be safe to, even in private, in case I slipped up in public. I would not let myself even *think* of him as 'Rex'. I would be *absolutely* discreet.

The girls were waiting up to congratulate me. I told them I had been praised for keeping the curtain up but that Mr Crossway had thought I was all wrong for the part. (This, if not his complete verdict, was at least true.) They admitted that they saw his point but loyally went on saying I was marvellous. And Zelle had sent a message that he ought to have divorced the leading lady and married me. We did not talk for long as I said I was tired. The truth was that I had a sudden longing to tell them everything that had happened, so felt I had better remove myself from temptation.

I lay awake for hours, remembering – and finding pleasure in the knowledge that I had a secret from the five girls sleeping so close to me. That made me wonder if being discreet might not actually be fun, apart from my dear's wishes in the matter. And it would not only mean not talking; I should need to do a lot of off-stage acting. I looked forward to that.

It began when I went into the office the next afternoon and felt I must pretend to be more unhappy than I now was about Mr Crossway's opinion of my performance. Miss Lester determinedly cheered me up and told me of her plan for getting rid of my 'excess of individualism'. She wanted me to go to a drama school. I told her I couldn't afford the fees, nor had I money to live on while I studied. She said that could all be arranged and Mr Crossway approved of her scheme and would coach me for the audition I should have to give at the school. And he would come up and talk to me about it during the afternoon.

I was on my own in the Throne Room when he arrived. He shut the door and said, 'Talk first. Affection, if any, afterwards.' He then told me he had agreed to Miss Lester's idea because coaching would give him the chance to see me without arousing her suspicions. Also he was anxious to be proved wrong about my acting. 'Besides, if you go to the school it will help you to get over this nonsense about me – as you must, you really must, my darling lunatic.'

By then, his lunatic was sitting on his knee, but not for long. After one not very lingering kiss he said, 'I will not make love to you when Miss Lester may come in any moment – or under the accusing eyes of my forefathers. Not that my father would have any right to cast a stone. He was far more disreputable than I've ever been.'

'You mean with women?'

'How worldly wise you sound! I did indeed mean with women. I fear they're an occupational

165

disease with actor managers. Now I mustn't see you alone again until I start coaching you. Miss Lester's finding out what you'll have to do for your entrance examination.'

'Couldn't you drive me home tonight?'

'I shan't do that again for some time; people so quickly notice that kind of thing.' Then he said he must go and have a last run-through with the official understudy of 'my' part. He had already rehearsed with her, in the morning. I asked what she was like.

'Dull, but safe – she won't climb on any footstools. Anyway, she'll have to play for several weeks.'

The poor girl who had been taken ill was having an operation for her appendicitis.

That night I watched my successor through the spy-hole. Her last scene did not get one laugh – nor did the scene that followed. Well, that was the way Mr Crossway and his leading lady wanted it, not to mention the author of the play. But I still thought it was a pity.

In a couple of days Miss Lester received particulars from the drama school. I should have to do two speeches from Shakespeare (there was a list to choose from) and one speech of my own choice from a modern play. I decided on Juliet's potion scene, a speech of Portia's, and a long speech of Darling Dora's from Shaw's *Fanny's First Play*. I already knew all these so I was ready for coaching. Miss Lester went round to see Mr Crossway during the matinée and he said he would start the next day. The job would have to be done quickly as the school was shortly to close

166

for the summer holidays. Normally I should not have been heard until the examinations before the autumn term, and it was only as a favour to Mr Crossway that the Principal agreed to hear me in a week.

My coaching took place in the stalls bar, not on the stage (the stage being a very un-private place). I began with Juliet's potion speech and was instantly absorbed in it. I thought of the bar as a tomb, all Juliet's horrors were real for me as I lived through them, line by line, until I drank my potion and fell senseless to the floor. During the entire speech I was oblivious of Mr Crossway, so it was something of a shock to sit up and find him groaning, with his head in his hand.

All he said was: 'Let's have a little light relief. Try Darling Dora. Perhaps God *meant* you to be funny.'

But he thought me even worse as Darling Dora– 'When you try to be funny, you aren't. Well, let's have a go at Portia. And take it calmly, quietly.'

This suited my conception of Portia – except that I thought her declaration of love for Bassanio should also be radiant. I made it *serenely* radiant. Mr Crossway told me I was both patronising and affected.

'I simply can't understand it,' he said despairingly. 'As yourself you haven't an ounce of affectation in you; it's your extreme naturalness that makes people take to you. And yet the minute you assume a character you're artificial. Are you imitating anyone? Your aunt, perhaps?'

But I had to tell him that Aunt Marion had

been considered a very natural actress. (I didn't mention that she had sometimes told me my acting was exaggerated. I had never for a moment believed her.) He then wondered if I had picked up bad habits from second-rate touring companies. But I had only been taken to see first-rate ones. He finally came to the conclusion that my bad acting was inborn, like original sin.

He did, then and later, try hard to coach me, taking me through speeches, sometimes quietly talking to me about them, sometimes making me repeat lines after him. But we got nowhere. When I stopped being what I called natural and he called affected, I became what both of us called wooden. The coaching sessions always ended by his telling me to come and be comforted; and as far as I was concerned, the comforting made up for everything.

On the day before I was due to go to the drama school he said I must forget everything he had told me and just be myself. 'I could be wrong about you – God knows, I hope I am. They may think you're a born actress. And so you are, in a way. But I'm afraid you're a born *bad* actress, my darling little Tich.' The rest of that session was entirely given over to comforting.

When I started for the drama school next day, I still was not sure whether or not I wanted to be accepted, as it would mean being away from the Crossway. But while I was waiting in the hall, reading the announcements of plays recently performed (the term had just ended) I suddenly knew that I did, very much, want to be a student here. It would give me my longed-for chance to act, lots and lots of parts. And surely I could show my dear he was wrong. He had accused me of so many things – affectation, over-acting, reciting, being a kind of single turn – and still never convinced me. I would go back to him in triumph, perhaps with a scholarship.

Soon I was conducted to a large room with a small stage at one end, where the Principal of the school and one woman teacher were waiting for me. They talked most charmingly, trying to set me at ease. This was not the school's real theatre, just a rehearsal room, said the Principal. 'We thought you'd find it more informal. And we wanted to know you as well as hear you.' I liked them greatly and felt they liked me. I went up on the little stage feeling happy and hopeful.

Portia, Juliet, Darling Dora: I did them all, in that order, and got only a quiet 'Thank you' after each of them. The final thank you was followed by a request that I should come and talk.

The Principal was still charming. He found things to praise: my vitality and ease of movement. The woman teacher spoke of my excellent enunciation. But I knew, almost at once, that they liked my acting no more than Mr Crossway did. And they soon began stressing how overcrowded the stage was and how few parts there were for anyone as small as I was. And the school was so full–

I said: 'You don't want me.'

The Principal said he did want me, would indeed love to have me– 'But we're so afraid it wouldn't be fair – to you. Still, let me think it over. I'll telephone Mr Crossway.'

He must have done so at once, because when I got back to the theatre Mr Crossway had already rung up Miss Lester.

'They liked you so much – as a person,' she told me. 'And the school really is very full. Mr Crossway's so very sorry. He says he'll drive you home tonight and try to comfort you.'

That prospect cheered me more than she could know.

After the performance she sent me down to wait in the car. No chauffeur was to be seen and I was pleased soon to discover that he was away on holiday and Mr Crossway was driving himself. However, the pleasure of being alone with him was offset by the fact that, while driving, he could only offer verbal comfort. When I pointed this out he laughed and said he'd try to do better– 'But only a little better. Making love in the back of cars is not one of my habits. Still, we'll get out of the traffic.'

He drove me up to Hampstead, where we stopped, looking down on the twinkling lights of London. But we still stayed in the front of the car and the only improvement as regards comforting was that he put his arm round my shoulders. This wasn't, in the circumstances, enough. He had relayed his talk with the Principal most tactfully, stressing every little compliment; but there was no getting away from the fact that I had been refused admission. And it now struck me that the coaching sessions would be at an end. Without a moment of pre-thought I said:

'Couldn't we go somewhere – perhaps back to your dressing-room? Couldn't we *be* together?'

He turned his head quickly. 'What do you mean?'

'I mean ... everything. Couldn't we, please?'

'We could not.' Perhaps he only spoke firmly but, to me, he sounded brutal. 'Good God, child, what am I going to do about you?' He started the car.

I asked if he was angry.

'Yes, very. But with myself, not with you. I never ought to have let this thing begin. And it's got to stop, my dear. It really has.'

For once I was past arguing. I just sat there, with tears rolling down my cheeks. He obviously didn't care for me, nobody liked my acting, there was nothing left. It was the first time in my life I had experienced misery.

After a few minutes he drove the car into a deserted, dimly lit street and said: 'Out you get.' For a bewildered moment I thought he was going to leave me there. Then I realised I was being invited into the back of the car. Once there, he said: 'I simply cannot bear to see mice cry. They're too small and their tears are too large for them.'

'And you didn't mean what you said? It won't have to stop?'

'Well, not just yet, anyway – unless you make any more immoral suggestions. I was deeply shocked. All you're going to get now is one chaste kiss on the forehead.'

What followed was the most comprehensive comforting I had come by, and completely restored me to happiness; though we returned to the front of the car sooner than I could have

171

wished and then drove straight back to the Club. When we got there, he advised me to tone down my expression before joining my little friends– 'You don't look at all like a girl who's come home by herself on a bus.' I went to the cloakroom to tidy up generally. Discretion had become something of a mania with me; so much so that I nowadays told the girls very little about my life at the theatre. I had never even mentioned that I was trying to get into a drama school.

Up in my cubicle I found a note from Lilian saying: 'Great news! Zelle got bored with being alone in her flat and is staying here for a while. We're all in room 44 – it's on the top floor. Come on up.'

I got into my dressing-gown and set out to find room 44. It turned out to be an attic, a very attractive one, with a deep window-seat let into its sloping outer wall. Zelle was sitting there with the window open behind her. Lilian was in the armchair, manicuring her nails. Molly knelt in front of the gas fire, toasting Veda bread which smelt marvellous.

I sat on the bed and listened rather than talked; and soon, thought rather than listened. It seemed to me extraordinary that two girls as strikingly pretty as Molly and Lilian should have only three uninteresting men between them and that Zelle, quite as attractive in her delicate, elusive way, should apparently have no men friends at all except an elderly, married cousin – while I had so recently been kissed by one of the most famous actors in London. I ate my Veda toast with much pleasure and gazed at the summer night sky through the open window, until I heard Molly say: 'Our Mouse is a hundred miles away.' But I wasn't as far away as that; I was in a dimly lit street somewhere in Hampstead.

10

As I spent so much time at the theatre I saw far less of Zelle than Molly and Lilian did, but even a few mornings and our late evening reunions were enough to convince me that Lilian had been right in thinking her puzzling; though I thought the word 'odd' was more applicable. I never felt there was any puzzle to be solved, simply that Zelle had an unusual character which was full of contradictions.

Sometimes there was a trace of grandeur in her manner; this was when she was launching into expenditure – usually on us – and wished to make it clear that the cost was of no importance. At other times she could be humble, slightly scared, and childlike. And though she dressed with a quiet sophistication that was almost elderly, compared with most young Club members, she was undoubtedly childlike in some of her tastes. She had brought with her from her flat a picture of a baby faun crouching over a fire in a misty landscape, at which she would gaze lovingly, making such remarks as, 'Look at his darling furry ears.' She had also brought some very impressive books, dealing with politics and world affairs – surprising reading for anyone who admired that faun, though perhaps not more surprising than *The Times*, which was the only newspaper she ever opened. I have a vivid mental picture of her sitting in the lounge, with her pony-straight legs neatly placed together, turning page after page. All the same, I was never sure if she actually *read The Times* – or the impressive books, though she sometimes handled them. What she certainly did read, swiftly and from cover to cover, was a copy of *Dracula* she found in the Green Room, a Members Only room where people often left their possessions lying about. She became so obsessed by this book that, for several very hot nights, she refused to have her bedroom window open in case Count Dracula climbed up from the street, four floors below, to bite her. She told this against herself, laughing; but she undoubtedly had a terror of the supernatural. When she heard that the top floor of the Club was said to be haunted she seriously considered moving to another floor. We were fond of her attic so Lilian assured her that the ghost only walked, if ever, on Hallowe'en, by which time Zelle expected to be back in her flat. It seemed that her guardian disapproved of women's clubs and had only agreed to her staying with us while he was out of England; he had recently taken his family to the Continent. 'In the autumn, I may study something,' said Zelle, rather grandly. 'That's all the more reason why I should enjoy myself now.'

Her main way of enjoying herself seemed to be treating people to meals, which was a godsend to

Molly and Lilian. They had now been promised work in the autumn but we were still only at the beginning of August and they had to be economical. (Molly's thousand pounds – referred to by her as 'bastard's pay-off' – had not yet arrived.) Zelle, overriding their mild protests, had taken them out to dinner almost every night since we had first met her. She also took them to theatres and a concert (both Molly and Lilian felt one concert was more than enough) and suggested Westminster Abbey for her first Sunday. The girls declined this firmly. 'Well, what *can* one do on a Sunday?' said Zelle, whose ideal was at least one entertainment per day. It was the scarcity of Sunday entertainments that led her to take the girls on an outing that changed all our lives.

I had known for some time that Mr Crossway had a younger brother, named Adrian, who was the vicar of the Suffolk village near which Mr Crossway had a country house. A few days after Zelle came to stay at the Club, Miss Lester told me that Adrian Crossway was about to give a garden party, in aid of his church, at which an entertainment would be performed by villagers. This happened every August. Mr Crossway always spoke the prologue and epilogue and read the lessons at the church services; the party had to be on a Sunday so that he could be free. Brice Marton stage-managed the entertainment, and this year he had asked Miss Lester if I could be his assistant, thus releasing Tom, who particularly wanted the day off.

Brice had been up in the office quite often since the night I had 'kept his curtain up'. (As pre-

175

dicted by Mr Crossway, the row between them had blown over.) He had been very pleasant to me and I now considered we were friends, so I was only too willing to help him and delighted to be in on the vicarage garden party. I happened to speak of it to Zelle, at lunch one day, and she at once saw a way of spending a Sunday – the party was open to the public. She decided to hire a car; and when I left for the theatre, she and the girls were discussing what they should wear.

It was now over a week since my happy excursion to Hampstead and, except in the presence of Miss Lester or through the spy-hole, I had not seen my dear. He had warned me that it would be difficult to arrange meetings but I had expected him to manage something before this and I was feeling starved. So I was thankful when he came up to the office that afternoon and found me alone, Miss Lester being out having her hair done.

It was damping to learn that he had come to see her, not me. And he did not at first show any wish to take advantage of this fine opportunity for affection. However, he succumbed quite soon, if only briefly.

While disentangling himself he said, 'This reminds me. I hear Brice is bringing you to my brother's garden party on Sunday. When we meet there, will you please treat me with the respect due to me from my junior secretary?'

I nodded resignedly. 'I suppose your wife will be there.'

'No, she's away, staying with her father. But all the village pussy-cats will be around with their very wide-open old eyes. So be a good child and behave discreetly, will you?'

I said it didn't sound as if I should *get* the chance not to.

'Well, you won't if I can help it. But one never knows what you'll be up to, especially as I shall be looking my best. I speak the prologue as an eighteenth-century squire – almost as ravishing as when I played Charles Surface, except for the corsets.'

'*Did* you wear corsets?'

'I did indeed. Doesn't that put you off?'

'It wouldn't put me off now if you wore a truss – whatever that is.'

This amused him so much that he again succumbed to affection and we narrowly missed being caught by Miss Lester. He carried things off well and at once began talking to her about business matters. Before he left he said to me: 'Well, I shall see you on Sunday. If I've a free moment I'll show you round my workroom. I've some models of stage sets that will interest you.' This raised my hopes of a private meeting.

Miss Lester told me that the workroom was in a converted barn, close to the house, and that he sometimes stayed there when working on a production. The house itself was seldom used now as Mrs Crossway did not care for it. Realising how little I knew of Mrs Crossway, I asked what she was like.

'Beautiful and charming. Beyond that, I know little. We've probably not met a dozen times in all the years I've been here.'

I found this astonishing. And I noticed Miss

Lester changed the conversation. My guess was that she didn't like Mrs Crossway.

On the Sunday morning I got up at six-thirty (wakened by the night porter, to the sleepy wrath of disturbed neighbours) and met Brice Marton at the station in time to have breakfast before we caught an early train. The journey sounded complicated; we should have to change from this train into a smaller one and then a car was booked to meet us. At first I thought it might be difficult to keep a conversation going but it got easier and easier – perhaps because Brice kept questioning me about myself and seemed interested in everything I told him. I questioned him, too, but for a long time the conversation kept sliding back to me.

Eventually we worked out that as he had lived in Manchester until he was fifteen – and I was eight – it was possible we might have been in a theatre at the same time; he and his mother had often had 'passes' and I had begun my theatre going very early. Apart from this, we had little common ground. He had never been in my suburb and thought of it as a luxurious place almost in the country. The 'slum' he had once said he was brought up in was the street where his mother, now dead, had been a theatrical landlady. He said residential streets in large industrial cities were apt to be slummy– 'But theatrical lodgings can be cosy. Old pros like Mr Crossway's father often preferred them to hotels.'

'Did he stay with your mother – Sir Roy?'

'Tour after tour. I first knew him when I was two years old. He was very kind to me – used to bring me toys. And soon after I left school he found me a job as a call boy.'

I said I had only seen Sir Roy when he was an old man, as Sir Peter Teazle; and though I realised he was a splendid actor I had thought his personality harsh. 'But perhaps that was the part. I expect you were fond of him.'

'That's where you're wrong,' said Brice Marton. 'I hated him like hell.'

'How extraordinary, when he was so kind to you. But then, Mr Crossway's kind and you're not exactly fond of him, are you?'

'Frankly, no. But I don't hate him like I hated Sir Roy. And as a matter of fact I'm fairly well disposed to Mr C. at the moment. I'm apt to be, for some weeks after we've had a row, because he behaves so well. There isn't another man in his position who would apologise to his stage manager.'

'Why don't *you* apologise, for a change?'

'Because I'm never in the wrong – I mean, with him; I apologised to you, when I was. Anyway, apart from the row, this is one day of the year when I almost love our Rex, because he's so much nicer than his horrible brother Adrian. Do you know why we're coming all this way? It's so that Adrian Crossway can say to people, "My brother puts his stage staff at my disposal." The villagers could manage quite well on their own but that wouldn't satisfy Adrian's sense of importance.'

'Is he like Mr Crossway to look at?'

'Much handsomer – you'll probably fall for him, especially when you see him welcoming the audience. He stands up on a mound under a cedar tree and stretches out his arms like St Francis blessing the birds. And then he turns into Christ suffering little children – he has all the smallest ones at his feet to watch that show. Sorry if that shocked you. I'm an atheist.'

I said I had been one at sixteen. 'Getting confirmed so terribly put me off God. But I think I've more or less slid into being an agnostic – a sort of Christian agnostic, really.'

He grinned. 'Mind you don't slide into being a full-blown Christian. You might, if you go to Adrian's service this evening. What with Adrian in the pulpit looking superb and Rex at the lectern sounding superb, and the church lit only by candlelight except for a stray gleam of sunset – if there wasn't a sunset I swear Adrian would fake one – the whole show would pack any London theatre. Of course the truth is that Adrian's a frustrated actor. He played a few parts and was shocking, stiff as a poker. Which reminds me, what did Rex say to you about your performance that night?'

'Well, he didn't say I was stiff as a poker, but he said almost everything else bad. He just doesn't think I can act.'

'You could get a job on tour if you tried hard enough. What's happened to all the drive you had when you butted into that audition?'

'I wonder.' And as I said it, I did wonder, but only for a second. Then I knew that I now wanted something far more than I had ever wanted a job on the stage, and every bit of my driving force was directed towards getting it. This was so startlingly clear to me that I almost feared Brice might read my thoughts – he was looking at me intently. So I changed the subject by asking what county we were passing through. He said we were just about entering Suffolk.

We had talked so much that I had hardly looked out of the window. By now we had changed into the little train and were passing through lovely country, unlike any I had seen before. Most of my childhood's holidays had been spent at the sea-side. 'The country', for me, had mainly meant Cheshire or Derbyshire, around which friends had sometimes taken me for drives. Here in Suffolk the trees were softer, somehow furry, their leaves a paler green. The whole landscape seemed to me gently blurred, with no harsh outlines; cornfields, water meadows, the thatched roofs of cottages and the tiled roofs of farms all merged into each other under the summer sun. And I kept mentally turning the real landscape into a painted landscape. I mentioned this to Brice, who said it might be because we were in Constable country. But Constable landscapes are darker, browner, than my landscape that day. I was painting it myself, covering it all with the hazy wash of my own happiness.

Brice had quite a lot to do with that happiness. I felt on such easy terms of friendship with him; and I had never before had a man friend. Also he was stimulating to talk to about life in general; we did not discuss only personal matters, as I always did with the girls at the Club. But I was shocked to learn that he rarely read a book. He said he had been fond of reading as a child but had lost the habit once he became connected with the theatre. I was even more shocked to realise that, since coming to London, I had not read a book myself – nor, until now, noticed that I hadn't; every day had been filled with its own interest. Though I had, since falling in love, repeated a good deal of poetry to myself while riding on buses: the only time, except when sleeping, that I was on my own.

After the little train dropped us at a tiny station we had a two-mile drive along a narrow road, mainly bordered by cornfields, until we reached the park surrounding Mr Crossway's old, gabled house, which was not as large as the words 'country house' had led me to expect; though Brice said it was the local Hall. I spotted the barn which must be Mr Crossway's workroom and wondered when he would show it to me. Then we passed the small, less old, lodge. A woman looked out of a window and Brice said she acted as care-taker, now the house was not used, and looked after Mr Crossway when he occasionally came down for a night.

A few hundred yards ahead was the church, very old, square-towered, and much larger than I had expected – as was the Georgian vicarage just opposite, which seemed to me more imposing than Mr Crossway's gabled house. The road had turned sharply before we got out of the car at the vicarage, and I could see the beautiful village street. I longed to explore it, also to go into the church and hear Mr Crossway read the lessons – the bells were still ringing – but Brice said we were due to meet the local stage manager in the vicarage garden. So we went in, through an arched wooden door in the high wall.

It was an extensive garden, at the side and the back of the vicarage, running down to a little stream where a wooden bridge led across to the park around Mr Crossway's house. Chairs for the audience were already set out on the lawn. Brice pointed out the quite high mound, topped by a cedar, where Adrian Crossway would stand to bless everyone; and then the local stage manager and his assistant came out of the vicarage. Except that one was middle-aged and one young and both were pleasant and efficient, I can't remember a thing about them, not even their names.

The entertainment was to take place on the wide terrace at the back of the vicarage, onto which a central door and four tall windows opened. The players – I gathered there were many – dressed in the vicarage bedrooms and had to get downstairs at the right moment to make their entrances. The method of achieving this was explained to me and then the four of us rehearsed it. Brice, in a kind of prompt corner hidden from the audience by a piece of scenery, held up cards with large black numbers on them. I, at an upper window where I could see him, called the number on the card to the local assistant stage manager stationed on a landing. He then warned the players needed for the next episode. When Brice turned the card over, so that the number was in red, I called 'Ready, One!' (or whatever the number was) and then the players concerned marched downstairs to the vicarage drawing-room, where the local stage manager waited in readiness to get them out on the terrace at the right moment. I was told again and again that it was absolutely simple.

At the end of the rehearsal somebody mentioned that there were many other players concealed in the yew walk – knights on hobby horses, folk singers, half a dozen monks – who would come on between some episodes (without any help from me, thank God). So many villagers seemed to be *in* the entertainment that I couldn't imagine how there could be anyone left to look at it.

Brice and I were coming out of the vicarage to get an early lunch at the inn when Mr Crossway and Adrian Crossway came through the lych gate of the churchyard and crossed the road to talk to us. Adrian Crossway was wearing a long and most becoming clerical garment, and I saw in a flash that his looks were all I had expected my dear's to be, that day at the audition – and which they had so depressed me by not being. Adrian's hair was thicker and fairer, his eyes larger and bluer, his nose straighter, his mouth more classical in outline. Also he was slimmer than Mr Crossway. I took pleasure in seeing them side by side and thinking that Adrian's good looks meant nothing to me – except that I rather resented them. And Brice's description had made him sound dislikeable. But I must say he couldn't have been nicer.

He apologised because the church service had prevented his being at the vicarage to meet us, regretted he couldn't give us lunch there as his housekeeper was busy with preparations for the garden party, and said he would look forward to meeting me during the afternoon. He even walked all the way to the inn with us, after Mr Crossway had gone to lay out his clothes in his dressing-room – which, he mildly complained, was the housemaid's pantry. One difference between them was that, unless Adrian was actually smiling, he looked extremely serious; whereas my dear Mr C. usually looked as if just about to see a joke. Anyway, he looked like that when he was with me.

After Brice and I were on our own at lunch he said, 'I can't decide if you've made a hit with Adrian or if he simply turned on his charm-the-woman manner. Tom would have only got the curtest "good morning".'

I had really quite liked Adrian, so I said, 'You're prejudiced, just because he's a Crossway.' But Brice wouldn't admit that. He said he found Adrian dislikeable in his own right.

After a scrappy meal we went back to the vicarage and did some more rehearsing with the black and red number cards. I had begun to fear I might wreck the show.

'Don't worry,' said Brice. 'When there's any hold-up I cue in the hobby horses from the yew walk and they prance round until I yell for them to go off.'

I felt I might be less confused if I knew what the entertainment was about; but Brice said that, after stage managing it for five years, he still hadn't any clear idea. He vaguely thought it dealt with the history of the village, with Boadicea and Queen Elizabeth thrown in for good measure.

By now the bedrooms were full of people dressing up. I had nothing to do until the show started so I stood on the front steps of the vicarage and watched the audience arrive. There were a good many cars parked along the village street and a steady stream of people paying their money at the door in the garden wall. Adrian Crossway stood there greeting people and escorting the local gentry to good seats. I hoped to see some pretty dresses but most of the gentry wore drab-looking silk, and the villagers wore drab cotton. Not one dress, in my view, qualified as a real garden-party dress. I remembered that Molly, Lilian and Zelle had worried about what they should wear; and I thought that, even if they wore their simplest summer dresses, they would look better than most of the audience.

I had been too busy all morning to think of the girls. Now I was on the look-out for them. I had begun to fear they would be late when a large, chauffeur-driven car pulled up at the garden gate and out got three absolute visions in fluttering printed chiffon. Molly's was mainly pale green, Lilian's was pink and mauve, and Zelle's was beige and white. All their dresses – and their hats – were the apotheosis of garden-party clothes. (I later learned that Zelle had bought them all, for the occasion.)

I reached the girls just as Adrian Crossway was introducing himself. He had been nice to me, but to them he was almost reverently admiring; they might have been three goddesses. As he took them into the garden I heard him say they were too late for front seats but he would find them a very special place.

When I got back to the vicarage, the local stage manager wanted to give me some last-minute instructions, so I only got to my open upper window as Adrian Crossway, tall and straight under the cedar tree on the mound, was about to address the audience. I then saw the 'very special place' he had found for the girls: they were at his feet, sitting on white skin rugs. On the lower slopes of the mound were the privileged village tots but they didn't have any rugs.

The minute Adrian said: 'Good people! My friends, one and all!' the audience stood and turned to the mound, as people in the chancel of a church turn to the east for the Creed. It would have been more impressive than it was if so many chairs had not been knocked over, but Adrian gave people time to pick them up. He then spoke well and I quite liked what he said about entertainments, as well as church services, having the right to be blessed.

After that, the audience turned towards the vicarage again, knocked over and picked up more chairs, finally got themselves settled; and the show began.

First, Mr Crossway spoke the prologue. Being above him, I could see little more than the top of his head. Anyway, I could neither look nor listen as Brice was already showing a number card. My job had started.

For nearly two hours I repeatedly dashed from my window-seat and up a flight of stairs, shouting my 'warnings' and 'readys', with no respite except during an interlude of folk song, during which I got the opportunity to have a good look at the mound. The girls were now not merely sitting; they were reclining, very gracefully, on the rugs. Reclining with them was Adrian Crossway and a large red-haired man rather like Henry VIII but better looking, and broad rather than fat. I was just wishing he would stand up so that I could see if he was tall enough for Molly when, up from the back of the mound, came Mr Crossway. I thought it unprofessional of him to mingle with the audience when he was still dressed as an eighteenth-century squire, but no doubt it would have been dull spending the afternoon in the housemaid's pantry. I saw him being introduced to the girls and then he, too, settled on the skin rugs. The whole group looked most picturesque and I watched it with interest until the folk songs stopped and my job started again.

When the entertainment mercifully ended I barely waited for Mr Crossway to finish the epilogue before I grabbed the chance to get into the bathroom to tidy up. I found I looked pretty awful. My hot face was shining and I seemed to have lost my powder compact. My grey linen dress with its spotless white collar ('like' a Puritan Maid, according to Aunt Marion) was creased and the collar no longer spotless. I felt in no mood to mingle with the girls in their chiffon glory. Anyway, I decided I must report to Brice. But when I got to the terrace he wasn't there; and as I happened to see the girls going into one of the marquees I hurried into the other and had two cups of tea. Then I felt better and went out to the lawn.

Already chairs were being stacked and people who were not at tea were wandering around. Almost at once I saw Mr Crossway coming towards me, still in his eighteenth-century clothes; many of the performers were still in their costumes. He said he had been looking for me.

'Any special reason?' I asked hopefully.

'In a way. Come and stroll with me. I've been talking to your very decorative little friends. Tell me about the dark one. Can she act?'

'Lilian? She's only been in musical comedies.'

'But she tells me she's played parts. I was wondering– Oh, dear, I'm afraid this may hurt your feelings.'

I found he was considering Lilian for the part I had played, that memorable evening. The girl who had been taken ill was not returning and he had never thought the understudy good enough. I felt a pang, but as there was no hope of getting the part myself I was all for Lilian having it. I suggested he should hear her read.

'That's what I thought. Is she teachable?'

'I'd say that's just what she is – very quick to pick up ideas. She'll be thrilled that you like her.'

'I don't know that I *like* her – except for the part; she seems a trine hard. The baby-faced giantess is a darling. She's made something of a hit with Hal Hammond, as you can see.'

Molly and the large red-haired man were strolling across the terrace and he was being most attentive.

I said, 'How suitable that his name's Hal when he's so like Bluff King Hal – though his eyes aren't so piggy.'

189

'And he hasn't acquired any wives yet,' said Mr Crossway. 'I must say they make a striking pair.'

'It's so splendid that he's tall enough for Molly.'

'He also has other advantages – including a good deal of money. He's a local landowner. If he's seriously attracted, your big little friend could do well for herself.'

'What do you think of Zelle?'

He said he'd hardly spoken to her. 'She was sitting next to my brother, who has persuaded them to stay for the evening service. Are you going back with them, or with Brice?'

'I suppose I couldn't drive back with you?'

'No, indeed. And I'm not going till tomorrow. I dislike driving at night. I shall sleep in my workroom.'

I asked when he was going to show me the workroom and he said he ought not to have put that idea into my head. 'When my wife's down and the house is open, people often wander over from here and I could have shown you round without its being conspicuous. But now it's out of the question. We can't walk across there all on our own.'

We had come as far as the bridge over the stream. I made sure there was no one within earshot and then said: 'But later – tonight – couldn't I visit you?'

'In your long black cloak, I suppose?'

'Well, I do have it with me.'

He chuckled. 'And after our interlude at Hampstead I take it that your intentions are entirely dishonourable. No, of course you can't visit me, tonight or any other night. This is a blood-curdling conversation to be having at a vicarage fete.'

'No one can hear.'

'I realise that now – but by tomorrow I shall fear some old lady may have had a powerful hearing-aid trained on us. Oh, you're a mad, bad girl and I'm so fond of you.'

'Even when I'm looking my worst, as I am now?'

He regarded me critically. 'Well, your nose is a bit glossy but what's a glossy nose between friends?'

'That's how I felt about you, that night when your face was covered in grease. Except that I felt more than friendly.'

'Well, so do I. But you really must get it into your darling head that I never seduce respectable young women, even when they don't want to stay respectable; and if any dowager has heard that through her hearing-aid I trust she'll set it to my credit. Now, as they say, we must mingle – with the others, I hasten to add.'

'Can I ask you one thing first?'

'You undoubtedly will if you want to.'

'I just want to know, if you didn't think it wrong, would you ... well, like me to visit you in your workroom?'

'Of course.' He said it very seriously and very kindly; then his tone became amused again. 'We'd better try to look less sultry as we rejoin the mob.'

'Are we looking sultry?'

'Well, you are. And I rather feared I might be, judging by the effect you have on me, you shameless girl. That's *absolutely* all for today. Let's find your friend Lilian and I'll ask her to come and read to me – tomorrow afternoon if she's free.'

We found both Lilian and Zelle strolling with Adrian Crossway. It turned out that he had asked all the girls to supper at the vicarage after the evening service, and he at once included me in the invitation, which I thought very kind of him.

'Do stay,' said Zelle. 'Then you can drive back with us.'

I said I must ask Brice if he wanted me to return with him. Adrian Crossway said I need not bother to let him know about supper. If I didn't turn up, he'd know I'd gone back to London.

I found Brice upstairs in the vicarage, checking and packing costumes which had been sent from London. He said of course I could stay and, though he would miss me on the return journey, I deserved some fun after my hard work. I helped him until all the clothes were packed except those that were still on people's backs; the local stage management would have to cope with them. Then Brice went to ask the housekeeper for a sandwich as he saw no chance of getting a meal for hours. I, too, had a sandwich because, if a plan I was already working on came to anything, I was going to be short of food before the evening was over.

Brice went off in the village taxi in time to catch the last train from the little local station. I went back to a bedroom and sat on a basket of clothes, thinking. By now I had decided my plan was practicable but I was not yet sure if I dared carry it through; and I still had not made up my mind when the bells began ringing for the evening service. I stood at the window and watched people going into the church, including Molly accompanied by Bluff King Hal, and Lilian and Zelle with Mr Crossway.

I could go to church too, and then to supper, and then home with the girls. But would I? I told myself I must make up my mind before the bells stopped ringing – no, it would be time enough when they all came in to supper; I could say I had been too busy packing costumes to come to the service. Then it dawned on me that my last chance of all would be when the girls drove along the road to London. I could stop the car, say I'd been for a walk and got lost ... or something like that.

This would give me more time for thinking and I had a sudden longing to be out in the country, all on my own. Surely I could find some little wood to hide in?

I waited until the bells stopped ringing and the last straggler had hurried into church. The little street was now deserted. I went quietly downstairs. A pleasant smell was coming from the kitchen; no doubt there was going to be a good supper but what cared I about food? The front door stood open. I dashed out and ran the short distance to the road that led to the station and London. Once I had turned the corner I was behind a hedge and out of sight from the village.

I could see no wood ahead of me but there were some tall haystacks in between me and Mr Crossway's house and on the opposite side of the road to the lodge. I went into the field, chose the best situated haystack and sat down behind it. Although I was only a few hundred yards from the church, and even less from Mr Crossway's lodge, no one could see me here. And it was a perfect place for thinking. In front of me stretched a patchwork of fields, divided by hedges dotted by tall trees and pollarded willows, and above me arched the vast twilight sky.

As a child I had been too happy and too occupied to be introspective but I had become so during my aunt's long illness, when I poured out my thoughts in my journal. Not one journal entry had I made since my first night in London and I had almost lost the habit of analytical thought about myself. Now I sternly told myself to concentrate.

Most of the concentration took the form of self-justification. My aunt's views on the emancipation of women were pressed into service, also the behaviour of my favourite Shakespearian and Shavian heroines, so often as much the wooers as the wooed; though I reminded myself of what he *really* wished – had he not said so? In such a case, when only his conscience was coming between us, obviously I must make the decision. Only ... it required courage.

I should have needed none if I could have acted on impulse, as I so often did. But with time to think, in this calm country twilight, I not only needed courage but also felt it ebbing away. Shocked, I reminded myself I might never again get the chance I had tonight. And I went on reminding myself. In the late dusk I got up and peered round the edge of my haystack. I was on higher ground than the village and could see both the church and the vicarage. I was surprised that there were lights in the church still – surely the service must be over by now? Then I saw that a group was forming in the churchyard and people in it were lighting lanterns; and I remembered hearing that the folk singers would end the day by walking the full length of the village, singing. I watched them troop out of the churchyard, swinging their lanterns, and for a moment I watched their progress along the street. Then the vicarage cut off my view of them but I could still hear their voices.

They were singing *The White Paternoster,* 'Matthew, Mark, Luke and John, bless the bed that I lie on.' I had often sung it at school. Listening, now, I had the most intense sensation of being a child again. It lasted for as long as I could hear the voices. Then I returned to being myself standing there by the haystack. I remember thinking, 'This is *me,* in this present moment. And it is wonderful to be me, entirely my own responsibility. And I shall do what I must.' Then the moment of acute consciousness passed and I was fully occupied with definite plans.

The lights in the church were out now and lights streamed from the vicarage. Would they have begun supper yet? I should have liked to be there, getting to know Adrian Crossway and Bluff King Hal; and in a secret, and therefore enjoyable way, showing off my dear Mr C. to the girls. I could still be there, in less than two minutes—

I sat down behind the haystack and watched the moon rise.

It must have been about an hour later when I heard voices and laughter, then the slam of a car door. I jumped up and looked towards the village. Now I could see the lights from a car in front of the vicarage; the girls must be leaving. The lights travelled forward, then turned onto the road near which I was. For a split second I thought of dashing out to intercept the car, but where I actually dashed was behind the haystack again. The car passed. Once more I came from behind the haystack and watched the rear lights for as long as I could see them.

Soon after they disappeared another car came from the vicarage. I dodged until it had passed me and then saw it turn in at the lodge gates of Mr Crossway's house. I looked across the park; and a few minutes later I saw lights in his workroom.

Now I need wait no longer and the moon was high enough to light me on my way. Then it occurred to me that if I arrived too soon he might bundle me into his car and drive me – where? Perhaps back to London. So I must still wait.

Sooner than I expected the lights in the workroom were out. Now I must get there as fast as I could. I ran along the road and in at the lodge gates, glad to notice that the lodge was in darkness. Leaving the drive, I raced over the grass to the workroom.

What did I do now? Knock on the door, tap on a window? At first I could see neither, except for the large double doors which had served when the building was still a barn. These were no longer in use; roses were growing against them.

Exploring, I found a French window open onto the warm, windless night. I tiptoed up to it and murmured into the darkness a very soft 'hello'.

Nobody answered. For a moment of blank disappointment I thought he was not there. Then the moon, like a very stagey bit of stage lighting, shone in on him and I saw that he was already asleep. He did not stir as I moved towards him.

He was lying on his side, facing me, one hand childishly under his cheek His left arm was outside the bedclothes. I noticed his naked shoulder; I had never before known that men sometimes slept minus pyjamas. I gazed down on him with love and great interest. He looked far younger than he usually did. This was partly due to the expanse of naked flesh but, even more, to his lack of facial expression. As a rule, his expression was one of controlled, sophisticated humour. Now, in utter repose, there was no control whatever, nothing but a youthful, slightly open-mouthed blankness.

I thought he must have been very tired to have fallen asleep so soon. It seemed unkind to wake him.

But I did wake him.

11

Less than twenty-four hours later I wrote:

How I wish I had kept this journal up since I came to London! Now it is too late. Even if I had time to write fully of all that has happened I could never recapture the flown moment, never be the me who lived it. Often I was happy – and I long for a record of that happiness. But if I made the record now it would be tinged by the sadness of farewell. Not that I am sad, exactly; or anyway, really unhappy. It is more that I am lonely, with a strange kind of loneliness which has nothing to do with being alone, away from people. Even if I could – and how I wish I could – be with him tonight I should still be lonely. Unless … yes, now I understand. It would be all right, even if we were apart, if he cared for me as I care for him.

But would it, quite? Surely even the most treasured (and legal) bride must feel a bit lost on discovering that belonging to a man does not make one feel closer but rather more noticeably separate? Or am I unusual? I only know that I felt much closer in the car at Hampstead than I did last night – when at one moment I found myself thinking it was a bit like my disappointment when I was confirmed. This may be blasphemous but I think not. For expecting to achieve union with God is similar to expecting to achieve it with man. Only I minded much more as regards man.

I don't remember doing much soul-searching after confirmation. I just became a cheerful atheist. And I can't imagine that any number of confirmations would improve matters. Whereas I do feel they will improve if I can be with him again – as, surely, I shall be soon, now there is no point in his having a conscience about me. He did look deadly serious this afternoon but I think that was mainly concern for me. The fact that I am here now is due to that concern. He said to Miss Lester: 'That child looks very tired. You should send her home early. She worked very hard yesterday.' He was standing behind Miss Lester when he said that, so she could not see his face. And as the remark could be said to have a double meaning I thought he would give me the nicker of a twinkle, but he merely looked worried.

Miss Lester sent me home at six. I could have gone out to dinner with Lilian and Zelle but I was too tired. Molly is out with Bluff King Hal – already; he drove up to London today. Lilian and I looked down on him from upstairs while he was waiting for Molly, and then rushed to tell her he was carrying flowers. I said, 'It's happened at last– "Roses in the hall"!' Then we sped Molly on her way, very happy for her. And Lilian was happy for herself as she has won her part at the Crossway. I was happy too – in a way; I am finding that out as I write. I am, somehow ... exorcising *the loneliness. It will pass, it will pass.*

But with it will pass someone I shall be a little sorry to lose: myself as I was before last night. Aunt Marion had a book of poems by Charles Cotton which she bought for the Lovat Fraser decorations, and in one poem are the lines:

She finds virginity a kind of ware
That's very, very troublesome to bear,
And being gone she thinks will ne'er be missed.

I think one will *miss it, but only for a very little while. Soon one will forget that it ever meant anything. Perhaps it never did; already I can almost accept that. The great plane tree outside my window is as beautiful as it was that May night when I last wrote in my journal, though its summer leaves are a little less green than the leaves of spring.*

When I settled here in bed, after the girls went, I planned to write very fully of last night while my memory of it is still vivid. (But surely it will always be vivid?) I meant to set down exactly what happened, without reticence. Why should sex, which is a part of love, be considered indecent when written about? Well, I still feel that. But before starting this paragraph I sat for a long time trying out words in my mind – and they didn't so much sound indecent as embarrassing, ludicrous and, above all, unlikely. I quite see why novelists fall back on asterisks; also I see why so many people make jokes about sex. It is, no doubt, wise to keep a sense of humour about it. Perhaps it would also be wise to keep one about love, but that is beyond me at present.

Anyway, though I can enjoy remembering what happened (though goodness knows it wasn't all enjoyable) I find I cannot bear the thought of writing one word about it. What I do want to record has nothing to do with sex.

I want always to remember:
Waking at dawn and hearing birds singing, and gradually seeing the room. I never before woke in a

200

place that was strange to me. There were rafters high above, and all around were many fascinating things, models of stage sets, drawings of theatrical costumes, photographs.

I should have liked to look at everything but I only allowed myself, once I was dressed, to tiptoe to a few of the models. It was so light by then and the birds were so noisy that I was afraid he would wake. I looked back, before I went out of the French window, and thought how young and defenceless he looked. I thought of many other things, too, things I cannot write about.

I want to remember the dew on the grass in the park, and patches of mist, and some mushrooms I saw, and great trees with gnarled boles-. It's strange how conscious of trees I was all yesterday. I don't remember noticing many flowers – which in London I am always noticing. Yesterday it was trees, trees, and the lofty Suffolk sky.

Once I was out of the park, on the road to the station, I saw a lark rising from the fields.

In spite of the early morning loveliness I did not truly enjoy the walk to the station because I was anxious about getting back to the Club, and even more, because it was hardly my morning for a long walk – though in a complicated and unwriteable-about way, I didn't mind that.

I might have guessed that the little station would still be closed. And there was a timetable, on a board outside, which showed there wouldn't be a train for hours. I stood there thinking that as I was an atheist I couldn't pray for help. Then I remembered I am now an agnostic, and I thought that entitled me just to toss a prayer up on the off-chance. And it was fantastic. Within seconds, a lorry loaded with vegetables came along – slowly, because the road was narrow. I was just going to hold up my hand and look beseeching when the driver slowed up on his own and asked if I wanted a lift. I would have accepted a lift to anywhere, so I climbed up beside him. And it turned out he was going to Covent Garden.

He was an elderly man with a kind face. We talked a bit about the morning and the countryside and then he said: 'What you been up to, little miss?'

I couldn't think of any convincing story so I said: 'Will you forgive me if I don't tell you?'

He said: 'That's all right, don't worry. But I think you've run away from school.'

I said gratefully, 'However did you guess?'

He said: 'Well, you're in uniform, aren't you? Was it an orphanage?' It must have been my 'Puritan Maid' dress and black cloak that gave him that idea. So I said yes, I was an orphan but I had friends in London who would take me in. He asked if I was sure they would, and if I would promise to go straight to them. And I said I was quite sure and I would promise. Then he said why didn't I have a bit of a nap? And I could lean on him if I liked. It seemed rude not to, though I didn't think I should sleep – but I did, almost at once, though I woke up a good many times. Each time I woke he said something encouraging. And when he set me down at Covent Garden, he made me promise that if my friends should happen to be away I would go to a police station for advice. If I live to be a hundred I shall remember his kindness.

I caught an early Underground train but still had to do some more walking to reach the Club. The doors were open so I got in easily, and managed to get to bed without waking Molly and Lilian. Anyway, I had a story ready for them that the little train had missed its connection with the London train and Brice and I had been forced to spend the night at a horrid little station hotel. I told this when Charlotte woke us with our breakfast trays. All they said was 'Poor you!' and then talked about themselves.

After breakfast I went to sleep in a hot bath and woke in a cold one. Surprisingly, there was enough hot water to warm it up.

This afternoon when I–

Lilian is back already. She has just called to ask if I will come up to Zelle's room, and I have said I will. I think I would like to be with people. And I could do with some Veda toast.

Everything will be all right. I am really very happy – anyway, I shall be, once I can have a little time alone with him, to talk quietly. Today I only had two minutes, just on the stairs. I will write of that tomorrow.

I find parts of this journal entry astonishing. They seem written by someone older than I remember myself as being, and certainly older than the girl who made the entry on my first night at the Club. The tinge of sophisticated humour about sex surprises me. Probably it resulted from life at the Club, where members (many of them not so unblemished as I at first thought they were) often broke their hearts over their personal sex-lives while treating the general subject of sex as a joke.

I am also surprised that I could tell myself I was happy. Perhaps that was bravado. No, on second thoughts, I believe that last paragraph was sincere; I did think everything would be all right.

Now memory is tinged by hindsight. I know, as the writer of the journal did not, what was just round the corner.

I did not write – next day, or ever – of the two minutes on the stairs but I remember them most vividly. Mr Crossway's ostensible reason for coming up to the office was to tell us that Lilian had read very promisingly and he was going to give her a trial. He talked for quite a while but no opportunity for seeing me alone arose. So when he went, he called to me from the stairs saying he wanted me to give Lilian a message. I hurried to him. He said nothing about Lilian, just looked at me intently and asked if I was all right. I nodded. Then he asked why I had run away without waking him and I said I'd thought it would be less trouble for him if I was gone when he woke. And I told him of my ride back with the cabbages – I thought that would amuse him but he said 'Good God!' under his breath and shook his head as if in disapproval. All the time, he was looking at me with an intimacy which I found valuable and exciting but I did wish he would smile. The only other thing he said was, 'I'll be in touch with you when I can.' He said this very kindly but still did not smile.

When I got back to the office Miss Lester asked what the message for Lilian was and I said it was to do with not learning her part until she'd had a rehearsal. Undoubtedly I had a talent for improvisation, even when hardly in the mood for it.

That was on the Monday. On the Tuesday I managed to be in the Throne Room on my own while Lilian was rehearsing. I looked through the spy-hole and saw that she was on the stage alone with Mr Crossway. He was taking her through the part line by line, making her copy his inflections. They were working on her long speech in the last act; and when they came to the end she said, 'Please give me time to make some notes.' He said, '*Can* you make notes on inflections?' She said yes, they would mean something to her. After she'd made the notes, they tried the speech again and she'd remembered every inflection. He praised her but added, 'They're a bit parrot-like.' She said, quite sharply, 'Well, give me a chance! I've got to work on them, make them my own.' He looked at her quickly, as if astonished by her tone, and then said, 'Good girl. That's exactly the right attitude.'

I closed the spy-hole feeling a new respect for Lilian, but also despising her a bit for copying, not creating.

The only other thing I remember about that afternoon was that Brice Marton came up after the rehearsal; he had been there, though I had not seen him. He told us Lilian was doing well, then he talked to Miss Lester, ignoring me. I was surprised, as we had got on so well only two days before. Just before he went he asked me if I had enjoyed my drive back with my friends. When I said yes, he said 'Good' – but so off-handedly that I wondered if he had really been annoyed because I didn't return with him.

When I got back to the Club that night Molly was out with Bluff King Hal again and Lilian was in a practice room, working on her part. I sat with Zelle in her bedroom – I think it was the first time we had been alone together since we had shared a room at the hotel. Being at the theatre so much, I saw far less of her than Molly and Lilian did.

She was eager to talk about the vicarage garden party and the evening service– 'And the folk singers with their lanterns, winding their way through the village. Somehow they made me long to be good.' It seemed strange that she and I had listened with such different feelings. Not that I thought of myself as being bad; still, I felt Zelle in her present mood would have been shocked at me. She had quite a holy look, perched on her window-seat in a madonna-blue dressing-gown, with her fair hair suggesting an aureole.

She kept saying what a wonderful man Adrian Crossway was, so I teased her by asking if she could fancy being a vicar's wife.

'It's not a thing you ought to joke about,' she said, almost angrily. 'The man's a saint. I wouldn't marry him even if he asked me to, which he never would.'

I said I agreed it wouldn't be a good idea to marry a saint.

'Oh, I didn't mean that. I meant I'm not good enough. But I do hope I shall see him again. I'm going to write and ask if he knows of any work I can do, to help people, especially children. I adored all those fat babies sitting on the mound with us. I've never done anything worth while in my whole life.'

'It sounds as if you've been converted,' I said, laughing.

'Yes, I have and it isn't funny. And I don't want

to talk about it. Promise not to say anything to Molly and Lilian.'

I promised, and said I hadn't meant to jeer. But I didn't take her conversion seriously, any more than I had taken her fears of being bitten by Dracula. I had never come near to knowing her well and accepted her as being irrational and sometimes a bit silly, but always charming and almost unbelievably generous.

Lilian came in then and asked if I would give her the cues for her part. She was word perfect, but not at all good in the first two acts, in which she had very little to do; I gathered Mr Crossway hadn't taught her these yet. In her important last act she seemed to me to have remembered all the inflections and also 'made them her own'. (I didn't, of course, tell her I had heard her intention of doing so.) A parrot she might be but she was a very clever parrot. I told her she was going to be excellent.

She said she was to have an Eton crop as Mr Crossway thought it would suit the part. 'We went to his dressing-room and I scragged my hair back and he studied me from all angles. He says a crop will suit me, as well as being right for the part.'

I felt a pang, thinking of her in his dressing-room, and to hide my feelings I asked, jokingly, if she'd fallen in love with him yet.

She said, 'I haven't dared to spare the time. But once I feel I'm safe in the part, oh boy!'

I was glad to remember he hadn't very much liked her, as a person.

I hoped to see him on the Wednesday but I

didn't; nor on the Thursday or the Friday. I hardly blamed him; he spent so much time rehearsing with Lilian and there was a full company rehearsal for her on the Friday. She was to go on at the Saturday matinée.

On the Friday evening, when Miss Lester and I were on our way to dinner at the pub, I happened to look in at the window of a dingy little print shop and I saw some small framed engravings of Regent's Park terraces. There was one of the terrace where Mr Crossway lived and, remembering how Lilian had admired his house, I thought the little picture would make a 'good luck' present for her. I had already arranged to send flowers with Molly's and Zelle's but I fancied sending something on my own, especially as I was feeling envious of her and did not like myself for it. The shop was closed but I went in on Saturday morning, bought the engraving and put a card with it saying: 'Little did we think when we walked round the park! All the good luck in the world to you.'

I left the parcel at the stage door and then went to lunch at the pub, expecting Miss Lester would be there, but she wasn't. It was barely half-past one when I finished eating and I was not due at the theatre for an hour; but I decided to get there early and put in some work, so that I could watch Lilian's last act from the dress circle. I knew that, anyway, Miss Lester would let me; but we were fairly busy so I felt I ought to play fair about taking time off.

As soon as I entered the hall of the office I saw, through the open door, that Mr Crossway was standing beside Miss Lester's desk with his back to me. I was on my way to them when I heard her say: 'How *could* you? She's eighteen and young for her age.'

I stopped dead, astounded more by her bitter tone than by her words – for a second, I didn't take in what they meant.

Mr Crossway said: 'You can't feel worse about it than I do. But if you knew the circumstances you might not blame me quite so much. There are times when it's kinder to do the wrong thing than the right one.'

'*Kinder?*' She still spoke with the utmost bitterness. 'Ah, yes, I ought to have remembered. You're a specialist in being kind to be cruel. Well, what happens now?'

Before he could answer, she looked past him and saw me. Instantly, she got up, came out of the office and through the hall without looking at or speaking to me, and went downstairs.

I dashed to him, asking what had happened– 'It was me you were talking about, wasn't it?'

'I'm afraid so. I was hoping to keep it from you – anyway, for the moment. But now you'd better know what there is to know. Don't worry too much. I'll keep you out of it somehow.'

He then explained that a letter from his wife, still away on a visit to her father, had that morning been delivered at the theatre and opened by Miss Lester – who always opened his theatre letters and winnowed out those there was no need for him to bother with. Mrs Crossway stated that she had received information from their lodge keeper that I had spent the night with him. The woman – I remembered seeing her when I drove past the lodge with Brice – had managed to find out my name. And she was prepared to swear I had gone into the barn and stayed there. Mrs Crossway now proposed to start divorce proceedings.

'She's threatened to divorce me for years,' he said, 'but I didn't think she'd set a servant to spy on me. Actually, I didn't think she wanted a divorce. I thought her threats were only meant to keep me at heel – she's always tried to do that, though I can't believe she still feels strongly about it. She used to, I'm afraid; but for some time it's been more a question of pride.'

He had seldom spoken to me about his wife but I had gathered they were very good friends. Now I felt I must have been wrong. Surely no friendly wife could spring such a thing on him just by means of a letter?

I said, 'Then you're not fond of each other any more?'

'Well, surprising though it may sound, I'd have said we were. I'm certainly fond of her, in spite of my goings on. She was extremely annoyed about my last affair but since then ... I'd have said everything was all right. But it's obvious from this letter that she no longer gives a damn about me. And it sounds as if she means business about the divorce.'

'And you don't want to be divorced?'

'I do not – for a great many reasons, one of which is that it would queer my chance of a knighthood, as she very well knows. My father was knighted, and I should very much like to be, and I've never known an actor who wouldn't, in spite of what some of them say. But I should mind far more about – well, losing her, and all the scandal of the divorce court. Of course, whatever happens, I shan't allow you to be involved in that.'

'But I don't mind being involved.'

'Well, I mind for you. And I don't fancy a co-respondent of eighteen who looks even younger.' For a moment there was a nicker of amusement in his eyes. 'Though I'm sure you'd be very funny in court – probably tell the judge what you thought of him. Anyway, she'll accept an arranged divorce, if I can't talk her out of the whole idea.'

I asked when he would see her and he said that was difficult, as the letter informed him she was coming to London but would not reach the house until two-thirty that afternoon and would be leaving again in an hour, after collecting some clothes. She would then join friends and she didn't tell him which friends, as she wished to be approached only through her solicitors. I suggested he should ring her up but he said he hardly could, during the matinée, especially as it would mean telephoning from the stage door – 'She knows that; and anyway, she'd probably hang up on me – you can see she's making things as awkward as possible. Oh, my God, look at the time! And I want a word with Lilian before we ring up.'

I had forgotten Lilian, forgotten the matinée. At first I had been almost glad about what had happened, willing and even proud to be involved in a divorce case. But though he had spoken kindly, not seeming angry with me, he had not shown me one spark of affection and I now felt what surely I must have at least suspected when I ran away from him at dawn: I had involved him in something he had never wished for and now bitterly regretted.

As he turned to go I said, 'It's all my fault. Is there anything in the world I can do to help?'

'I'm afraid not, my dear. But there's something I ought to tell you now – God knows I hate to be so unkind but Eve Lester's just told me my idea of kindness often turns out to be cruelty, and she's probably right. Anyway, there's no getting away from this. If I do manage to talk my wife out of a divorce, you'll have to leave the theatre.'

I nodded. 'And if you don't manage to?'

'I think you'll still have to leave. Surely you can't stay on – not now Eve Lester knows? And I doubt if she'll still want you here.'

I said I understood. For a moment he looked at me unhappily. Then he hurried away.

I sat there, very still, not so much planning what I was going to do as knowing I was going to do it.

12

I got to the house soon after half-past two. I thought of the curtain going up at the theatre, with Lilian waiting in the wings for her first entrance. I also thought of the print of the house I had given her. The message, 'Little did we think...' now applied far more to me than it did to her.

I rang the bell and a butler – the first I had ever seen except on the stage – opened the door. I asked for Mrs Crossway and he asked if I had an appointment. I said no, but I had to see her about something very important. He looked so dubious that I prepared to push past him, before he closed the door against me, and dash upstairs – where, presumably, she would be, as she had come to collect clothes. But after a second's hesitation he held the door open for me and said he would make enquiries. And just as I entered the hall she came downstairs.

I had seen her at the Crossway first night, but only from a distance. She had then been in gleaming white; now she wore the type of tweed suit right for town or for country. She was, as Lilian had once described her, 'tall, dark and *very* Society'.

The butler turned to her and said there was a young lady asking for her. She gave me a quick glance, then told him she would cope. As he went, she came towards me, not smiling but not looking annoyed.

'You shouldn't come to people's private houses,' she said, but quite nicely. 'Do you really want to see me, or is it my husband? If it's an autograph–'

I interrupted her. 'It isn't. And it's you I want. I *must* talk to you, please!'

'Well, I can't think what about. Still, come in, little girl.'

She was smiling now and I guessed why. I was wearing one of my youngest summer dresses ('like' Kate Greenaway girls) made of a chintz sprinkled with daisies, and I had a wreath of daisies round my turn-down straw hat. She had, as my kind friend the lorry driver had, mistaken me for a child.

We went into the dining-room, a very formal room with eighteenth-century furniture. There was an oil painting of Mr Crossway, much younger than he now was, over the mantel. Mrs Crossway pulled out a chair for me and we sat facing each other.

'Now,' she said pleasantly.

For a moment, words failed me. I had imagined having to force myself on her, saying things like, 'Please, please you must listen!' Faced with encouragement I didn't know how to begin. But at last I managed: 'I'm the girl you wrote the letter about.'

She looked blank. 'What letter?'

'The one you sent to the theatre this morning. I saw it – because we open his letters to save him trouble. Perhaps you didn't know that.'

'I knew Eve Lester might, but I didn't give a damn about that. Do you work in the office too?

214

Oh–!' She broke off, staring hard at me.

I said again, 'I'm the girl. The one you thought...' I let the words trail.

'The girl the lodge keeper saw? It's not possible. Is that what you've come to tell me – that it wasn't you?'

'It was me,' I said miserably. 'But nothing wrong happened – nothing at all happened, really. He doesn't even know I was there. Oh, if only I could make you believe me!'

She gave me a long look, then said: 'Of course I believe you. Now stop worrying and tell me everything. What the hell were you up to?'

'I just wanted to see him.'

'Are you in love with him?'

'Yes, terribly. But he's not in love with me, not one bit. And though he's kind, he hardy ever lets me be alone with him.'

'Does he know how you feel?'

'I told him. I couldn't bear not to.'

She nodded sympathetically. 'I can understand that. So you thought you'd go to the barn just to be alone with him. But it was pretty late for a visit, wasn't it? How did you plan to get back to London? Oh, I suppose you were staying in the village.'

I had felt from the beginning that unless I kept *almost* to the facts I should tie myself in knots. So I said, 'No. Somehow I've got to tell you. I hoped he'd let me stay with him.'

To my astonishment, she laughed. 'Well, you *are* a naughty little girl. Though I gather your courage failed. Was that it? Tell me.' She said it almost coaxingly.

'When I got there he was fast asleep – I could see him through the French window. I did just go inside but I couldn't bring myself to wake him. I was so afraid he'd be angry. I stood there quite a long time, willing him to wake up. But he didn't. And at last I went out and sat on a seat built round one of the old trees.'

'At the back of the barn. I know.'

'There'd been a moon but it had clouded over. I couldn't go away until there was a little light. I sat there hours – till the dawn came. Then I walked to the road and got a lift back to London with a load of cabbages. All very ludicrous, really.'

'Not to me, you poor baby,' said Mrs Crossway. Then she looked at me speculatively. 'I wonder what would have happened if you *had* wakened him. Frankly, I don't think you'd have had any luck. With all his faults, he wouldn't consider you fair game. Besides, for years now, he's only fallen for bitches. I suppose I oughtn't to say that of him to you, but you know from my letter that I'm through with him. However, I'm not getting free at your expense – and for once, it wouldn't be fair to him. Did anyone but you see the letter?'

I shook my head 'Miss Lester happened to be out of the office when I opened it.'

'Have you got it with you?'

Where *was* the letter? Still in the office? No, he had taken it with him. I hastily said I had hidden it as I'd had no chance to put it in my handbag.

'Well, you can go back and destroy it. This is going to remain just between you and me.'

'Do you mean it's all right?' Without a moment's warning I dissolved into tears. I think it was partly due to relief and partly to her kindness; also I hated having deceived her. They weren't just a few quiet tears but the uncontrollable, gulping kind that I hadn't cried since childhood. They embarrassed me horribly.

She said, 'Why cry now, you silly girl? Though I suppose you've plenty to cry about. It's hell being in love with someone who doesn't give a damn about you.'

She got up, went to a dumb-waiter, blew down a whistle and asked for some coffee to be sent up. Then she sat down again and said: 'Mop up, ducky. Remember you have to go back to that theatre and behave as if nothing's happened. I'll tell you something that'll cheer you up. He does give a damn about you. It's just dawned on me that you're the girl from the office who helped him at rehearsals – and went on and played one night. Didn't you jump on a footstool? I should have liked to see that.'

'He was furious. And he thinks I'm a hopeless actress.'

'He was amused, really. And he's told me again and again how much he likes you.'

She went on talking, repeating things he had said which had made her like the sound of me. I think she was giving me a chance to control myself. When I'd managed to, she said briskly, 'Now can't you settle for being someone he thinks of as a real friend? Can't you cure yourself of – well, having a crush on an actor? Oh, I do realise it seems more than that to you.'

'How can one *want* to cure oneself of caring for anyone?'

'I know what you mean.' She no longer sounded brisk. 'Sometimes I wish I still cared. I used at least to be happy between his affairs. He's such a very, very nice man – he has all the virtues except fidelity. But now ... you see, I now don't care enough to make putting up with things worth while. I've stopped finding his unfaithfulness heartbreaking; I just find it infuriating. And I'm absolutely through with standing for it.'

She was telling herself this, as much as telling me. I asked if he understood how she now felt.

'Well, I've warned him but he doesn't believe me. Of course I haven't told him I've stopped caring. Anyway, I haven't completely stopped; I'm still fond of him, as he is of me. But I've got to get out, before I'm too old. My father's made me see that – I was staying with him when I got the letter about *your* goings on, you bad child.' She gave me a quick smile. 'Well, that was a false alarm but I shan't have to wait long. His last mistress left England some months ago so he's sure to start something soon. And I shall never again turn a blind eye.' She went to get the coffee from the dumb-waiter and brought it to the table. 'All the same, I'm not spying on him. The woman at the lodge did it off her own bat; she's by way of being devoted to me – used to be my maid. I'd like him to know I didn't–' She broke off. 'How silly! I was forgetting he doesn't know anything about it.'

I, too, had forgotten he was not supposed to; and I saw how easily I could make some slip. I must say as little as possible and get away as soon as I could. Glad though I was of the coffee, I wished I did not have to stay and drink it.

After that, she pulled herself up by saying she'd talked too much about herself and said things she oughtn't to have said– 'But somehow you're easy to talk to.' Then she began asking me about myself, where I came from, where I lived and so on. While I answered, another fear came to me. Suppose he did ring up from the stage door, in the first interval – before I had warned him to know nothing about the letter? He could be private enough if he turned the stage door keeper out. Just as I thought of this, a telephone rang in the hall. I waited in terror, expecting the butler to come and say Mrs Crossway was wanted.

Nothing happened. And then I saw by the clock on the mantel that it was too early for him to have telephoned. The first act would not be over yet. But, oh, I must get away! And the coffee was so very hot.

A moment later, I made a slip. She asked if I had given up my plan to go on the stage. I said, 'No, I'll try again, now I have to leave the Crossway.' She asked why I had to leave and I opened my mouth to say 'Because he says I must'; I even got as far as 'Because'. Then I managed to break off and finish, 'Well, surely you want me to, don't you?'

'Because you're in love with Rex? As if I minded – except from your point of view, you poor kid. I'd hate you to leave on my account. You stay on but do try to be sensible about him. By the way, you can tell him I shan't go away, as I said I would. I shall be here when he gets home tonight.'

I stared at her. 'But surely I mustn't tell him anything?'

She slapped her forehead. 'Of course you mustn't. If I don't watch my step I shall muck up our conspiracy. Let's get it straight. You say nothing, you do nothing – except destroy the letter. And *I* say nothing. And we never admit we've had this meeting. Perhaps someday we can meet officially. I hope so.'

I said I did too. It wasn't true, much as I liked her. If we met again I still might give something away.

At last my coffee was finished. I got up, thanking her for being so wonderful to me, and then took a last look at the portrait over the mantel. The hair line was that of the number two toupee. She noticed the direction of my eyes and said, 'That was painted soon after we married. We were so happy. He was faithful to me for nearly a year – or rather, it was nearly a year before I found out he wasn't. You know, even now, if he'd pull up... But he won't, probably can't. And women would never let him.'

We went into the hall. She opened the door for me and, just before I left, said: 'I think it was very brave of you to come here, and I'm grateful. It'd be pretty silly if I'd tried to divorce him when, for once, he isn't guilty. He'd be grateful to you, too. It's a pity we can't tell him.'

I was dead set on telling him as fast as I could, before he got in touch with her and wrecked everything. So I didn't linger.

I took the first turning out of the park and managed to pick up a taxi. The first interval would now have started but he was on at the end of Act I and at the beginning of Act II and had a change of clothes between them; if he was going to telephone, the second interval was the dangerous one as he had more time then.

Back at the theatre, I dashed up to the office and said to Miss Lester: 'You may not be on speaking terms with me but you've got to help me, if it's for the last time.' And then I told her what I'd done, and asked her to warn him at once. I didn't dare do it myself as it would mean talking to him in the wings and I knew he would hate me to do that. She took in everything I told her, then just nodded and got the key of the pass door. When she went I still did not know how she felt about me.

But when she came back she left me in no doubt. After telling me she had made Mr Crossway understand, she said: 'Now listen. If you want to talk to me about this whole wretched business I'll do anything I can to help you. But if you like, we'll just pretend it never happened.'

I looked at her in astonishment. 'Aren't you angry with me? Don't you want me to leave? He said you would.'

'How little he knows me, after twenty years. Perhaps you ought to leave, for your own good, but I shouldn't think you want to, do you?'

I said I thought I'd die if I had to.

'Well, we can't have you dying. Do you know, when I came back to the office and found you'd vanished, I wondered if you'd gone out to throw yourself under a bus?'

'*Me?*'

She laughed and said she was glad to see me look so astounded. 'I might have known you're not a girl to bow out of things. Let's go down and watch Lilian's last-act scene.'

We went down arm in arm.

Lilian really was very good. For the first time I saw how Mr Crossway wanted the part played and why he was right about it. I suppose it was because he had trained her to carry out his ideas exactly. And the Eton crop suited her wonderfully well. It somehow accentuated the beauty of her eyes and, surprisingly, made her look not boyish but even more feminine than usual.

When we got back to the office Miss Lester told me to wait in the Throne Room as Mr Crossway would be coming up to see me after the matinée. 'He wants to hear everything from you, so that he gets the complete hang of it and to thank you, of course.'

'Thank me?'

'Well, you pulled off a miracle. Tell me, didn't you mind having to lie? You've always struck me as truthful.'

I had always struck myself as truthful. But when I came to think about it I found that, though I hated deceiving Mrs Crossway, I had not felt conscience-stricken about the lying itself and I still didn't. It seemed to me just a way of protecting my dear. I said I hoped the end justified the means.

'Anyway, don't think I'm judging you,' said Miss Lester. 'I haven't the right to.'

Then one of the programme girls came in for something and I went off to the Throne Room.

222

I sat at the long table staring at the spoke-like metal work of one of the round windows. I still did not know if he would let me stay. And when he came in he looked almost grimly serious. But he did thank me very kindly. Then he listened while I told him everything I could remember. I finished by saying:

'She doesn't want me to leave. And Miss Lester doesn't. And I don't want to go. But I will if you still wish it.'

He was silent so long that I felt sure he did wish it. Then he smiled. I don't know if he changed his mind or if it was due to his fatal kindness, but what he said was: 'Then that's four of us who want you to stay. But will you be good? Will you stop playing Delilah to a poor old shorn Samson?'

I laughed at that but said I would, truly; and then I held out my hand and quoted:

'Shake hands for ever, cancel all our vows,
And when we meet at any time again,
Be it not seen in either of our brows
That we one jot of former love retain.

–Not that there were any vows, and the love was all on *my* brow, but you'll note that my intentions are excellent.'

His expression was relaxing more and more; the old amused look was back in his eyes. He said, 'If it wasn't love on my brow, it was something remarkably like it.'

'Even when we were "ill met by moonlight"?'

'Most of all then – wrong though that was. If only I could make you understand how genuinely fond of you I am.'

We stood looking at each other and I was suddenly sure that with very little effort, I could be in his arms with everything starting again. And I didn't make the effort. Was I trying to play fair? Or did I, for once, want to retreat instead of pursue? Even when I thought about it afterwards I could never quite understand myself. But whatever the reason, I broke the moment of intimacy by saying briskly, 'What have you done with that letter?'

He took it out of his pocket.

I said, 'Then let's top the great farewell scene with the great letter-burning scene.'

There were matches beside the large glass ashtray on the table. I lit the corner of the letter and it promptly went out; but at last I reduced it to ashes. He watched with amusement and when I had finished said, 'By rights, shouldn't the great farewell scene have ended with one kiss on the brow?'

Again I retreated. 'Not on *my* brow – or love might be seen there again.'

He said, 'Good child. Still, keep just a little love for me, under that nice thick fringe.'

Then he went, quickly – leaving me happier than, only a few minutes earlier, I could have believed possible. And in my mind, I went on with the Michael Drayton sonnet to my great satisfaction. Both the poet and I had been premature in accepting love as being on 'his bed of death'.

Now if thou wouldst, when all have given him over,
From death to life thou might'st him yet recover.

But the word 'might'st' expressed an uncertainty I refused to feel.

13

For the next two weeks I allowed myself to be reasonably happy. I say 'allowed' because I only maintained something approaching peace of mind by constantly telling myself there was nothing I need *do*, no step I ought to key myself up into taking. I felt sure it would be best just to wait, in calm, recuperative confidence.

I was well aware that I needed to recuperate; sudden renewal of hope hadn't wiped out the strain of the last weeks. I told myself I really was a bit young for such goings on, and treated myself in a kindly, almost motherly way, giving myself small treats such as flowers in my cubicle and chocolates in the bath.

And I took to reading poetry again. One of the few books I had brought to London was *The Oxford Book of English Verse;* and while verifying my memory of Drayton's 'The Parting' I came across the Epigram, *'Respice Finem'*, by Francis Quarles:

My soul, sit thou a patient looker-on;
Judge not the play before the play is done:
Her plot hath many changes; every day
Speaks a new scene; the last act crowns the play.

I memorised this and said it to myself again and again. It did not strike me as unreasonable to want my crowning last act to be played while I was still in my 'teens, as the act I had in mind was that my dear should realise how much he loved me and proceed to marry me (no unkindness intended to Mrs Crossway, as she now wanted to be free). As far as I was concerned, that last act could start now and continue for the rest of my life.

I did an immense amount of 'thinking things out'. This took the form of remembering everything that had happened and then visualising what might happen when things came right. There was no end to the ways in which the coming right could come about. I thought best while walking so I often walked both to the theatre and home to the Club at night. I liked to walk through back streets, often getting lost, which worried me not at all; sooner or later one struck a main thoroughfare. No man ever accosted me however late at night I was out, and I don't even remember noticing any men; I was too occupied with my thoughts.

Neither Lilian nor I suggested we should go home together and we were seeing less of each other; she had dropped our occasional morning walks in favour of looking at shops with Molly. I could have gone too, but never did; and I sometimes skipped the nightly toast-making sessions in Zelle's room. One reason for this was that it upset me to hear Lilian talk about life on her side of the curtain. And it really infuriated me that she, as an actress, could call my dear 'Rex' while I, as a secretary, couldn't. (Even in our most intimate moments I never had; I hadn't called him anything.) I began to let myself at least think of him as 'Rex' instead of 'Mr Crossway' or 'my dear' – or just 'him'. It was some small compensation.

During those two weeks I met him three times, when he came into the office to see Miss Lester. On the first two occasions I just said, 'Hello,' cheerfully, and went on with what I was doing. The next time, I went off to the Throne Room where I had press cuttings in hand. I had a faint hope that he might follow me but he didn't. However, I got my reward when I went back to the office after hearing him leave. Miss Lester said: 'If you can keep this up you'll pull off another miracle. He asked me to give you his love and say how grateful he is.'

Since that Saturday when she had opened Mrs Crossway's letter this was the only reference Eve had made to the matter. (It was around this time that she told me to call her Eve instead of Miss Lester.) She had said I could talk about it or not, as I pleased; and I had chosen not to talk. We had worked together just as we always had, though I had been conscious of a little extra kindness in her manner. She encouraged me to eat enormous good brown dinners at the pub, and her after-dinner brews of coffee became stronger and stronger. By now I was as much a coffee addict as she was.

Brice Marton often joined us at dinner. I had thought him off-hand at our first meeting after the vicarage party, and it had been a week before I saw him again – not surprising, as he had always been in attendance while Lilian was rehearsing. Then, on the Monday after what I now thought of as Black Saturday, he had come to the office just as Eve and I were going out for our meal and asked if he could come with us. Since then I had seen him frequently and he had always been pleasant, but I had never felt so much at ease with him as on our train journey. He now seemed slightly guarded and I sometimes caught him looking at me in a puzzled, almost resentful way; but as soon as our eyes met he would switch his expression to one of casual kindness.

At the Club my main stand-by was Zelle, with whom I usually spent the mornings, Molly and Lilian so often being out together. There had been a slight change in the relationship of the four of us. Now that Lilian was occupied at the theatre and Molly with Bluff King Hal, Zelle was no longer playing the role of Fairy Godmother, probably because no such character was at present needed. And it seemed to me that Zelle had stopped being the lonely child in need of playmates.

She had become more serious and spent much of her time reading; often we sat together reading rather than talking. I read poetry; she read books on religion suggested by Adrian Crossway. They had exchanged several letters and, towards the end of my second recuperative week, she said he was soon coming to London and would see her about some work she might do.

I did not think her interest in religion and good

works was entirely on their own account. And Adrian Crossway's letters, from what she told me, were long and personal. I felt that she, as well as Molly, had 'started something' at the vicarage party.

As regards Molly, we were all anxious to know just *what* she had started. Bluff King Hal was coming to London almost every day to see her. He was taking her out to meals, theatres, night clubs and for drives in the country; and providing enough 'roses in the hall' to stock a shop. Obviously he must be going to propose something but Lilian feared it wasn't going to be marriage, particularly as Molly had told him she was a byblow.

'I felt I had to,' she explained to us. 'You see, he comes from an old county family. And he used to be in the regular army like my father. If Father didn't care to marry an actress, Hal certainly might not care to marry an *illegitimate* actress. So it was only fair to warn him. He just laughed – that is, he laughed at me being called Moll Byblow – and it didn't stop him asking me out again. But no doubt it sank in.'

'You're a damned fool,' said Lilian. 'I can understand your wanting to be honest but why couldn't you wait till he'd proposed?'

'Because then he could hardly back out,' said Molly.

'Exactly,' said Lilian.

'And the awful thing is that if he asks me just to have an affair with him I know I shall succumb, because I'm so much in love with him. And after all, I am my mother's daughter.'

'Your mother was a damned fool too,' said Lilian. 'I often wonder if any man would marry any woman if she didn't make him.'

And then, just under three weeks after Molly and Hal first met, she irrupted into Zelle's room one night officially engaged and with an appointment to go out next morning to choose the ring.

'Hal thinks an emerald,' she said blissfully. 'And then he's driving back to discuss the wedding with Adrian Crossway. It should really be in the bride's parish but I don't even know what mine is, and it'll be lovely having a country wedding. I do wish you could all be bridesmaids but Hal has masses of small nieces panting to trot up the aisle and make me look a giantess.'

'I don't see how I can even be there,' said Lilian, 'though I might if you don't choose a matinée day. I wonder if Rex will go? Perhaps he'll drive me down – and you too, Mouse.'

I was far more envious of that casual 'Rex' than of Molly's happiness.

Two days later, Zelle gave a lunch party to celebrate the engagement. It was Sunday so I did not have to go to the theatre.

No psychic tremor warned me that this was to prove an important occasion but I remember it vividly. I can recall my awe on entering the hotel – much the grandest I had ever been in – and then our gradual relaxing into ease as we were received and waited on as if we were, at least, four young peeresses in our own right; though we never relaxed to the extent of making as much noise as we usually made when all together. It would have been too much like shouting in a cathedral.

We were given a table at one of the tall windows and I was so placed that, by turning to my right, I could look out on the park in the bright September sunlight; and, by turning to my left, see the beautiful, very formal restaurant. Everyone there was behaving as decorously as we were – we remained decorous even when we toasted Molly in champagne, for which she thanked us with dignity. All her pre-byblow confidence had returned. The backwards tilt of her head, when she looked serenely round through her lorgnette, was superb and she several times addressed me as 'child'.

I was feeling far from child-like but I was surprisingly happy. The sunlit park, the gracious restaurant, perhaps the radiation of Molly's happiness, and certainly the champagne all combined to lull me into a mood of 'wait and watch the world go by; all will yet be well'. Lilian must have been similarly conscious of the atmosphere because, towards the end of the meal, she said: 'I do love this place. I know I shall remember this party as long as I live.'

Molly, Zelle and I said we would, too.

'In a way, it's a sad occasion as well as a celebration,' said Lilian. 'I shall miss you terribly, Molly. Nothing will ever be the same as it has been this summer. But we will all keep in touch, won't we? Let's make a vow to meet here this day next year. My party then – if only I've enough money.'

'No, mine,' said Molly, who obviously had no

231

doubt she would have enough money.

Judging by the prices on the menu the meal was going to cost Zelle more than I earned in a month so I did not enter the competition to play hostess; nor did I take Lilian very seriously. But she was certainly taking herself seriously, because she got a pocket diary out of her handbag and made a note. Then she said:

'No, next year's too early – and we'll probably meet lots of times in the near future. What we've to guard against is slipping away from each other as the years roll by. We'll lunch here every five years, on and on through our lives–'

'Till it's forty years on,' Molly broke in cheerfully. 'Can't you see us all doddering in on sticks or in Bath-chairs?'

'Don't!' said Lilian, shuddering. 'Though it might be rather beautiful, four exquisite old ladies looking back on their youth. And do you know what? If we lose sight of each other I shall put an advertisement in *The Times* Personal column just "Four Friends Reunion" and the date. And then you must all come or at least send a telegram.'

'But I never read *The Times* Personal column,' said Molly.

I said I didn't, either.

'Then you must start tomorrow and read it every day of your lives,' said Lilian.

Both Molly and I expressed our doubts about that.

'I'll read it for you, Lilian,' said Zelle kindly.

Lilian, already emotional, now became indignant. 'You won't! Nobody will help me! Nobody wants us to go on being friends.' Then she began to giggle. 'Oh, dear, I've had far too much champagne. Now you must all talk of something serious, like politics, while I calm myself into a state suitable for my surroundings.' She took a long drink of champagne to help her.

Soon after that something occurred which made far more impression on me than anything Lilian had said. Not long after we came in I had happened to notice four people at a table some distance from us: a man, a woman and two schoolboys. The man had his back to us but I had a good view of the woman, and I looked at her several times because her face seemed familiar. As I could not place her I decided she must just be someone I had seen in the foyer of the theatre. These four people were now getting up to go and, as the man turned towards the door, I saw his face.

Instantly I knew why the woman's face had seemed familiar. The two of them were the original of the large oil painting we had seen in the house where we first met Zelle.

I turned to point them out to her but as I opened my mouth I saw that she had flushed deeply and was gazing at the man with dismay. I looked towards him again, at the exact instant when he saw Zelle. He, too, seemed dismayed. Then his expression went blank and he continued on his way out. For a second, Zelle's eyes met mine. Then she looked down and opened her handbag.

Molly and Lilian were not in a position to see the man. And as they were talking, I did not think they had noticed Zelle's flush. She took a hand-kerchief from her bag and pretended to blow her nose, not very convincingly. By the time she had finished, the flush had receded.

My first guess was that she and her guardian had cut each other because Zelle did not get on with his wife and would not want to meet her. My second guess so startled me that I pushed it aside for later consideration.

Coffee arrived then and when we had drunk it Zelle paid with an impressive number of pound notes and we left the hotel.

Back at the Club, we went to the Green Room; being a Members Only room we usually had it to ourselves on Sunday afternoons, when most girls either went out or entertained friends in the lounge. There were two vast sofas, long enough for two people to lie full length on each of them, provided legs were tactfully disposed. I have particularly pleasant memories of Sunday after-noon naps in the Green Room – I almost always seemed to be short of sleep.

When we had settled down Lilian said, 'Not many more afternoons like this for you, Molly. Sometimes I wish we'd never gone to that vicar-age party – I mean, from a selfish point of view.'

'But you got your lovely job there,' said Molly. 'Aren't you happy about that?'

'I suppose so,' said Lilian. 'It's just that I've a sort of end of summer feeling. You'll soon be going too, won't you, Zelle? Back to your flat.'

'Yes, but I shall often come here to see you,' said Zelle.

'Not the same, not the same at all,' said Lilian gloomily. 'Well, we'll just have to console each other, won't we, Mouse?'

I agreed but without feeling it was important to me. The companionship of the girls had meant less since I had fallen in love. Now I wanted Lilian to shut up so that I could think my own thoughts. Did I wish we had never gone to the vicarage party?

Somewhere above us a gramophone was playing 'Japanese Sandman'. I remembered hearing it sung in a seaside concert party on one of my holidays with my aunt. It seemed a suitable song to fall asleep to. I followed the words in my mind until I came to 'Then you'll feel a bit older, in the dawn when you wake', which I at once pressed into my own service. *Had* I felt older? It was one of those questions which could only be answered by 'Yes and no'. Soon I drifted into sleep.

I slept until a late tea, organised by Lilian, was being brought in. I was sharing a sofa with Zelle, who was still asleep. And as I sat up, I felt my lunchtime suspicions must be wrong; her pale face might have been that of a saint.

'Wake up, Zelle,' said Lilian briskly. She seemed to have slept off her gloom.

'Why not let her sleep?' said Molly.

'Because her tea will go cold. Besides, I hate being in a room with sleeping people – unless I'm sleeping myself.'

Zelle unresentfully woke up and had her tea, but she seemed to me quieter than usual.

Lilian began talking about Molly's trousseau; by now, Molly had received 'bastard's pay-off' so could afford to launch out. Lilian, after commenting on this with satisfaction, remarked:

'Molly, did it ever strike you that your being a byblow worked out all for the best with Hal and you really were very wise to tell him?'

'Of course I was,' said Molly. 'I couldn't possibly not have told him.'

'Oh, I'm not thinking of your conscience,' said Lilian. 'I'm thinking of the effect on Hal. If he did have the idea of asking you to have an affair, as we were afraid he would, well, he could hardly have done that after he saw how much you minded about your mother not having been married.'

Molly's baby face crumpled with worry. 'Do you mean that, if I hadn't told him, he wouldn't have asked me to marry him?'

'We shall never know that, shall we?' said Lilian. 'And anyway, it doesn't matter. The great thing is, he did ask you.'

'But of course it matters!' Molly now looked horrified. 'I don't want him to marry me because he feels he ought to. Perhaps he thinks I told him just to force him to propose.'

I said that was nonsense. 'You told him so soon – long before he proposed.'

'Perhaps he went on hoping he wouldn't need to. There was one time, later, when he got very matey – out in the country. But I didn't, well, rebuff him. It was he who pulled up.'

'That proves he respects you,' said Zelle.

'No, it doesn't. Perhaps it was knowing what happened to Mother that made him feel he couldn't take advantage of me.'

'It would have made some men feel just the opposite,' said Lilian. 'They might have thought your mother's daughter would expect to be taken advantage of.'

'Not Hal,' said Molly. 'He's the soul of honour. That's all the more reason I wasn't sure a byblow was good enough for him.'

'But you're being utterly illogical,' said Lilian. 'It's because he's the soul of honour that he proposed. And everything's all right.'

'Not if he *only* proposed because he's the soul of honour and didn't really want to. It's as if I tricked him into proposing.'

'It is not!' we all yelled at her, but we didn't have any effect. And the more we argued, the worse things got, the truth being that there really is no way of deciding if an honourable man is less or more likely to treat a girl honourably because her mother wasn't treated honourably.

At last I said: 'Surely an honourable man treats a girl honourably however her mother was treated.'

'Of course,' said Lilian. 'And if hearing about your mother made Hal a bit extra honourable, well and good. Anyway, it's now signed and sealed with a whopping emerald, so why worry?'

'I find your attitude ... distasteful,' said Molly, choosing the word carefully. During the discussion she had stopped looking like a worried baby and became more and more haughty. 'One is not a gold-digger or a go-getter – or whatever one calls a woman who forces a proposal from a man.'

'One just calls her sensible,' said Lilian.

Molly, ignoring this, rose. 'Excuse me, please. I shall have a bath before dinner.'

She stalked out looking enormously tall and every inch the daughter of a D.S.O. in the regular army – even if he hadn't got around to marrying her mother.

We stared after her. Lilian said:

'What the hell do you make of that? Is she doubtful of Hal or just angry with me? And why be angry? When she first fell in love with him we talked like mad about ... well, tactics for getting him to propose. I suppose she's now joined the ranks of women who've landed their men and she wants to forget any landing was needed. Oh, God, I hope she won't do something silly.'

But we couldn't see anything she could do, except perhaps have it out with Hal, in which case he was bound to reassure her.

'Still, I wish I hadn't put the idea into her head,' said Lilian. 'It must have taken the edge off her happiness.'

I said, 'Not for long, I shouldn't think. She's got such a lot to be happy about.'

'All the same, I'll try to have another word with her before she goes to her bath. My theory is that when people have anything to gloat about they should be helped to gloat a hundred per cent.'

The minute Lilian had gone Zelle said, 'I want to talk to you – not here; someone may come in. Let's go to my room.'

But when we got to the fourth floor she said, 'No, not my room in case Lilian comes up. We'll go to the roof.'

We went up a narrow staircase and stepped out onto a large, flat roof surrounded by a parapet. I had never been here before so I looked around with interest. We walked over a notice chalked in giant letters saying: 'Do not tap dance here. I am asleep underneath.' A little further on was another notice: '*Nor* here, *I* sleep, too. Follow the arrows.' The arrows led to a part of the roof that was over bathrooms. Zelle said the tap dancers usually came at dawn when they were full of zest. She herself often came up at night, to look at the stars.

We went over to the parapet. One got no sensation of giddiness, because part of the fourth floor jutted out below so that nowhere was there a sheer drop to the ground. We stood leaning on the parapet, looking towards the western sky where the sunset was just beginning.

For a few minutes we talked casually about the view and the faint smell of hay – I thought it must come from the heat-dried grass in Regent's Park, though it surprised me that the scent should blow so far. At last I asked Zelle what she wanted to talk about. She was silent for a moment. Then, not looking at me, she said: 'You saw him today, didn't you? You knew who it was.'

'You mean your guardian – your cousin, Bill?'

'He isn't really my guardian, or my cousin. Did you guess?'

I said uncomfortably, 'Well, I did wonder, but only today. It was so odd that you didn't take any notice of each other.'

'We couldn't, with his wife and the boys there. They don't know I exist. Did Molly and Lilian notice anything?'

I told her I was almost sure they hadn't.

'Anyway, they probably know about me – though if so, they've been wonderfully tactful and never given me any hint.'

'Nor have they to me. I handed on everything you said that night at the hotel and they accepted it. I expect they still do. Why didn't you want us to know the truth?'

'Well, who would? I thought it might put you all off being friends with me, specially you. Does it?' She turned her head and looked at me.

'Of course not – whatever it is; I still don't quite understand. Was nothing you told me true?'

She was looking away from me again, staring into the sunset. 'Bits, here and there. Most of the time I was just inventing. You said you were an orphan so I said I was, too. You said you had been brought up by an aunt so I invented a grand-father. It was true that I lived in a Welsh village.'

I asked about the crumbling old house she had described so fully. She said the house was there but it wasn't crumbling and she hadn't lived in it. 'I lived in a wretched cottage, we hadn't even a bathroom. My father was usually out of work; he drank. My mother did odd jobs when she was well enough; she's dead now. I went to the Plas – the old house – to do cleaning, and sometimes I helped to "maid" women who stayed there. I was terribly envious of their clothes. Then I was taken on as nursemaid. I went to picnics if the children did and that was how I met Bill – he often stayed at the Plas. A year ago he brought me to London and set me up in a flat. Well, now you know. You *are* shocked, aren't you?'

I swore I wasn't. But I was, a little. My aunt's broadmindedness had extended to women who lived with men who couldn't marry them ('George Eliot did'), to emancipated women who refused to marry the men they lived with ('One doesn't necessarily agree with them but they *are* making a stand about something'), even to prostitutes ('They are often driven to it'). But she was prejudiced against 'kept women' – unless they were great courtesans or in history, when it didn't count – and she had handed on her prejudice to me. Besides, it distressed me that anyone who looked like Zelle should be kept by an elderly, ugly man. But perhaps she loved him; if so, I should feel better about it.

I said, 'I expect you're fond of him.'

It was some seconds before she answered. 'I ought to be. He's wonderfully generous – and so considerate; he puts masses into my bank account so that I can pay my own rent and all my bills and never need ask him for money.' She gave a little laugh. 'Poor Bill, he's in for a shock when he finds I'm overdrawn and haven't paid the rent. But he won't mind. He'll be glad I've had a happy summer. It's been the happiest time of my life.'

I said it seemed dreadful she'd just spent so much on the lunch party when her bank account was overdrawn.

'Well, I wanted to have one last fling before I leave the Club. Oh, God, I wish I didn't have to go. I hope you're right in thinking the girls haven't guessed about me. If they have, Molly might tell Hal and he might tell Adrian Crossway. He's coming to have tea with me on Tuesday, to talk about the work he's found for me in an East End Settlement.'

It seemed peculiar work for a kept woman but I held my peace about that and said I couldn't imagine Molly talking to Hal about her. 'She wouldn't think it fair and anyway they'll only be interested in each other.'

'And the girls might understand, they've been around quite a bit. It was you I worried about most. You're so untouched.'

I wondered if it would help her to know the true facts about me but I was still being discreet. So I just said I was as fond of her as ever. And it was true. I was shocked *for* her, not *at* her; shocked she should have to live a life so unsuitable for her. Thinking of this I said, 'Zelle, wouldn't you be happier if you gave Bill up? Couldn't you, if Adrian Crossway gets you a job?'

'Oh, it isn't a paid job. I'll only be able to do it because Bill's keeping me. What I hope is that doing worthwhile work will make me feel better about Bill. Let's forget it all and have dinner somewhere nice. We'll go down and find the girls.'

We found Lilian in her cubicle. She said Molly had stonewalled all attempts to reassure her about Hal, by saying: 'The subject is closed.'

Molly was still in her bath so Zelle and I went along and thumped on the door and Zelle asked her out to dinner. Molly said, 'Thank you, child, but I intend to have a quiet Club dinner and go early to bed.' The tone was icy for a girl lying in hot water.

I whispered to Zelle, 'It sounds as if she's taken her lorgnette into the bath with her.'

14

The next night, when I got back from the theatre, I decided to miss the gathering in Zelle's room and go up on the roof; I had taken a fancy to it and there was a good moon. I went to the place where Zelle and I had stood, and leaned against the parapet.

After a few minutes I heard someone calling my name. It was Lilian's voice, I thought; I turned and could see her by the staircase door. She saw me then and joined me.

'Zelle thought I might find you here,' she said, 'as you weren't in your cubicle. The most awful thing's happened. Molly's just informed me she's going to spend a night with Hal. She won't say when but I gather it's to be soon. She's terribly upset but absolutely determined to do it.'

'But why? Did Hal ask her to?'

'No, she asked him. She more than asked, she insisted – said she wouldn't marry him if he didn't agree. And now she doesn't think he'll want to marry her afterwards and neither do I. Could you have believed any girl would have been such a fool?'

Lilian then launched into a description of what Molly said she had said to Hal and what Hal had said to her. It would have been funny if only we hadn't felt it would result in disaster.

It seemed that after the idiotic conversation in

the Green Room Molly had planned to ask Hal if he really did want to marry her, but she had come to the conclusion (just as Lilian, Zelle and I had) that he could hardly say anything but 'yes'. So she had decided to convince him he didn't *have* to marry her, by pretending to be modern and dashing and asking him to take her away on a trial trip.

'Can you imagine it?' said Lilian. 'Molly pretending madly and poor old Hal being horribly shocked; he's the last man to do anything modern. And then he got touchy and said she didn't have to marry him if she had any doubts. She thinks his final idea was that she wants to find out if she likes sleeping with him, before she ties herself up. As if anyone could find out in one night! You have to take things on trust and hope for the best. But now, with Molly in this mood and Hal disillusioned about her, things are sure to go wrong and they won't get a chance to come right.'

I asked if there was any hope of getting Molly to change her mind but Lilian said she didn't think it would help now. 'I gather she was weakening a bit by the end of the evening, but by then *he'd* begun to be for it; or rather, he was dead set on her not marrying him unless she was sure she'd stay married. He said his family didn't go in for divorces. What a mess it all is! And I started it – by what I said in the Green Room.'

'Well, you didn't mean to.'

'God, no! And yet I keep harrowing myself by feeling I may have been sort of unconsciously trying to bitch things for Molly because I envy her so.'

I was astonished to hear Lilian say that as I knew she found Hal extremely dull. Was she merely envying Molly for making a wealthy marriage? (If the poor girl was still going to.) I was trying to puzzle this out when Lilian went on:

'I'm terribly unhappy. Would you mind if I told you about it? I haven't said a word to anyone else because he asked me to be discreet. But he certainly isn't; I bet lots of people at the theatre know. Do you?'

I said, 'I do now. Go on, Lilian.'

Surprisingly, after the first sharp pang of jealousy, I didn't mind very much – that is, I didn't then; I expected to, later, but was determined to defer misery, otherwise I should give myself away to Lilian. And of course I was curious; that helped. I even found some pleasure in listening because everything she told me concerned him.

She said that though she had often joked about her interest in him, it was a joke; and she had started rehearsals with only one idea: to make a success of her part. Never had she planned to attract him and when, during rehearsals, he had showed her he was attracted she had been flattered and excited but not in the least in love. Then–

'Once I'd opened in the part, you can't imagine what it was like,' she told me. 'He'd take me out to lunch and to supper and get me to come to his dressing-room after matinées. It was wildly thrilling – I fell for him instantly though I did try to hold out; I didn't want to seem easy to get. But I don't believe women ever do hold out on him and he must have seen how I really felt. Anyway, one afternoon – it's just a week ago – we went to a secret flat he has. We've been there three afternoons since.'

I said, 'Then why aren't you happy?'

'Because he doesn't really give a damn for me – doesn't even pretend to. We're supposed just to be playing a delightful game. If I give him even a hint that I care for him he gives me much more than a hint that he doesn't want me to. He likes me to be hard; that attracts him. You wouldn't think a man could make love so devastatingly and yet never show any tenderness. And somehow he always manages to make me feel it won't last. Oh, God, he can be cruel!'

'I don't understand. He's the kindest man I've ever known.'

'He's not kind in love,' said Lilian.

He had been kind to me. He had shown me tenderness. Surely that proved he cared more for me than he did for her?

'Oh, I know he can be kind-hearted,' she continued. 'He still is to me, sometimes, at the theatre; and in a way it means more to me than what happens at that flat. He's very fond of you, by the way; did you know? He often talks of you.'

'Really? What does he say?' I tried not to sound eager.

'Oh, that you're a darling and intelligent and amusing; and brave, too – I suppose he meant that night you went on in my part.' She smiled and spoke as if being nice to a child. 'Sometimes I'm quite jealous of the things he says about you.'

'You needn't be.' I meant to say it casually but

it came out sounding bitter.

She looked at me quickly. 'You're not – you've always said you're not – you're not just a bit in love with him yourself?'

I reminded myself that I had to be discreet (his word, and he had used it to her too). I had often longed not to be – in a Club where most girls gossiped about their love affairs, to the Club maids, if no one else was handy – but I was proud of resisting the temptation and meant to go on doing so. I intended to say, 'No, of course not,' and laugh Lilian's question off. But this sudden temptation was too much for me. I told her everything.

From the beginning she was far more distressed than I expected her to be. She kept interrupting me to say things like, 'I can't believe it. Why didn't you tell us? We might have helped you, advised you.' When I told her about the night in the barn she was so horrified it was almost funny. I said:

'Really, Lilian! You sound like someone's grand-mother. Why are you so shocked on my account when you're not on your own?'

'You're years younger than I am. And I've had other affairs.'

'Have you, Lilian? You never told me.'

'Well, of course not. You were such an innocent. Molly and I always tried to protect you from – well, knowing too much about things like that. Anyway, I've only had two other affairs and one didn't count; we were engaged.'

'Has Molly had affairs, too?'

'No, she hasn't and that's why this spending a night with Hal is such a catastrophe. Oh, God, what hell life is – for Molly and me and now you! Well, if it's any comfort to you, Rex is liable to tire of me any minute.'

I had already been comforted by thinking that. I knew I should be deeply sorry for her when it happened; but that didn't stop me from being thankful it *would* happen. Only momentarily had she shattered my hopes. I was now engaged in rebuilding them.

She took me back to my story, wanting to know about the next few days after the vicarage party. I guessed she was trying to fit in the end of my affair with the beginning of hers, so I made it quite clear that they didn't overlap. She said, 'If only I'd known about you! Still, I can't pretend it would have made all that difference – because I'm so terribly in love. I never knew I would feel like that about anyone. Though I could almost hate him on your account.'

I said, 'Well, don't. Because *I* think he's treated me wonderfully. Everything was my fault, yet he wasn't angry even when I landed him in real trouble.' I told her about Black Saturday.

When I was in the middle of my visit to Mrs Crossway, Lilian interrupted. 'No wonder he thinks you're brave. And how grateful he must have been! He hates her to find out about him, even though she'll never divorce him.'

'But she's longing to.'

After I'd handed on the complete gist of my talk with Mrs Crossway, Lilian said, 'He must have told me she'd never divorce him just to stop me from entertaining false hopes. Oh, I wish I had your courage. *I'd* go and see her and tell her everything. If I was the co-respondent he'd have to marry me – except that he wouldn't if he knew I'd told his wife. He'd hate me too much.'

'Anyway, you wouldn't want him to marry you against his will, would you?'

'Wouldn't I just!' said Lilian. 'I'd have some claim on him then, however unfaithful he was. As things are, he can just turf me out for good. Besides–' She began to giggle school-girlishly. 'Once I was married I'd have that lovely house. Why didn't you tell his wife the truth? Then *you'd* have had the house. And you'd have made the sweetest little co-respondent. Perhaps we could *both* be co-respondents – and share the house and him. I'd mind less with you than with anyone.'

By now I was laughing too. Everything seemed lighter, easier. I no longer felt jealous; we just seemed companions in misfortune. Lilian controlled herself first and said, 'Stop or we shall get hysterical. Oh, it's such a relief to talk to you and it somehow helps to know you're in love with him too. Though I can't think why it does, especially as I'm madly envious of you.'

'*You're* envious of *me?*'

'Of course. Because he's fond of you. That's something you can count on.'

'Still, you wouldn't swop what you have for that.'

'Well, not yet,' said Lilian, laughing again, 'but you wait till I'm out on my ear. We'll help each other now, won't we? I'll tell you all the nice things he says about you.'

'But how can I help you?'

She was silent so long that I wondered if she had heard. At last she said, 'I think you *have* helped me.'

I asked in what way. Again there was a silence before she answered. Then she spoke quite casually. 'Oh, by being friendly. Let's go to bed now.' She looked around at the moonlit roof. On its grey surface the shadows of the chimney stacks were densely black. 'Rather nice up here – though it's probably filthy. Anyway, it's somewhere one can talk without being overheard.'

As we went down, we wondered if we should go in and talk to Molly about *her* problem. 'At least she's off her high horse with me now,' said Lilian, 'and she may need company.' But Molly's light was out.

'Though I daresay she's lying awake worrying,' Lilian whispered. 'And we probably shall, too.'

But I didn't. The guilt I felt at having talked to Lilian was as nothing compared with the relief it had brought. Discretion is too heavy a burden for eighteen-year-olds.

I was due at the theatre the next morning, so that Eve could go to a fitting of one of her admirably cut suits (doomed to be treated like a very old rag). I would willingly have worked on through the afternoon but she sent me off duty immediately after lunch; only in exceptional circumstances would she let me work morning, afternoon and evening. I sat reading in Regent's Park, on the far side from the Crossway house. I had a horror of meeting Mrs Crossway, and had never ceased to feel unhappy about deceiving her.

About half-past four I went back to the Club

for tea and as I entered the lounge I saw that Adrian Crossway was having tea with Zelle. They were so much absorbed in each other that neither of them noticed me, and I was careful to choose a table some way from them. Here I was hidden from Zelle by a pillar but I could still see Adrian Crossway in profile – a very handsome profile. He was wearing a suit of clerical grey flannel and looked to me like a stage clergyman of the disarmingly human type, one who plays a splendid game of cricket. I dimly remembered such a character in a play I had seen done by amateurs; and another character had been a 'fallen' woman whom he had treated with gentle tolerance, telling her in effect to go and sin no more. (My dear aunt had remarked that it was no use telling the woman that, when he didn't tell her how to earn a living.) What would Adrian do if he learned the truth about Zelle? And could she really let her 'fallen' state by night sponsor her good works by day?

I was thinking this might make a much more interesting play than the one I remembered, when Lilian came from the writing-room at the far end of the lounge. She joined me and I offered her a free cup of tea in my slop basin, an economical habit much favoured by Club members and much frowned on by the Club management. As I was pouring it, she noticed Adrian Crossway and turned to me in astonishment. I told her he had come to see Zelle about the good works she was planning to do.

'How extraordinary!' Lilian shot another glance at Adrian Crossway. 'He doesn't look to *me* as if he's discussing good works. Heavens, do you think he's fallen for her?'

I said this was only the second time they'd met.

'Still–' She broke off, gulped her tea and said she must go and post a letter. 'And I won't be back because I've some jobs to do.' It was Club protocol never to barge in on a girl entertaining a man so I was not surprised that she whisked out of the lounge with her head averted from Adrian Crossway.

Soon he rose to go and Zelle went with him, presumably to see him off. As they crossed the lounge I noticed how vividly pretty she looked, with more colour than usual. When he held the door for her he smiled in a way that might have been merely due to clerical benevolence but certainly looked more than that.

I hoped to ask her how things had gone but she did not return. And soon it was time for me to go to the theatre.

I did not get home until late, having walked; I had as yet nowhere near finished all the 'thinking things out' called for by Lilian's disclosure of her affair. There was a note from Zelle in my pigeon hole, asking me to come up to her room and saying: 'Don't let the girls know as I've told them I have a headache.' Luckily they weren't around as I went up to the fourth floor.

I found Zelle, in her madonna-blue dressing-gown, reading the Bible. She said she had hated it as a child– 'I hated everything to do with chapel. But it's different now.'

We sat together on her window-seat and she told me about Adrian Crossway's visit. He had been marvellous– 'Goodness simply radiates from him, though he doesn't talk about it much or keep mentioning God. Somehow he makes goodness seem fun – we kept on laughing. I wish you could have seen him.'

I said I had and he had seemed as happy with her as she was with him. 'He looked terrifically interested in you, Zelle.'

'He'd be interested in anyone who wants to be good. I don't flatter myself it's more than that, though he did say that even at our first meeting he'd felt we were going to be friends. He's coming to London again on Saturday and we're going to this place in the East End, and then I'm having dinner with him. And soon I'm going down to stay at the inn, so that I can go to his Harvest Thanksgiving Service. He says the church will look lovely.'

Who was I to decide she wasn't a suitable friend – or even a wife – for a clergyman? Particularly as I wasn't religious. I tried to sound enthusiastic. 'You'll enjoy that, won't you?'

She gave me a quick glance. 'Don't worry. I've the right to do it now. I've given Bill up.'

'Zelle! When?'

'Tonight. I was due to meet him at the flat. It was awful.'

It certainly sounded awful. She had so disliked the idea of leaving the Club that she had asked Bill if she might keep her room on and only go to the flat when he could be with her. 'And he didn't mind a bit – he was glad I'd made some friends. But of course he wanted me to stay on at the flat for the night. Well, I'd expected that and

I thought it would be all right. I'm fond of him and I've never – well, *minded*. But I couldn't go through with it, I simply couldn't. And I never will again.'

I asked her if she'd told Bill that and she said she'd tried to but he'd kept on saying it would all come right. 'At least, he said that after I swore there wasn't anyone else, which there isn't in the way he means. I just said I wanted to live a decent life.' There was a sudden glint of humour in her eyes. 'You should have heard me piling that on. You see, I meant to make him feel guilty so that he'd put my bank account straight. And he did ruin me – as I gently reminded him.'

'Goodness, do people still talk about girls being ruined?'

'They do where I come from,' said Zelle. 'Anyway, poor old Bill got properly harrowed and said I wasn't to worry about anything. And he'd go on paying my allowance and be very, very patient. So I relaxed a bit. And then suddenly–! Patient! I had a free fight to get out of the flat. I'll never go back there. I'll never see him again. It's finished.'

'But what will you do – without an allowance?'

'I'll get a job. Perhaps Adrian can get me one. I shall tell him on Saturday that I've lost all my money.'

'Won't you tell him about Bill?'

'No, never. I couldn't bear to disillusion him. He thinks I'm good – he said so, today, when I was telling him I longed to be. He said, "The longing is the goodness, and one can see that in your eyes." Wasn't that wonderful?'

I thought it embarrassing, when said during tea in the Club lounge. But perhaps Adrian Crossway had not said it as emotionally as Zelle did. I felt sure her longing for goodness was mainly a longing for him, whether she knew it or not. Then I accused myself of cynicism and did my best to be sympathetic.

We went on talking until nearly two in the morning; that is, she did, with very little prompting from me. Again and again she went over the scene in the flat, telling me what she had said and what poor old Bill had said. (I discovered he was nearly sixty.) I found her hard-headedness about Bill and sex, combined with her emotionalism about Adrian and goodness, a bit dislikeable; but I still liked *her,* and felt sorry for her. I also felt sorry for Adrian Crossway and I could not imagine how things would work out.

At last, to my relief, she asked me to go. She said she wanted to read some more of the Bible before she went to sleep.

On my way downstairs I thought how extraordinary it was that Molly, Lilian, Zelle and I were all at the same time involved in difficult love affairs. But I soon saw it wasn't in the least extraordinary. As I went along dimly lit landings, past the doors of rooms and the archways leading to 'villages' of cubicles, I could think of any amount of girls sleeping within them who were involved in love affairs, few of them satisfactory. Words dropped into my mind: 'It is our time of life for them.'

Then, for a philosophical moment, I tried to project myself into a future when I should be as old as the oldest Club member, whose room I was then passing. (She was around sixty, a cheerful soul who enjoyed half-crown flutters on horses.) But I hastily returned to the present, finding the thought of aged peace unattractive; and knowing that, whatever the agonies, I would not willingly have skipped one day of my time of life.

15

After our midnight session on the roof I had expected Lilian to want more confidential talks, but she showed no sign of it. And though she, Molly and I always exchanged words over the cubicle tops while we had breakfast, the words had become fewer. We weren't at all unfriendly but it seemed that none of us welcomed questions or wanted to volunteer information.

The day after Zelle kept me up so late I fell asleep after breakfast and woke only in time to get down for lunch. Molly and Lilian were out. I wondered if Lilian would be spending the afternoon at the flat. Then I tried to get my mind off that subject; but even if I had been able to, it would have been brought back to it in the evening, by a talk I had with Eve Lester.

She had been out of the office settling some problem in the dress-circle bar. When she came back she said: 'I'd better tell you – before you pick up some gossip; the whole theatre's buzzing with it. But perhaps you know already. I mean about Lilian and Mr Crossway.'

I said I did know and she asked me how. 'Brice promised not to tell you. Was it one of the programme girls?'

'No, it was Lilian herself.'

'Well, one can't expect her to be discreet when he isn't. I suppose she's cock-a-hoop.'

There was a hard note in Eve's voice which was not like her. So I told her how unhappy Lilian was.

Eve's tone softened. 'Poor kid, one ought not to decide girls are hard just because they look it. Funny how hardness attracts him these days. Perhaps it makes him feel less guilty.'

'*Does* he feel guilty?'

'Well, not morally. But he minds hurting people and I think he tries to protect himself by choosing hard women and making it clear that he doesn't really care for them – which often makes them keener than ever, poor devils. But I can't fuss about Lilian's future miseries. How's this affecting *you?*'

'She hasn't taken anything that was mine.'

'And won't,' said Eve. 'He'll go on being fond of you after he's fallen for, and tired of, any number of Lilians. I just wanted you to know.'

I thanked her and then sat quietly while she talked about him, mainly excusing him, saying his susceptibility to women was part of his equipment as an actor, and that his affairs were a form of stimulant – which he could no more resist than some men could resist drink. She told me the theatre staff always got to know and heartily approved – 'Except Brice, of course; he's always furious – but he's furious about almost everything Mr Crossway does. The others think of it as part of a romantic Don Juan-Casanova story and like father, like son; though the old man was much more dashing, often ran several affairs at once. Well, there it is and I'm thankful you're being so sensible about it.'

She wouldn't have said this had she known I had convinced myself that neither Lilian nor her successors could prevent my Last Act from crowning my play as I wished it to be crowned.

The next day – the Thursday of that memorable week – Lilian and I had lunch together at the Club. She told me Molly had just departed carrying an overnight case. 'And when I asked her where she was going she said, "Mind your own business, child." So I suppose she's off with Hal and I bet it wrecks everything. But I've too much on my mind to worry about her. If you knew…!'

I thought I soon should, but then Zelle joined us; and as she did not know about Lilian's problems and Lilian did not know about hers we only talked about Molly's, which we all knew about. Lilian and I soon went off to the theatre – it was matinée day – and the bus was no place for confidences. But after we got off Lilian asked me if I ever prayed. I said I tried not to, but sometimes one could not resist a vague 'please make it all right, God'. She said: 'Well, mention *me* to him, will you – just for the next few days? Believe me, I need it.'

I asked her if she was praying herself, and she said she was half demented with it – 'There's a voice in my head that goes on all the time, saying "Please, please, please" to someone somewhere. I'd love to talk about it but I daren't. It might be unlucky.'

That afternoon I worked in the Throne Room. Eve had rescued a play from the scripts turned down by the official play-reader and was convinced Mr Crossway ought to read it. But it was very badly typed. So she had asked me to re-type it and set it out properly, fitting the work in when I could. Its hard-up young author had recently called on us and I had said I would get my copies – I was taking carbons – finished soon. I have reason to remember that job as, only a few days later, it altered the course of my life. (This was more than it did for the life of its author as the play was never produced; though he did eventually have some success.)

But at the moment I was merely thankful to be on my own with interesting work to occupy my mind, though it was not too occupied to prevent my watching Lilian's last-act scene through the spy-hole. She played it exactly as she had been taught, without one changed intonation. But Rex had certainly changed his performance. He made it clear that he was attracted by her. This actually improved the scene and did not detract from the scene which followed. I wondered if he had changed deliberately or if he did not realise what he was revealing. Either way, it would be a change noticed by Brice Marton or anyone watching from the wings. No wonder the theatre knew of his interest in Lilian.

When I got back to the Club that night I went

to my cubicle without going to Zelle's room. Lilian, too, skipped the Veda toast session. She and I talked a few minutes, lamenting over Molly's empty cubicle. Then Lilian said, 'Don't forget. Pray, pray, pray!' And though I dimly felt that what benefited her might not benefit me, I dutifully did pray.

Nothing special happened at the theatre next day – that is, nothing special happened to me; plenty was happening to others and doubtless Eve knew about it by the evening. Had I been in the office she might have told me, but I was shut away with my scripts except when I came out for coffee and then she was not there. I worked on until the curtain was down, when she looked in on me to say she was going home and would I close the office when I left? I said she looked tired and she admitted she had a headache.

I walked home and intended to go straight to bed but there was a note in my cubicle from Lilian saying, 'Come up quickly – marvellous news about Moll Byblow. And I'm happy too – but not a word about that until we can talk privately.'

When I opened the door of Zelle's room I had a sudden memory of my first sight of it. Now, as then, Zelle was on the window-seat, Lilian in the armchair and Molly in front of the gas fire making toast. Now, as then, I sat down on the bed. But my mood was very different, for then I had come back from being made love to in the dimly lit street in Hampstead.

Molly had already told her story, but was more than willing to tell it again. She and Hal had, the previous day, driven a long way into the country and gone to a small hotel. From the outset Hal had been almost silent, Molly embarrassed and miserable. They had barely exchanged a word during the drive or at tea in a lounge where people stared at them.

'We didn't go up to the bedroom until after tea,' said Molly, 'and then poor old Hal did try to be a bit more cheerful. He said, "Well, this is very jolly," but soon relapsed into gloom and sort of whistled through his teeth all the time we un-packed. He put out his pyjamas and I put out my nightgown. He looked at the nightgown and said, "Jolly, what?" then quickly looked away from it. I said what about a walk before dinner and he seemed quite pleased at that idea so we went out and traipsed round the village. He kept saying it was jolly pretty and I kept agreeing. Then I noticed the huge figure of a man carved in the chalk of a hill, so I said what about going to have a look at it? Hal said jolly good but it was some way off so we'd need to go in the car which we did, and drove to the foot of the hill. Then we walked. It was steep and Hal kept pulling me up and saying "Ooops a daisy". I can't remember that he said anything else till we got up to the chalk man.'

Molly explained that the chalk man only looked like a man when viewed from the distance. Close to, all she saw were white paths deeply cut in the grass. Anyway, she was too puffed to be much interested so she just flopped down by one of the paths to get her breath. Hal sat down too, and they both admired the view; and then they said nothing for so long that Molly felt she really must try to make conversation.

So she began to talk about the chalk man, asking Hal if he thought he was prehistoric– 'I mean the man, not Hal of course. He said it was jolly likely but he wasn't much of a one for any kind of history. Then I thought I'd try to puzzle out the shape the chalk paths made, so I opened my lorgnette and set to work. I made out his head and his two arms and his body – they were higher up the hill than we were – and I found his legs, which were lower than we were. And then, my dears, I found that at the top of his legs there was just everything there; usually it's down there only it was *up* there and wildly exaggerated – unless prehistoric men were very extraordinary, which they well may have been. Of course I realise they didn't mean to be indecent but you would think that, since those days, someone would have let the grass grow tactfully or carved out some tiny pants – though they'd have to be enormous pants, really. And the awful thing was that I'd plonked myself down beside the most indecent path of all.'

I asked if Hal had noticed this and she said he had and she discovered that he thought she'd done it on purpose. 'Just as I was gazing at where we were sitting, he said he thought he'd better take me back to London – because, though he quite understood I was a modern girl who wanted to try things out, I'd now got him so nervous that he didn't think he'd give satisfaction, not that he'd been found wanting up to now.'

Then there had been a period of wild misunderstanding, with Molly accusing Hal of accusing her of being sex-mad and Hal not even denying it– 'Though he said he was all for it, *within reason.*' And then the truth had gradually come out that she'd feared he didn't want to marry her and she had been trying to show him he needn't.

'Of course it was frightfully complicated,' said Molly, 'and the more I explained, the less sense it made. But he finally *saw* – and said he'd like to wring Lilian's neck for putting the idea into my mind, not that she meant to. And then he was marvellous, and we laughed and laughed about the chalk man. And then we quietened down and watched the sunset and Hal actually said he loved me – which he's never managed to get out before. And I said, me too, right from the beginning. And he said him, too, right from the beginning. And then he said he'd been a fool and I said, no, I had. Really, you'd have loved it, Mouse, because we were practically poetic.'

I asked where they went for the night.

'Oh, back to the hotel,' said Molly. 'Hal said that was quite all right, now that he understood. And everything was blissful – anyway, it will be. I did get an *inkling.*'

They were to be married as soon as possible. 'And we both want *hundreds* of children,' said Molly. 'Now I must concentrate on toast-making. I'm ravenous.'

She knelt in front of the gas fire with her two long red plaits dangling down her back. The quality of her happiness went particularly well with toast-making and toast-eating. Lilian was far more excited and though she talked only about Molly I could have guessed – even without her note – that she was excited in her own right. Zelle said very little. I wondered if she was thinking about seeing Adrian Crossway the next day.

Soon Molly said she must go to bed and get a long night's sleep. I would have gone too, but Lilian asked me to wait while she had another cup of tea. She gulped it down the minute Molly was out of the room and then got up to go, so I realised she had stayed just to give herself a chance to talk to me. The minute we were out on the landing she said, 'Up on the roof, quick!'

It was chilly on the roof after the warm room; as we walked over to the parapet I hoped Lilian would not keep me out long. Then she began to talk and I forgot about being cold, forgot about everything except what she was saying. With triumph and delight she informed me that Mrs Crossway was bringing a suit for divorce.

'She had a detective watching the flat on Wednesday afternoon. He actually came to the door and rang the bell. Of course we didn't answer but he could easily have heard us talking before he rang – he could have listened through the letter-box. I didn't know it was a detective then, but when we came out there was a man in the corridor looking furtively casual, so I had hopes – I asked you to pray, remember. Anyway, Mrs Crossway had it out with Rex this morning and he admitted everything. He said it was no use denying it. And the marvellous thing is that he doesn't mind – well, he did at first but he seemed to change when he saw how wildly hopeful I was. Suddenly he was his very kindest self. He's never been as sweet to me as he was today.'

I asked if he was going to marry her.

'Well, of course. I'll be named in the case. Mrs Crossway wouldn't hear of an arranged divorce. She's left the house for good and I'm going to see it on Sunday. He says we might as well come out into the open now.'

I longed to get away without saying anything but I did manage: 'I hope you'll be very happy.' Presumably I didn't make a success of it for she instantly said: 'Oh, God, you *mind!* You shouldn't, you really shouldn't. It'll make no difference to his fondness for you. And I'll be in a position to help you. Perhaps someday I can persuade him to give you a part.'

'No, thank you, Lilian. He says I can't act.'

'Well, why can't he teach you, the way he taught me? Anyway I can make sure you meet lots of interesting people and find the right man to marry – somebody young. I want to ask you something. Promise you won't be angry.'

'I shouldn't think I would.' I was too stricken to imagine having the spirit to be angry.

'When you went to the barn that night, are you sure that anything really happened? It's so hard to believe it of Rex – with you. And you're so innocent you just might think– Well, I once knew a girl who believed she'd been seduced when there'd been nothing that actually *counted*.'

I was surprised at the roundabout way she was

putting it – she who could be almost crudely blunt. Then it dawned on me she was still treating me as an innocent because she so wished me still to be one. She wanted to get me off her conscience and, in her own mind, off his too. So I let her believe what she wanted to. It needed some embarrassing inventions and I had to endure much relieved laughter from Lilian, who promised to buy me a book on sex. I thanked her, feeling deeply apologetic to my dear aunt who had, on my fifteenth birthday, presented me with valuable works by Dr Marie Stopes.

Before we dropped the subject Lilian swore she would never mention it to Rex. Then she said she was cold and we ought to go in but there was something else she needed to say – 'It's about Zelle. We must all of us be very kind to her. You see, I had to tell Rex what she is. I loathed doing it, because I'm really fond of her, but it was only fair to let him warn Adrian.'

So Lilian knew about Zelle. Still, I wasn't going to admit that I did, not yet. I just said: 'What about?'

Lilian, in her hardest voice, said: 'I'm going to stop treating you as an innocent. Bill isn't really Zelle's guardian. He keeps her. Molly and I guessed almost from the beginning but we didn't want to disillusion you.'

It seemed pointless to pretend I hadn't known, and I was quite pleased to say Zelle had told me. I also said I couldn't see why Adrian Crossway had to be warned, as he had his wits about him and anyway was only helping Zelle to do something worth while.

'Rubbish,' said Lilian. 'He was very much attracted – he admitted it when Rex telephoned him. And he was more than grateful to be told the facts.'

'Does that mean he's going to drop her?'

Instead of answering, Lilian quickly looked towards the entrance to the roof. There was someone standing there, but whoever it was instantly turned and went down the stairs.

I said, horrified, 'Was it Zelle? She does sometimes come up here at night.'

'Anyway, she couldn't have heard, surely? Not right across the roof, when we were talking so quietly.'

I said it was more likely she thought we were having a private conversation and didn't want to butt in– 'If it *was* Zelle.'

'Molly and I must have it out with her and make her realise we like her as much as ever. You must have had a shock when she told you the truth. What about your *princesse lointaine?*'

'In a way, I still see her as that. And she's given Bill up now she's interested in good works.'

'You mean now she's interested in Adrian,' said Lilian. 'But, oh God, has she? Then she really must be in love. That's damped my spirits. Poor Zelle! Come on, we must be mad, staying up here in this wind.'

The next day I had to be at the theatre in the morning, so that Eve could go to her hairdresser. But when I got to the office I found she had cancelled her appointment and was there, waiting to break the news; she said she hadn't felt she could face telling me the night before. She was relieved when she heard I knew already and even more relieved when I said (trying to sell the idea to myself as well as to her), 'I've no right to mind and I don't intend to. If it hadn't been Lilian it would have been somebody else.'

'Quite true,' said Eve, 'once Mrs Crossway was determined to find grounds for divorce. Still, it's worrying on his account. What kind of a wife will Lilian make him?'

'Admirable, I should say. She'll run his house well and put up with his affairs – which is what he asks of a wife, isn't it?'

Eve gave me a surprised look. 'That sounds ugly, coming from you. But there's no denying it.'

I said I hadn't meant it to sound ugly. 'I wasn't condemning. He is as he is and I was just accepting it.'

'Which is what I've done for twenty years,' said Eve.

She told me to take the afternoon off but did not argue when I said I'd prefer not to. I think she was as glad of my company as I was of hers.

Shortly before the curtain fell she mentioned that Mr Crossway would be coming up to see her after the matinée; so I cleared off to the Throne Room and worked on the play I was typing. I felt sure he would leave without seeing me. But he came in and closed the door. I was so at a loss that I just went on typing. He sat on the table and, after a few seconds, said: 'Could I, at a convenient moment, have your attention?'

I looked up, met his eyes, and in the same instant felt both agonised and completely at ease with him. The ease, the sense of intimacy, somehow increased the agony, but I managed to say quite lightly: 'We *have* played our farewell scene.'

He smiled. 'No, we haven't. And as far as I'm concerned we never shall play it. We only said farewell to ... to an interlude that should never have happened. And I want to say now, as I said then, that I'm deeply fond of you.'

I said: 'You didn't mention "deeply" before.'

'Then perhaps absence has made the heart grow fonder. Anyway, the "deeply" was sincere. And we're going to meet very often, I hope. Lilian is devoted to you. She doesn't, I take it, er – know about us?'

I shook my head. 'And never will, from me.' I didn't explain just what she didn't know; it seemed better not to, as she had promised never to admit she knew anything at all.

'Thank you. By the way, I'm considering a play which has a number of very small parts, little better than walk-ons, I'm afraid, but if it would amuse you to play one–'

I laughed, quite genuinely. 'Would that be a consolation prize or a booby prize?'

He laughed too, then said: 'Oh, my dear, absurd child, I'm not sure I ought not to send you away for your own good, but I should so hate to lose you. You have a genius for making im-possible situations delightful. See you again very soon – that is, if you're willing?'

I said: 'Lilian permitting.'

'Lilian encouraging, I assure you. She's going to arrange a lunch party.'

He gave me one last most intimate, affectionate

smile and went.

Was he again – I had never forgotten that over-heard phrase of Eve's – being kind to be cruel? I only knew I had been given back enough to live on. And dimly, dimly, I began to see a new Last Act to crown my play.

16

When I got back to the Club that Saturday night I went straight up to Zelle's room wondering what had happened at her meeting with Adrian Crossway. Getting no answer to my knock, I thought she must have gone up on the roof or to have a bath; it was most unlikely she would be out as late as this. So I opened the door intending to go in and wait for her.

I switched on the light and then thought I must have come to the wrong room. This one was obviously unoccupied; not a personal possession was to be seen. I stepped back to look at the number on the door. But I had made no mistake and, when I looked again, I saw one trace of Zelle: the nail she had, against Club rules, knocked into the wall so that she could hang up her furry-eared baby faun.

I stood staring, remembering the room on the previous night with the girls strewn around, the gas fire glowing and the warm air filled with the smell of Veda toast. Now the room not only felt cold; it even smelt cold and as if a thorough cleaning had ousted all association with previous occupancy.

I went down to the village and found it in darkness. Molly, I knew, had gone with Hal to visit some of his relations. Lilian would be with my dear; I imagined her entering some restaurant, triumphantly radiant. Was there anyone I could ask about Zelle's sudden departure? The other three occupants of the village – now probably asleep – hardly knew her.

Then, as I switched on my cubicle light, I saw a letter from her on my dressing-table. It said she had heard Lilian talking to me on the roof, so had not been surprised to get a telegram from Adrian Crossway saying he was 'unavoidably detained' in the country. He had added 'writing' but she doubted if he would. 'Still, if any letter does come, please hang on to it for me, in case I send you an address. But I probably won't. In a way, I'd rather not know if he writes or not. As long as I don't know, I can pretend he has and that he's said something nice. He might, as he's such a marvellous man. Love to you all. I will always remember this summer. Don't worry about me. I can always go back to being a char. Zelle.'

I felt terribly sorry for her. And I was sorry for Lilian, too, because I knew she would be harrowed. I didn't blame her for making sure Adrian Crossway was warned, I even admired her for it; though I couldn't have done it myself.

When I woke in the morning Lilian still hadn't returned. I wondered if she had already installed herself at the Regent's Park house. No, it was more likely she was at the flat. Darling Charlotte the Harlot brought my breakfast and advised me to have a long Sunday sleep; but I had other plans ahead of me and was thankful to have them.

For the first time, I was going to the office on a Sunday. I had told Eve I wanted to finish work on the young author's play; the typing was done but I still had to sort and bind the copies. She had demurred until I said I wanted a job to occupy my mind. Then she handed over the keys. I did want a job and I did want to finish the play; but even more I wanted a place where I could put in some uninterrupted thinking, and I wanted that place to be the Throne Room.

It was a sunless day, cold and windy for September; suddenly it seemed out of the question to wear a summer dress. I put on my grey woollen dress and black cloak, and remembered I had worn them together for my very first visit to the Crossway.

The bus was nearly empty, as were the streets with their closed shops. And when I let myself into the foyer, the closed theatre felt most unlike its usual self. It had felt much the same during the period when it was 'dark', but I had never been alone in it then. Today, even after I was up in the office, the atmosphere seemed almost uncanny.

Binding the scripts took me over an hour. Then, having stacked them neatly and tidied up the Throne Room table (a sort of clearing the decks for action) I settled down to think.

First I considered my re-constructed Last Act.

It was now out of the question that Rex would ever marry me – because, however unfaithful he was, Lilian would never divorce him; she had made that clear during our first conversation on the roof. So the best I could now hope for was that some of his unfaithfulness would be with me. If so, should I feel guilty to Lilian? I doubted it – and anyway, had she not almost indicated a willingness to share him with me? I felt sure she had not expected to be taken up on that; but if she was prepared to put up with infidelity she could at least include me in the general amnesty.

I then wondered if I was fooling myself by believing he would ever feel more than a kindly affection for me. And I was sure that, even now, there was something more than that. Here in the Throne Room yesterday I had been conscious of it. And that night in the moonlit barn Samson hadn't argued with Delilah. Anyway, not for long.

No, provided I willed it, he would – now and then – succumb. But could one build a life on that? Undoubtedly one ought not to. And undoubtedly one was – almost – determined to.

I thought how much my aunt would have disapproved of such abjectness. I was sure no Shakespearian heroine (except, perhaps, the spineless Mariana) would have put up with such a life. I felt guilty to George Bernard Shaw, whose works had so much conditioned my upbringing. I ruefully remembered myself, so splendidly independent, when I prepared for the conquest of London. But again and again I came back to the fact that I now wanted what I wanted. And it seemed one could combine abjectness with an iron determination to have one's own way. (Perhaps Mariana wasn't so spineless, after all.)

Still, I did try to interest myself in a nobler course of action. Suppose I arose, fearless and free, and left the Crossway? Well, apart from facing the emotional wrench, I wasn't keen on facing being jobless and incomeless. I had already spent this year's tiny income from my aunt's estate. And just as the security of my childhood had left me with a terror of 'the law', it had also left me with a terror of being penniless. And I had lost faith in myself as an actress; anyway, lost faith in convincing other people I was one. As for continuing as a secretary, in any job but my present one, the idea appalled me.

It then struck me that if I got what I wanted I might then lose my job. My love would have slung me out had Mrs Crossway wished him to; no doubt he would do the same if Lilian demanded it, as well she might. Tolerance towards him would hardly extend to his partners in crime, even me; I could not really count on that 'all girls together' attitude towards sharing her husband. And I was fond of Lilian. I no more wanted to lose her as a friend than I wanted to lose my job; and both losses seemed likely if I borrowed her husband.

Was there no way out I could face? Suddenly I saw a glimmer of one. Suppose I stayed – but renounced any further claim on him? I could still go on loving him – even my aunt would not have disapproved of that. Couldn't I find happiness in working for him and being his un-demanding little friend? I doubt if I then knew the word 'sublimation' but it was something near the meaning of that word which I offered to myself as an ideal.

I could – just – imagine building a life round that kind of love. And I had a good model in Eve Lester. She wasn't in love but her devotion did amount to love, selfless love; and she probably had more lasting value to him than any other woman. Could I, in time, be so valuable? And if so, could I be satisfied?

I then offered myself compensations. There was the part he had mentioned; he would never trust me with much more than a walk-on, but even walking on would be a pleasure. And while typing the play I had just finished binding, it had occurred to me that *I* might write a play. Suppose I left the Club and took an attic bed-sitting room and wrote in my spare time? Perhaps one day my dear would produce a play of mine and I should sit with him in the stalls as an author, not a secretary. And if his admiration for me got out of hand would I backslide from nobility? No! I would make him see we must not spoil our partnership as playwright and pro-ducer.

I had sold myself the idea: I would stay, love undemandingly, perhaps act, certainly write a play. I would build a life my aunt would have been proud of. (As for G.B.S., my play would be very Shavian.) *This* was the Last Act that would crown the play of my life – and go on crowning it.

I looked up at the paintings of the Crossway family. I had come to take them for granted but now – was I not going to serve their theatre as well as Rex Crossway? I gazed at his portrait, trying to see warm approval in the painted eyes. I couldn't; they were too badly painted to do anything but stare blankly. The eyes of the barnstormer, King Crossway, were even worse painted and suggested that his interpretation of Hamlet had included a squint. But the Sargent portrait of Sir Roy was a very different matter. Here the eyes were alive; the whole face was. I had always thought Sir Roy handsome, if satanic – or did 'sardonic' describe him better? I felt he took a cynical view of my resolutions. I said aloud: 'You wait and see!' Then exaltation made me feel hungry and I decided to go out to an early lunch. Would the pub be open for meals on Sunday?

As I went into the hall of the office I faced a narrow door which led to the roof. I had seen it dozens of times without taking any interest in it. Today, perhaps because I had recently liked the roof of the Club, I felt inclined to explore the roof of the theatre. I unbolted the door and stepped out.

This roof, unlike the used roof of the Club, gave me the sensation of being in a place where it was abnormal to be. At the front, the solid stone balustrade was too high for me to see over. At both sides, the balustrade was pillared and raised up on a plinth. By standing on the plinth I could see over and down to one of the narrow old streets below which was quite deserted.

I then decided to walk to the far end of the roof, which was very long – covering, as it did, the front of the house, the auditorium, the deep stage and the dressing-rooms. I strolled as far as I could go and then climbed up on the plinth and sat on the balustrade. There was not, as at the Club, any jutting-out floor below but I was un-worried by the sheer drop to the street and proud of being so. I sat there in the grey, windy morning deliberately exulting in the mood I had worked myself up into.

Perhaps the wind chilled me. Perhaps the Sunday emptiness all around was depressing. Perhaps my high mood was a fake. I only know that it was succeeded, with shattering suddenness, by intense dejection. I saw myself as an undersized, talentless little oddity who had made a fool of herself over a middle-aged philanderer who found her nothing but an embarrassment. The fact that I thought of him as a philanderer (I considered 'rake', which I thought a more attractive word, but I wouldn't let him have it) did not prevent my believing I should love him for ever; but it made my plan to serve him selflessly far less worth while. *Nothing* was worth while. I quite simply wished I were dead.

I then told myself I wished no such thing. 'If you did, you would jump off the roof.' But I still went on hankering for death. Suppose one did jump, how long would it be before one was dead? I took a penny out of my handbag and dropped it, counting while it fell. It reached the pavement at the count of six. I then imagined myself jump-ing, counted, imagined hitting the pavement, looked down and imagined seeing my dead body. Of course, I might not die instantly: an uncomfortable thought. Still, I probably should; it was a long way down. Just six seconds and everything would be over.

I have never known if I seriously thought of jumping. All I am sure of is that I became both giddy and utterly horrified of falling. I longed to make the small jump necessary to get from the balustrade to the roof, but I felt incapable of it. All I could do was to close my eyes and grip the balustrade. And once my eyes were closed I felt even giddier.

It was then that I heard someone calling me from below. Surprise vanquished giddiness and I was able to get down onto the roof. The voice called again. I stepped onto the plinth and looked over the balustrade. At an open window of the top floor of one of the little houses on the opposite side of the street, Brice Marton was standing. (I knew he had rooms close to the theatre but I had never known exactly where.) He called loudly: 'I want to see you – it's something important. Come down to the foyer and let me in.'

I called back, 'All right,' and went down, wondering what he could have to tell me. When I opened the door to him I saw he was very pale. I said, 'Did you think I was going to jump?'

He looked at me searchingly. 'Were you?'

'I was considering it – but only considering what it would be like. And then I thought I was going to fall.'

'I know. You swayed. It was terrifying.'

'I'm so sorry. It was really quite a useful experience because I'm now sure I never shall kill myself. I knew in that awful giddy moment how furious I should be afterwards. What did you want to tell me?'

'It can wait a bit. Just at present I want a drink.'

We went up to the office. Eve kept quite a lot of drink to offer people. Brice helped himself to whisky and suggested I should have some. As a near suicide, I felt entitled to; but it tasted filthy so I never finished it. After Brice had gulped down some of his, he said:

'I'm not going to beat about the bush. I know why you're unhappy. And I know where you spent the night after Adrian Crossway's blasted garden party.'

I thought of saying I didn't know what he was talking about but I felt sure it would be useless; so I just asked *how* he knew.

'Lilian let it out at her first rehearsal. Oh, *she* didn't know. But she chaffed me about being stranded with you and having to go to a hotel – you'd told her that. I guessed in time so I didn't give you away.'

'That was kind. Well, I suppose you were suitably shocked?'

'Not morally shocked. But so appalled *for* you. And I could have prevented it if I'd asked you to come back with me.'

'Only for the moment, Brice. Sooner or later I should have got what I wanted.'

'No, you wouldn't,' said Brice. 'Not once Lilian was around. You happened to catch Rex between affairs.'

That infuriated me. I said angrily, 'How about minding your own business?'

'Anyone I like as much as you *is* my business,' said Brice. 'Particularly when they've considered jumping off a roof. I'd be interested to know your plans. You won't, presumably, stay on here just hoping for crumbs from the rich Lilian's table?'

I told him I intended to stay, but without hoping for anything that was Lilian's. Indignation had helped to banish my roof-top dejection and I was determined to recreate the high mood that had preceded it. Grandiloquently, I described it to Brice, trying to make it valid for myself as much as for him. He listened so patiently that I felt he was impressed. But when I finished – by saying, 'After all, Eve's made a life worth copying,' – he said:

'You poor deluded infant, don't you know you'd drop all this high thinking if Rex gave you a quarter of a chance? As for Eve, it's true her devotion's selfless but she does get something in return. She's been his mistress, on and off, for twenty years.'

I didn't believe him. 'Then why couldn't Mrs Crossway name *her* in a divorce?'

'Mrs C. condoned the affair many years ago, and probably doesn't know it still goes on – as I assure you it does, if only occasionally. I should have thought you'd have guessed Eve wasn't just a patient drudge.'

'I never thought of her as that but– Oh, poor Eve!'

'She's happy enough. I doubt if she minds any

more about the other women. All that matters to her is Rex's happiness.'

I said determinedly, 'Well, *I* can live for that, too.'

'At eighteen? She's over twice your age and she's had twenty years of – well, it is a kind of devotion he gives her; and she knows she can count on it. What can you count on? And do you fancy joining her as the nucleus of a small harem, patiently waiting for a night? I should even have thought you'd hate the idea of robbing her, however you may feel about robbing your friend Lilian.'

'But I've told you. I'm not hoping to rob anyone. Why can't you believe me?'

His tone, which had been harsh, became kind. 'I do believe you. I'm sure you're sincere. But I'm equally sure that you're fooling yourself. Now listen. When I shouted across the street that I wanted to tell you something, it was to get you down from the roof. But there *is* something I've been planning to talk to you about. For a long time I've been thinking of leaving the Crossway and now I've got the chance of running a repertory company. It's at Whitesea, a one-horse seaside place but the theatre's charming and I could manage, direct and pretty well do what I please. I'll take the job if you'll come with me as a secretary. And you could help with the stage management. You might even act sometimes, which you never will here.'

'That's where you're wrong,' I said with dignity. 'I may get a small part in the very next play.'

'There won't *be* any next play for at least a year.

281

You come with me.'

He said it very nicely, and it was pleasant to feel he wanted me with him, so I thanked him politely before explaining that I couldn't face the wrench of leaving– 'At least I can *see* Rex here – if only through the spy-hole. Why do *you* want to leave?'

'Because it isn't right for me to stay, feeling as I do about Rex. After I found out you'd spent the night with him I was positively murderous; and you may remember I have a disastrous temper. Eve says I've inherited it from my father – presumably I got Rex's share as well as my own. He flares up sometimes but no one could call him bad tempered. As you're a bad guesser I suppose you've never realised he and I are half-brothers?'

I literally gasped. 'Brice! Is that true?'

He said he'd never been sure of it himself and could just as well be the son of a conjurer or a trapeze artist as his mother had been friendly with so many of her lodgers. 'All that's certain is that I'm not the son of her husband as he hadn't been around for years. But Sir Roy believed I was his son. And Rex believes it. That's why he puts up with so much from me.'

Now I could see a resemblance to the Sargent portrait. I said so to Brice, who said he could not see it himself.

'It'll be more obvious when you're older,' I told him. 'Anyway, it will if you fill out a bit. Sir Roy's face is so much heavier. But there's something in the eyes – that is, when you smile; which isn't very often.' What I really meant was that his

282

expression was usually grim. 'Anyway, *I'm* sure you're his son. Fascinating! Why do you mind so much? You do, don't you?'

'Yes,' said Brice.

I nodded sympathetically. 'I have a girl friend who's illegitimate, and *she* minds.'

'Oh, it's not the illegitimacy that worries me. But I've never been acknowledged. And my mother warned me that if I ever claimed relationship the old man would not only chuck me out but also stop her allowance – which he paid her until she died; he was pretty generous. And I suppose he was kind to me. But he treated me – well, as the call boy I was. Rex never did, though. If I didn't loathe Rex I'd love him.'

I said, 'Surely, now Sir Roy's dead you and Rex could admit the truth to each other?'

'Only if he opened the subject,' said Brice. 'And he never will. Eve says it's partly out of respect for his father and partly because Adrian's so bitterly against it. And I can see that openly accepting their bastard half-brother might be embarrassing. But they could do it privately. Well, now you know why I loathe all Crossways.'

'All the same, you must be proud to *be* a Crossway. I know I would be.'

'I hope I'm acquiring some of the family glamour for you,' said Brice, actually achieving a smile.

I considered this. 'Well, I do find it exciting.'

'*How* exciting?' said Brice.

And then, to my utter astonishment, he grabbed hold of me and kissed me. I resisted, but only for a few seconds; then I kissed him in return.

When he released me at last, he was looking very much surprised.

I said: 'That was involuntary. Doesn't mean a thing – except, probably, that I'm a bad lot.'

'Rubbish,' said Brice. 'What you really are is a schoolgirl whose crush on a matinée idol got out of hand. At least, that's what you *were*. Now – well, you've been left in mid air. Oh, I don't flatter myself you've suddenly discovered I'm the real man in your life. But you'd better let me have a shot at being him, or you'll tumble into a worse man's arms.'

'I won't tumble into anyone's arms,' I said indignantly – and again found myself in Brice's. This time he didn't stop at kissing me and we ended up on the sofa, dislodging a pile of scripts. I can't recall offering any opposition and it was Brice who eventually got up and said: 'Well, I'm dead keen on getting my bloody half-brother out of your system but not here. We need a bit more style.'

I rose and smoothed down my dress. 'If you think I was going to let you– And anyway, it means nothing, nothing, I tell you. I still love Rex.'

'I'll overlook that,' said Brice. 'Now let's have lunch and then go down to Whitesea. I'll show you the theatre. And we can spend the night at a hotel.'

'No, thank you.'

'Oh, separate rooms. And you can lock your door if you, er, change your mind. We'll spend tomorrow morning in the theatre and come back in the afternoon. Eve won't mind your being away, in the circumstances. I'll write her a note. Do you need a little more persuading?'

I backed away from him. 'No. You write your note.'

He sat down at Eve's desk and I went to get the copies of the play I had typed; I wanted them to be in the office for Eve to find next morning. While I was in the Throne Room I had a long look at the Sargent portrait. Sir Roy was certainly Brice's father and he was looking more sardonic than ever – or did I detect a gleam of understanding in his eyes? If anyone understood bad lots, he ought to.

As I carried the scripts to the office I thought that, if I hadn't come into the theatre to finish them, none of this would have happened. Was I sorry it had? I sat wondering, while Brice finished his note. Did I even *like* him? I wasn't at all sure. But I was quite sure I wanted him to kiss me again – wanted it so much that, when he looked up, I hastily turned away, afraid my expression might tell him so; not that he didn't know already.

I put my scripts on Eve's desk and he put his note on top of them and told me to leave the theatre keys there too, as he had his own keys and would take me out of the stage door; he wanted to pick up a coat from his office. We went down and across the dust-sheeted stalls to the pass door. Brice unlocked it and stood back to let me through. Halfway up the steps to the stage I turned and looked down, remembering the day I had crashed into the audition. My memory of seeing Rex in the stalls, through the pass door, was so vivid that when Brice slammed the door after him I felt he was slamming it on Rex. A second later, Brice said: 'Do you remember that first day, when I threw your cloak and umbrella after you through the pass door?' It was a queer kind of shared memory, Brice thinking of his first meeting with me while I thought of my first meeting with Rex.

We got Brice's coat and then went out of the stage door and along the alley. The wind was almost a gale and the baskets of geraniums at the front of the theatre were swinging madly.

'I'll have to take these down,' said Brice, and went back to the stage door for a chair to stand on. To shelter from the wind I stood close to one of the glass doors to the foyer. Through it I could see the painting of my dear as Charles Surface. It now meant little to me compared with his present, far less handsome self, but it served to focus my thoughts back to him. And I was conscious of a devastating sense of loss.

It would be exciting to let Brice make love to me – it was a comfort that anyone wanted to, after all the blows my pride had suffered. It would be interesting to work in a repertory theatre; obviously I ought to jump at the chance. And yet I *knew* it would be a mistake, somehow a crossing of my fate. But even so, it was fated; for I felt quite sure Brice would not let me change my mind. And it gave me pleasure to feel this, for it was the ruthless force of his character that attracted me. He came back with a chair and lifted down the baskets, and I helped him to carry them to the stage door. Then we set off again. He gripped my arm through my cloak and marched me along. Even the grip of his hand excited me. I took one last look at the theatre, knowing that – though I should be back next day and it might be weeks before Brice and I finally left – this was my real farewell.

BOOK THREE

'Every Day Speaks a New Scene...'

1

By the time I got back to the hotel Molly and Lilian had left the window table in the restaurant and were waiting in a stately and almost deserted lounge to which the head porter conducted me. Lilian looked up so eagerly that I hated telling her Zelle had eluded me; but I had made up my mind that – for the present – it was the best thing to do, best both for her and for Zelle.

I had thought out my story and was careful to account for all the time I had been away. I described how my taxi-driver had lost Zelle's bus at traffic lights and how we had caught up with it later and followed it a long way, only to find that Zelle was not on it. 'She must have got off before we caught up with it.'

Lilian accepted this resignedly. 'I felt you wouldn't catch her. It *was* Zelle, or she'd never have run away.'

'What we don't know,' said Molly, 'is if it was Zelle in disguise or Zelle as she really is now.'

'And we never shall know,' said Lilian.

I longed to console her. 'We might, Lilian. Perhaps she'll come to our next reunion.'

'There won't be another. When I put "This may be the last reunion" I didn't mean it, but I do now. We three can meet any time we like, so there's no point in working oneself up like this when Zelle's shown she doesn't want to come.

Besides, forty years on is my limit. Forty-five would be an anti-climax.'

'Forty years on isn't as I expected it to be,' said Molly. 'I thought we should all be doddering.'

'So you said at that first lunch,' I reminded her. 'And Lilian thought we should be exquisite old ladies. Instead of which well, we're not really old at all. Just elderly.'

'Such a boring, stodgy word,' said Lilian. 'Sometimes old age has a kind of harrowing beauty. But elderly – ugh!'

I said, 'Well, don't let's think of ourselves as that. As a matter of fact, whenever I speak of myself as elderly, something within me protests.'

'I don't wonder,' said Lilian. 'Seeing the way you sprinted after Zelle. But then you're just an infant – still in your fifties. What puzzles me is this: When my grandmother was my age she did seem old – you couldn't have called her anything else, though she was strong as a horse; lots of old ladies are. Now, did she *feel* older than I do, because one thought of her as old? Molly, do your grandchildren think of you as old?'

'I haven't the faintest idea,' said Molly. 'But I'm almost sure *I* see myself as older than you two see yourselves. Perhaps that's because even to be a mother, let alone a grandmother, one needs to pretend one's a bit old. It's a pity you two haven't had any children.'

'Not if they make you feel older,' said Lilian.

'I must go,' said Molly. 'I've some shopping to do for Hal before I collect him at his club.'

She took her shopping list from her handbag and got busy with her lorgnette which nowadays contained both reading glasses and long-distance glasses; these shot out when she pressed the right button but she usually pressed the wrong button first. In all the years no normal pair of spectacles had been allowed to rest on that delicate nose. 'Come with me, dear children. I don't like shopping all alone.'

We went out into the sunny September afternoon and trailed around while underwear for Hal was bought, or rather, ordered; nothing offered was ever large enough. We finally left Molly on the steps of his club where her affectionate regret at parting from us was obviously outweighed by her loving eagerness to be with him. 'Poor dear, he'll have been so bored,' she said. He had driven her up to London and put in a day merely waiting to drive her home again.

Lilian, as we walked away, remarked, 'They say no one's completely happy but she's always come pretty close to it.'

'I don't know, Lilian. With a family that size, even the small anxieties must be enough to take the edge off happiness.'

'I doubt it. If all's well with Hal – and all usually is, touch wood and God bless the dear, dull man – then all's well with Molly. I think home, now.' She hailed a taxi.

Regent's Park was looking as beautiful as it never failed to look. I said so to Lilian, as we stood on the steps of the newly painted house while she found her key.

'I don't seem to notice it much now.' She let us in.

Passing the dining-room I glanced through its

open door. Rex, at thirty, was still over the mantel. Rex, now eighty, would be above in the drawing-room. In between these two, as we went upstairs, I tried to visualise Rex at forty, the Rex I had thought of as my dear, hoping it would help me to be tactful and patient.

'He's looking forward to seeing you,' said Lilian. 'That is, if he hasn't forgotten you're coming.'

We found him seated in an armchair near one of the tall windows, gazing across the park; though, judging by the blankness of his expression, he was gazing without seeing. He did not turn his head until Lilian said: 'Look who's here, Rex.' Then he gave me a quick smile.

'Ah, how delightful! Lilian should have told me you were coming. Then I could have enjoyed looking forward to it.'

She did not point out that she *had* told him. She merely said she had a few things she must see to– 'Unless there's anything I can do for you, Rex?'

He frowned and shook his head as if pushing the question away. Only when the door had closed behind her did he give me his welcoming smile again. I pulled up a chair and sat facing him; then said brightly, 'Well, how are you, dear Rex? You look wonderful.'

He did, indeed. As an old man he was far handsomer than he had been in middle age. He was thinner and the fineness of his features was no longer obscured by a slight pudginess. His once fairish hair – really no-coloured – which had stopped receding in the days of his number one toupee, was glossily white and looked much more luxuriant now that he no longer took stern measures to flatten its wave. His fair skin was remarkably unwrinkled; even the laughter lines at his eyes and mouth seemed to have been ironed out. I have heard that some faces look younger after death; in Rex's case it was a lack of life while still living which gave him a fictitious youth. But for the moment he seemed fully alive.

He said he was well enough– 'But bored. That's my complaint. And there's nothing one can do about it.'

He had been saying this to me at all our meetings for the last five years. Usually I suggested radio or television programmes which might interest him, or told him of books I had liked. But it never did much good. He complained that radio and television so often sent him to sleep – 'Though perhaps one should be grateful for that' – and books were so dull that he could not remember the thread from page to page. He did read newspapers but disliked the news.

Today, knowing that Lilian sometimes persuaded him to go to first nights, I asked what plays he had seen. He could not remember their names but said they had been dreadful or unintelligible or both. 'And our new star performers are exhibitionists who face front and shout.'

I suggested he should come back to the theatre and show them a thing or two. The topic momentarily interested him. 'But where could I find a play? Drawing-room comedies are no longer written. And one's hardly a kitchen-sink man.'

I said classical comedy was popular– 'More so than when you retired. And you've never yet played Sir Peter Teazle. There's an idea for you.' It was nonsense, of course. He could not conceivably memorise any part; it was his growing difficulty in memorising, far more than any change in public taste, that had caused him to retire in his early seventies. But at least the subject was still giving pleasure.

'Then you must be my Lady Teazle,' he said, looking at me with a flicker of his old amusement. I quickly began– 'Do you remember...?' and it was as if a veil had been lifted. We chatted gaily about our first meeting and his memory was almost better than mine. Then he remembered several details incorrectly and I tactlessly pointed this out. He brushed my correction aside irritably and then lost interest; I had made the mistake of nagging his memory.

However, his affection for me conquered his irritation and he was soon asking me questions about myself. But he took little interest in what I told him and finally dismissed my present doings by saying he could never understand why I had exiled myself to the country. 'But then, you always were an incalculable little creature. And such a mishmash you've made of your life – acting, writing, book shops, dress shops; I've lost count of your goings on. Of course you should never have deserted us at the Crossway. You had great things ahead of you there.'

This was news to me. 'Such as? Hardly as an actress. Surely you haven't forgotten how hopeless you thought me?'

He chuckled. 'No, my memory's not bad enough for that. But there would have been ... other things for you, if you hadn't run away with Brice – not that I haven't always liked and admired him. Remarkable man – though formidable, nowadays. Have you seen him lately?'

'Not for months. I hope to see him tonight.'

'Give him my love. Yes, I missed you both when you bolted together. I suppose it turned out all right for him, leaving the Crossway. But not for you. I was thinking of it only last night, in the small hours. I often wake then and scout round for something pleasant to think about. You'd be surprised how often I choose you. But naturally I think of you as you were then, not as you are now.'

I said it was cheering to know that for someone I was still eighteen. Actually, I found it harrowing.

'Charming child you were – and still are, as my little companion of the small hours. Of course you have some glamorous competition for my attention but you usually win.'

It was a curious victory to have, forty years too late.

Tea arrived then, brought by one of Lilian's two Italian maids. (I was convinced that, as long as there was any resident 'help' left in London, some of it would be in Lilian's employ.) The girl's dark dress and muslin apron made a gesture towards the uniform of a parlour maid and the tea tray was worthy of one of Rex's drawing-room comedies. I was thankful that Lilian arrived to officiate as I should certainly have got into difficulties with the silver spirit-kettle.

Rex, surveying her with rather more approval

than usual, remarked that he had once taught her to pour out tea and she had never forgotten.

'What you taught me was how to get some very tricky laughs while I poured it out,' said Lilian.

I remembered that play, the last she had acted in with Rex, all of thirty years earlier. Around this time I could see there was some rift between them, though I did not know what had caused it. For some years Lilian acted with other managements but with no great success, for without Rex's teaching she was no actress and he would no longer give her even a minimum of coaching. Still, they had gradually reverted to being on reasonably good terms and she had always, as I had once predicted, made him an admirable wife, putting up with his infidelities while remaining (as I could not have predicted) completely devoted to him. On the whole, I thought they had been fairly happy. But of recent years, boredom and patchiness of memory had rendered him liable to an irritability which, when directed towards Lilian, sometimes amounted to an ill-temper utterly unlike such a sunnily natured man. And she bore it with a patience that was unlike a not very patient woman.

During tea he was at his best because his memory was good (though only about the past; he twice forgot things I had told him since I arrived). What pleased me most was that he was charming to Lilian as well as to me. I think he saw us as our youthful selves; he kept referring to us as 'you girls'. His mood held until he went off to take his pre-dinner nap, having first made sure he would see me at dinner.

Lilian turned to me eagerly. 'You've done him good. All he needs is stimulation. He's wonderfully young for his age, really – his doctor says there isn't a trace of senility. This memory trouble is a kind of laziness and probably a way of escape.'

'From what, exactly?'

Her cheerfulness ebbed. 'Me, more than anything. I get on his nerves. But if I so much as suggest a weekend away from him he raises objections.'

I said he depended on her so much.

'He does, really. But I don't think he admits it even to himself. Let's go up to my room. I want to show you something.'

During the early years of her marriage Lilian had been too impressed with the house to make many changes. She would have preferred a bedroom that reflected her personality rather than that of the first Mrs Crossway, but Rex had liked it as it was so she had kept it much the same even when it had to be re-decorated. But after he had finally moved out on her, to a room of his own, she had compensated by an orgy of interior decoration. This had been in the 'thirties and the bedroom had come to resemble a setting for a Fred Astaire-Ginger Rogers film. Off-white and pastel satins had abounded. Lilian's bed was raised on a silver-leafed platform and surmounted by a canopy held by silver-leafed cupids. I remember telling her she had at last done Madam Lily de Luxe proud. And I did, then, admire the spacious luxury; it was such a contrast to the theatrical digs I had been living in while touring as a highly unsuccessful actress.

Since then, Lilian had made many changes though she had kept her ornate bed, and the furnishings had always been carefully planned to go with it. But for some time now, she had taken to dotting photographs and souvenirs about. And when she opened the door today, I saw there were now so many knick-knacks that the room was really untidy.

She said, 'I know this is a mess but I've a craze for having bits of the past around me. I spend a lot of time up here, especially in the evenings; Rex usually goes to bed soon after nine. This seems the only place I can feel at home in now. It's funny how I've bowed out of the rest of the house.'

'And you used to love it so.'

'Too much. I sometimes think this house is to blame for everything. Do you remember this?'

It was the little print of Regent's Park I had given her on her first appearance at the Crossway; she had kept it hanging in her dressing-room as long as she acted there. She said, now, that she had recently unearthed it from a box of things connected with her stage career. 'Look, I stuck the card you sent with it on the back. "Little did we think when we walked round the park!" Funny, when you wrote that you didn't know I'd ever live in this house. Do you think one can force things to happen, just by wanting them terrifically? *I* do. I think the powers that be said, "All right! The girl shall have her house – no matter how many lives she wrecks in getting it."'

'Lilian, what rubbish! And whose lives have you wrecked?'

'Oh, my own and Rex's and yours and Zelle's, though Zelle's had nothing to do with my wanting this house. I'm just a natural life wrecker.' She had wandered over to the window. 'I used to love this view. Now I find it sad.'

'Then stop looking at it and let's try to sort this nonsense out. First of all, me: I've had nothing but kindness and generosity from you since we were girls. How have you wrecked *my* life?'

'By marrying Rex, of course. If I hadn't, he'd have married you in the end.'

I burst out laughing. 'Lilian, you're crazy. He never had the remotest intention of marrying me.'

'But he would have had it, later. Eve Lester thinks so, too. You can ask her tonight, if you like. Did I tell you she's coming to dinner?'

'No, you didn't and I'm delighted to hear it. But I shan't ask her anything so idiotic. Oh, I know Rex has always been fond of me, but as a wife – well, he'd never even have considered me. I was too small, not pretty enough, and utterly unimportant. We didn't use the phrase "status symbol" then, but the idea operated all right. And I didn't measure up.'

'You're unjust to him,' said Lilian. 'The real trouble was that he thought of you as a child, even though you spent that night with him.' She had learnt the truth about that soon after she married; trust Rex to be indiscreet.

I could see she now had an *idée fixée* about his feeling for me so I just said, 'Anyway, why blame yourself? You didn't chase Rex. He chased you.'

'But he never meant to marry me. I forced him to.' She had left the window but still not come to anchor. Now she perched on the arm of a chair and looked at me intently. 'Did you never guess? I wrote his wife an anonymous letter. That's why she had him followed.'

My main concern was not to show I was shocked. I found the very words 'anonymous letter' automatically shocking, like the word 'blackmail'. But I managed to say, 'Well, that wasn't a very ghastly crime. She was bound to find out eventually and she wanted to divorce him. No, I never guessed. Does Rex know?'

'I told him ages ago. It was really that which – well, made him clear out of this room for good. We were having one of our rows. He was telling me for the umpteenth time that I had no initiative and no courage – comparing me adversely with you, as a matter of fact; you were always tops with him for courageous initiative. Well, sending that letter was the bravest thing I ever did and I thought it rated a few good marks for courage – and for loving him enough to do it. So I upped and told him. My God, that was a world record error of judgement.'

So that had been the cause of the rift between them. I said lamely, 'People are so prejudiced about anonymous letters. Sometimes the circumstances justify them.'

'I doubt if you really believe that,' said Lilian. 'And the ironic thing is that I got the idea through you, that night on the roof, when you told me his wife wanted a divorce. Do you remember?'

I did. And there was still a shadowy pain in

remembering. But the pain – if it was poignant enough to deserve the word – was due to a sense of vanished youth, not to remembrance of youthful misery. I said: 'Lilian, it's forty years ago. None of it matters any more.'

'It does to me,' she said sombrely. 'Sometimes, for me, time telescopes. Then is as real as now. There's lots about it in books I've read. You suggested some of them.'

The whole room was littered with books; the one small bookcase had long ago overflowed. There were books on the great religions, the panacea religions, panacea books which left religion out (the 'think hard and you'll get it' type), books on mysticism (they were the ones I had suggested; it was the only form of religion that had ever interested me), on metaphysics, astronomy... I had often wondered what they all added up to in Lilian's mind.

I said, 'I doubt if it's wise to let the past loose in the present. And obviously it can't do any practical good. Even if one annihilates time metaphysically, one can't change what's happened.'

'I don't agree,' said Lilian sharply. 'I'm not at all sure one can't change what's happened. If you get your thinking absolutely right it can work both backwards and forwards.'

'Well, lovely, lovely. Let your old pal in on the trick.'

She smiled affectionately, then became intense. 'No, no. I'm dead serious...'

As far as I could follow, she believed that if one could recollect the past completely – could, as it were, re-possess it – and then re-think it, regretting one's mistakes so intensely that one somehow got absolution for them, then they would cease to exist and wouldn't, in fact, have happened. She wasn't sure how this would affect one's present life; perhaps it would merely reconcile one to it; perhaps the real improvement would come only when one lived one's life again – or reincarnated; she favoured both ideas. But if time did not exist, 'then' would be 'now' and one would be living a different life while living the present one...

Much of it might be nonsense but she had certainly stretched her mind in some interesting directions. Still, I couldn't see how it could help her. She obviously thought it could for she finished by saying, 'That's why I so wanted to meet Zelle. You see, I can't get absolution about her, from myself, unless I get it from her first.'

'Surely you can't mean absolution for letting Adrian Crossway know the life she'd been living? No one could blame you for that.'

'*I* blame myself,' said Lilian sternly. 'I told Rex partly to gain face, I'm sure I did. She might have kept it from Adrian for ever. Perhaps I sinned against him too. He's remained a desiccated celibate.'

'Hardly desiccated. He always strikes me as unctuous – not that I've met him for years.'

'Well, I don't worry too much about him,' said Lilian, with the flicker of a grin, 'seeing that he's ended up as a bishop. But I've always worried about Zelle. And lately I've felt I shall never let myself off unless I can tell her I'm sorry. You see, it's the letting oneself off that counts – if, as I believe, one somehow governs everything that happens to one. If I could feel less guilty, I'd stop punishing myself.'

Should I weaken and tell her where Zelle could be found? No, I was still sure I mustn't – yet. Instead, I asked her if she had forgiven herself about the anonymous letter. 'You should, darling. Even if you did wrong – which I'm not saying – you've more than atoned, these last years, by being so good to Rex.'

She shook her head. 'A few years' patience isn't all that important. But the fact that my life's such hell now does atone a bit. It would be easier if I didn't care for him; then I could be matter of fact, like a nurse. As it is, he so often *hurts* me as well as infuriates me. But what I want to know now is, do *you* absolve me – about the anonymous letter? By writing it I wiped out your chance with Rex.'

I was silent a few seconds, not in doubt about my feelings but wondering how I could describe them forcibly enough. At last I said: 'I can only tell you from the bottom of my heart that I'm grateful. The thought of being married to Rex fills me with horror. Honestly, I think I'd rather die.'

'Ah, but you're thinking of him as he is now. Can't you see he wouldn't be like that if he'd married you?'

I felt momentarily impatient. 'But I've told you, he *wouldn't* have married me. And anyway, you over-estimate what I felt for him; it didn't survive my affair with Brice. And you're just being egotistical, blaming yourself for everything. Why not blame Zelle for taking you to the party where you met Rex, or me for telling you Mrs Crossway wanted a divorce? Things just happen. Nobody's to blame.' But even as I spoke I blamed myself for telling her about Mrs Crossway. Never before had I realised how that long ago indiscretion had affected both Rex's and Lilian's lives, let alone my own.

'There are different kinds of happenings,' said Lilian, her eyes fanatical. 'Some are fated, some we force to happen. I'm a forcer – or I was, during that little period of our lives. How strange it was, the way the four of us were linked! I once thought it might be due to astrology, but none of us were born in the same year, let alone the same month.'

'Oh, God, Lilian – not astrology!'

She giggled endearingly. 'I know – I'm a bloody fool. Perhaps all my ideas are nonsense. But sometimes, when I've been alone here for hours, I've seemed to glimpse a way to make sense of everything, if only one could will it with all one's mind.'

I said: 'The trouble with you is that you're a woman of enormous energy that's never found its right outlet. It's my belief you're a hussy *manquée*.'

'A what?' She looked interested.

'You remember hussies – in novels and films. Girls who were bad but likeable; they always wiped the floor with the innocent heroines. You started off in fine style by bagging Rex, and you should have gone on like that, taking lovers and probably leaving him for a millionaire. Instead of which you had to adore him *and* develop a conscience. Well, no doubt it'll get you into heaven.'

'I don't want heaven. I just want this life the way it ought to have been.'

'Who doesn't?' I felt we needed a new topic. 'Got any new clothes to show me?'

She said she hadn't bought any for ages. 'I make myself take care of my hair and skin but bothering about clothes doesn't go with the books I've been reading. Not that I've got anywhere, really.'

I guessed she was in need of a new interest. Art, music, literature, languages, flower arrangements, even tap dancing... I had lost count of the subjects she had studied, not one of which had remained important to her.

'Don't give up yet,' I said, having no new idea to offer.

She went to draw the curtains and put the lights on, saying she found twilight depressing. To me, the sea-green walls in the dim, concealed lighting were more depressing than the twilight. Passing her dressing-table she picked up something from the midst of scent bottles and cosmetics. 'Do you know what this is?'

'Looks like a piece of rubble.'

'So it is, but very special rubble. I got it when they were demolishing the Club. I happened to pass one evening, just after they began – on the gentlemen's cloakroom, actually; never did I expect to see inside that. Most of the building was still intact, with the front door locked. I looked through the letter box. Then I stood back and tried to decide where our "village" was.'

'On the second floor.'

'I thought so. I spotted your window. The glass was broken. It was the queerest feeling, standing there in the dusk. Though I daresay it would have meant even more to you, as you were there so much longer than I was.'

I had usually stayed there, when in London, until well on in the 'thirties, when the Club gave up those premises. I had hundreds of Club memories and could recall the names, faces and even the voices of well over fifty Club members. But no memories were as vivid as those of my first summer and, among Club members, only Lilian and Molly had become my lasting friends. There was indeed something inexplicable about the linking of our lives.

Lilian, gazing at her piece of rubble, added: 'Do you believe objects can have a sort of power in them? I once slept with this under my pillow, hoping it would make me dream of the old days.'

'Must have been uncomfortable. And I do think you were asking a lot of a bit of rubble from the gents'.'

'Well, it was the only bit I could get.' She put it back on her dressing-table, where it looked absurdly out of place, and began asking me about myself. As always, she showed more understanding of my way of life than most people did. Before long, the maid came up and said Miss Lester had arrived

Lilian looked at her watch, then at me. 'You have a chat with Eve while I urge Rex back into circulation.'

Eve Lester still lived in her Covent Garden

maisonette. She had retired when Rex did, but he remained her only real interest in life, though she had acquired some others in the hope of their interesting him and would bring him news of her doings much as one offers toys to an invalid child – or, as she once remarked after an offering had been spurned, like a faithful dog dropping a dead rat at his master's feet. She came to see him almost every day and was often urged by Lilian to live with them. But it was Eve's theory that she would lose her value for Rex if she was always on hand. In my opinion, Eve was the only woman he had consistently cared for.

I found her standing by the drawing-room fire. Only two years younger than Rex, she was now grey-haired and very thin but she still retained both her elusive, faded beauty and her air of casual elegance. The casualness, as always, was due to the way she wore her clothes, the elegance to her extreme good taste – though she ignored present fashions. She reminded me of the *grande dame* actresses I had seen in my childhood; perhaps, as the heyday of her youth had been before the First World War, she had then decided how an elegant old lady should look. Tonight she was in a long, clinging grey chiffon dress which made me feel I looked like an elderly beatnik. I told her so.

She said she was probably overdressed– 'But Rex likes this kind of thing. You look sweet, really; very funny, of course, but you always did and we always loved it. Though nowadays it's you who are fashionable – just like a teenager.'

'Oh, dear! I do try to resist teenager clothes,

but they so often fit me well and I must admit I adore them. My secret vice is that I sometimes wear black woollen tights. Our vicar found me in them and said I looked like an imp.'

She laughed and then began talking about Rex. How had he seemed to me? Had I been able to interest him in any topic? Oughtn't I to see him more often as I was one of the few people he liked to see? I tried to answer tactfully and refrained from pointing out that my life did not revolve round him, as hers and Lilian's did. But she must have known what was in my mind for she finally said, 'You never *really* cared for him, did you? Well, I suppose that was a good thing – for you.'

Rex and Lilian came in, saving me from having to answer.

Dinner went off fairly well. At first Rex treated me as the guest of honour. But only when he could chaff me or talk about his earliest memories of me did he seem to enjoy himself; when I mentioned any present-day matter – concerning me or the world in general – he showed little interest. At last he turned to Eve and they bickered cheerfully for the rest of the meal. There was no irritation behind his bickering when Eve was his partner. Only with Lilian did he ever bicker with real ill temper – and mercifully, that didn't happen at dinner.

I ate the excellent food and thought of the dozens, even hundreds, of meals I had eaten in that room – and doubted if I had ever been in it without remembering my first sight of it, on Black Saturday, when I had talked to Mrs Crossway (dead long ago, and I wondered if she had much enjoyed her post-Rex life; she had never married again). The eighteenth-century furniture was just as it had been then; merely forty years more valuable.

Soon after dinner I said I must go. Rex did not try to stop me but he smiled very sweetly and said, 'Dear child, always running away from us, aren't you?' I hoped he would soon forget my present self in favour of his 'little companion of the small hours'. Lilian had telephoned for a taxi. She saw me into it and begged me to come again soon– 'And write or ring up – anything.' I promised to be in touch with her very shortly. As the taxi drove off I looked out of the back window and watched Madam Lily de Luxe return to her house, where now only her untidy bedroom seemed to her like home. I felt a pang at leaving her – but only great relief at leaving Rex.

2

When I got to the Crossway the empty foyer had that air of being both deserted and expectant which I always feel in theatre foyers when a performance is taking place. The man in the box-office (I knew none of the theatre staff now) did not raise his head as I went towards the stairs. I paused at the back of the dress circle, listening to a roar of laughter from the house. Then I went on up to the offices. The one Eve and I had used was in darkness; Brice seldom kept his secretaries in the evening. He himself used the Throne Room.

He rose to welcome me, from behind the large desk which had replaced the long table, then settled me in the chair opposite him. He sat with his back to the wall of portraits where, ousting the mediocre painting, Rex as Charles Surface had joined his father and grandfather. No one, now, looking from Brice to Sir Roy, could have doubted that they were father and son.

Once, in his thin youth, I had seen Brice as a Manchester Terrier. If he still resembled any dog it was a far fiercer, weightier one, a Dobermann Pinscher. How right Rex had been in describing him as formidable, nowadays! But had he not always been formidable? Certainly his career had been one long series of battles – which he had almost always won; and his greatest victory had been in getting a lease of the Crossway when Rex retired.

He had fought then not with Rex, whose lease had expired, but with 'the bricks and mortar boys', in this case the ground landlords, who saw no reason why a rickety old theatre should not be replaced by a gorgeous cinema or an office block, especially as the rickety old theatre had not paid during the last years of Rex's tenancy. But Brice, having – against all odds – got hold of it, had made it pay. He had kept it alive by a series of raucous farces which had often seemed to me a fate worse than death – often, but not always; the play now running was a black farce about teen-agers which fully deserved its great success.

At first we talked in the curiously casual way

one so often does with one's oldest friends on meeting them after some considerable time. How were we? Was the show still doing well? How had I found Rex? (Long ago, persuaded by me, Rex had spoken to Brice of their relationship, happily accepting it.) And while we chatted, I noted that Brice, though he still looked a brown-skinned, black-haired man, was a little pale and beginning to go grey at last; and that if not yet heavy, he was no longer slim. Also a silent film of memories passed before my mind's eye, of scenes we had played together here in the Crossway offices, in various dingy professional lodgings, and one rather grand flat when he had launched his first successful West End play. Rows and reconciliations, partings and comings together again – over what must have been nearly twenty years – had been followed by twenty years of friendship. Perhaps its closeness had sometimes been due to the distance between us; still, I was fonder of him than of anyone in the world. And it was pleasant to feel sure I always would be fond of him; and that I knew him through and through and nothing he could do, whether good or bad, would ever astonish me.

He was asking if I wasn't tired of vegetating. What was it all about, really, this shutting myself away in an isolated cottage? I said I didn't quite know– 'I thought I did, when it started. I'd saved enough money to live on for a few years without taking a job, and I wanted to do something worth while, just for once. I never have, you know: just messed about at acting, writing, dress-designing, God knows what-all. I'd an idea that, granted perfect peace, I could write a decent novel.'

'And have you?'

'I shouldn't think so. Anyway, it's not finished – one reason for which is that I *haven't* been granted perfect peace. I've too many friends. There's the vicar, who doesn't mind that I never go to church; and the doctor, who doesn't mind that I'm never ill – touch wood – and a young nuclear disarmer who doesn't mind that I agree with him, blast my elderly impertinence.'

'Are you having an affair with any of them?'

'What a shocking question to ask a respectable old lady! Though I do sometimes wonder if the nuclear disarmer had a fixation on his grand-mother.'

'You could pass for forty.'

'That wouldn't help as he's only twenty-six. Still, thanks.'

'You must have been there two years. Haven't you spent all your savings yet?'

I was within sight of it but I said airily, 'Oh, I can manage even when I have. Quite a bit of income dribbles in. Amateurs still do my one play, which you so kindly lost money on. And the shares my dear aunt left me have gone up so much that she must be dancing in heaven. And anyway, there's plenty of secretarial work to be had locally. But what I really want now is to have a shot at painting.' I described my recent ambition very fully.

After listening patiently he said: 'Utter non-sense, of course – except that, in your case, it just might not be. I'd never put it past you to turn into a Granny Moses. But you could paint in

London. Why not come back? Take a little flat.'

'Even little flats are ruinously expensive.'

'Well, I can always give you work. Would you like to adapt a German farce for me?'

'You would never produce my adaptation of a German farce. When I want you to support me I'll demand it – for past services.'

'You wouldn't have to demand, as you've always known. I'll find you a flat, if you like or...' his tone became histrionically casual, 'you could share mine. You know how large it is.'

I did indeed. He now occupied one of London's earliest mansion flats, so archaic that one felt there ought to be a preservation order on it. All its front rooms had bay windows, all its back rooms looked on to a well; it was as inconvenient as it was hideous and his only reason for living in it was that, in the eighteen-nineties, it had been lived in by Sir Roy Crossway – not that, even to me, Brice had ever admitted he had any feelings about that. I thanked him for the suggestion but said people would think it very funny if we set up house together.

'Well, if you minded that, we could marry.'

So he *could* still astonish me. I hastened to explain I hadn't meant that kind of funny. 'I just meant comic. And our getting married would be even more comic. Still, I'm grateful for the offer, belated though it is.'

'You've always known I was ready to marry you.' He grinned. 'That is, whenever we were on speaking terms; and even when we weren't, really.'

'Still, you never mentioned it. Nor did anyone

else. I can't remember having one respectable proposal.'

'You discouraged them in advance.'

'Could be. But it's nice to have one to chalk up, even at my age. Was it a sudden impulse?'

He said he supposed so. 'It was so pleasant, sitting here talking together. And I'm fonder of you than anyone in the world.'

'You take the words out of my thoughts. Well, I can't turn respectable now but I will consider the loan of part of your almost historic flat. It depends on how Granny Moses progresses. I may want to go on and on painting the view from my window.'

'Is there nothing in London you fancy painting?'

'Teenagers, perhaps – the scruffier the better. They strike me as gloriously paintable. Can I see a bit of the show?'

He looked at his watch. 'It's almost the end of Act II.'

'I'll watch through the spy-hole.'

I slid open the panel and looked down over the dark, crowded gallery to the bright oblong of the stage. In a composite set showing attics, garishly decorated with Pop Art, a group of teenagers were coming as near to raping each other as a broad-minded censorship permitted. The show was really a bedroom farce in which no one shut the bedroom doors. I liked it much better than the first play I had seen through the spy-hole.

'Lovely,' I said to Brice, when the curtain had descended. 'Especially your leading lady. She's no taller than I am. Her head, like mine, is too large for her height. And she's overacting to high heaven. Was I simply in advance of my time?'

'No, love,' said Brice affectionately. 'If you were young now you'd still be all wrong, somehow.'

'I see. Just a freak, at any period. Brice dear, how very well you've directed this show. I must see the whole of it again.'

'It's slipping. And I'm losing control of the kids. The trouble is, I've grown to like them. They quite approved of me when I bullied them, but if one softens towards them they think one's trying to get in on their act, hand oneself a second helping of youth. They resent that.'

'Well, God knows *I* long to get in on their act – I'd love to be a teenager now. But the few I know don't seem to resent me.'

'Even the ruthless young are sometimes tolerant to freaks,' said Brice. 'Besides, in some odd way, you're still stuck in your own teens.'

It was something I often felt myself. I could look in the glass and note the signs of age with calm disinterest, as though they had nothing to do with me. Frequently I reminded myself not to 'act young' when people were present. When quite alone I was liable to dance. Oh, yes, I was a freak all right. Absurdly, I had not really felt complimented when Brice said I could pass for forty. I had never felt anything like as old as forty.

I said I knew what he meant. 'I'm not merely a freak. I'm a mentally arrested freak.'

'Still, you're old enough for a drink and I've

forgotten to offer you one. What'll you have?'

I told him I'd had more wine at dinner than I care for. 'Shall I send down for some coffee?'

'No, thanks. Do you remember Eve's black brew?'

He smiled. 'I wonder the office isn't haunted by the smell of it – which was much better than the taste. Poor old Eve.' He always combined affectionate admiration for her with intense disapproval of her life. 'Sixty years devoted to Rex.'

'I was thinking of that this evening.'

'And also thinking, "But for the grace of God there went I"?'

'It might have been *by* the grace of God.' Why had I said that? Surely I didn't mean it?

Brice obviously didn't think so. 'That's nonsense and you know it. I'll have to leave you now, for a few minutes. I told my stage manager I'd see him in this interval.'

'Is he anything like you were?'

'Much fiercer. Will you wait? Then we'll go out to supper.'

I said it would make me too late. 'I ought to leave now. I've someone else to see before I start for home.'

'Oh?' Brice sounded curious.

'A woman. I don't think you ever met her. Come on, or the interval will be over.'

We went down together. There were a good many people in the foyer, most of them in day clothes: 'Unglamorous audiences, nowadays,' said Brice. 'Still, they do cough less.'

He sent the commissionaire for a taxi, repeated his offer to share his flat, adding, 'Just try it –

even if you hang on to your bloody cottage as a bolt hole,' then hurried off towards the pass door. I went outside to wait for my taxi. Leaning against one of the pillars of the portico, I wondered how long he could keep the Crossway from demolition. He had satisfied a lifetime's ambition by getting control of it but he never admitted to any strong feeling for it; instead, he insisted it meant much to Rex and must be kept standing as long as Rex lived. I did not think it mattered to Rex now and I even doubted if he had ever felt emotional about it or about the Crossway family. Basically, Brice was a far more emotional man than Rex had ever been.

Once in the taxi, I wished I did not feel I must try to see Zelle. I dreaded it, rather; also I wanted to think about my own affairs. Should I share Brice's flat? Should I even marry him? (No, I should not. But I was complimented to have the chance, particularly as, of recent years, he'd had some very attractive young women in tow; I doubted if any of them had had *him* in tow.) Also, a puzzling thought had stirred in my mind while I talked to him and I wanted to investigate it. Well, that must wait.

Soon I was at the block of tenement flats where Zelle lived. Could I really knock on all the doors and enquire for her?

I didn't have to. As I walked towards the entrance to the block I looked down at a basement room where the curtains had not been drawn. It was lit only by a gas fire, in front of which, stiffly stuck out, were two pony-straight legs. My sight line was such that I could not see the rest of their

319

owner, but they were unmistakable legs. I was glad to see they wore good stockings and that the slender feet were well shod.

I went down dimly lit stairs and rang the basement flat's bell. Zelle opened the door. My first impression was of greyness, grey hair, pale skin, grey sweater and skirt. She was no crone; just an elderly, neatly dressed woman, rather too thin.

She smiled and said: 'Oh, hello! I'm glad you've come. I was terrified you would, this afternoon – you followed me, didn't you? I saw you jump in the taxi. But when you didn't turn up, I was disappointed. Come on in.'

She took me into the gas-fire-lit room and switched on a lamp. It was red-shaded, kind both to her and to the drab little sitting-room with its dull, inexpensive furniture. I told her I had recognised her legs. She laughed and said they were getting very skinny, then told me she'd just come back from baby-sitting and had been too lazy to draw the curtains– 'I was wondering if I'd go to bed at once.'

I asked if she did much baby-sitting and she said she had four regular nights a week. She preferred it to day work, though she still did that occasionally– 'I don't mind sewing or silver polishing but they will try to edge in cleaning and cooking. Cleaning tires me now and I've never been much of a cook. But I quite enjoy baby-sitting and my nicest job of all is sitting with a dog. Anyway, it's all very well paid so I do quite well. Did you think I was down and out? I borrowed those clothes from an old actress who has the flat opposite – they're from what she calls her "character wardrobe". Of course I never expected you to recognise me.'

'Why didn't you join us? Oh, I know you hardly could, in that get-up, but why didn't you come as yourself?'

'Well, I did think of it. And then I felt I'd rather just have a look at you all. Not that I'd have disgraced you – I've some quite nice clothes. The woman whose dog I sit with often gives me things. It was her copy of *The Times* I read the advertisement in. I couldn't believe my eyes.'

'Did you never see any of the earlier ones?'

'Were there some? No, I never saw them. Funny, I've kept the name Zelle – always tell people I'm called that, though I'd almost forgotten where it came from. And I'd quite forgotten Lilian's idea of having reunion lunches – though I remembered it after I'd read the advertisement, and lots of other things too. That was a nice room I had at the Club.'

I asked if she still had her picture of the baby faun, and at first she couldn't even remember it. Then it came back to her. 'Now what happened to that? I probably left it behind somewhere. For years and years I was moving around; I used to do resident jobs, mother's help and housekeeping; and I was in a factory during the war. Not long after that I got this flat and I've stayed put. It's central and I like the church in the square. What's been happening to you? I saw your name in the papers once or twice. You had a play on, didn't you? But I haven't seen anything about you for years.'

'There hasn't been anything to see.' I found I could give her a résumé of my life as briefly as she had told me about hers. She said mine sounded exciting– 'Anyway, you've had lots of change. Tell me about Molly and Lilian.'

I told her, and said how anxious Lilian was to see her. This astonished her so much that I tried to explain. She looked amused and said, 'Fancy old Lily de Luxe with a conscience – and after all these years! Actually, I thought she did the right thing. Oh, I was bitter for a while, but it was only fair he should be warned; otherwise he might have got out on a limb over me, poor man, because he was on the way to being smitten. I suppose you'll laugh when I tell you I really was converted.'

'*Religiously* converted?'

'Well, don't look so horrified. I remember now, you didn't believe in religion. I always did in a way, but I hated it until I met Adrian Crossway. That changed my whole life. You'd be surprised how moral I've been, not that I take much credit for it; that year with poor old Bill sort of put me off anything else – well, for quite a long time. Later, I did meet a few men I liked. I could have married one of them. But it'd have spoilt what I felt about Adrian Crossway. That wonderful man! Well, let's have a drink. I think I've some gin.'

'Couldn't we have some tea – as we used to, in the old days?'

She went to get it. I had asked for it only because I wanted a few minutes alone, to think. In my handbag was a letter from Adrian Crossway to

Zelle. As instructed in her farewell note I had hung on to it, awaiting the forwarding address that never came. I had brought it to all the reunion lunches, in case she turned up. And now … should I hand it over? It might well be disillusioning. If so, could it not – even after all these years – do real harm? She had built her life round something she had got from Adrian; might not the letter damage more than just her idealised memory of him? But it was a letter intended for her and she had asked me to take care of it, if it came, and let her have it if she gave me the chance to.

Perhaps I ought to take it away and steam it open. I loathed the idea – and how could I judge if the contents would hurt her? I no longer felt I knew her. Once or twice a note in her voice had reminded me of the Zelle I remembered, but most of the time she had seemed just a thin, grey, elderly woman, very matter of fact – except about Adrian Crossway. I looked round the dull little basement room, trying to learn more about her from it. There were no books; just a pile of women's weeklies and parish magazines. The few pictures were framed colour prints of bluebell woods and the like. What a setting for the *princesse lointaine* who had poured out money on us all! But perhaps I had never really known her. Was she not basically a poor girl from a Welsh village, used to hard work – and with religion, probably, in her bones? Her year with a rich elderly man, culminating in a few months with us, represented only an odd little quirk in the mainstream of her life.

I was still undecided what to do about the letter

when she came back with the tea and made the decision for me by saying, 'I suppose – I've often wondered – I suppose no letter came for me after I left the Club? I mean, from Adrian Crossway. But it's silly to ask, really. You wouldn't remember.'

That settled it; she must have her letter. I took it out of my bag and handed it over.

She sat staring at the envelope. 'Such beautiful writing ... goodness, it does feel extraordinary, after all these years. It's a George V stamp. Well, here goes.'

After a couple of minutes she looked up and said, 'It's a marvellous letter. I'd like you to read it.'

In my opinion it was a swine of a letter, pompous, sententious and oh, so guarded! Adrian wrote of unexpected parish work which would debar him from an immediate visit to London. Also he had decided that the work in the East End he had suggested for her would not be suitable– 'We must think again, and forgive me if this takes a little while.' He regretted that he could not get her accommodation in the village for the weekend of his Harvest Festival and mentioned some churches in London she might like to attend– 'Remember, God is the same God both in town and country.' Finally, there was a paragraph of obviously valedictory good wishes concluding with: 'You were kind enough to say that coming to my church had meant much to you. I trust that any little help I may, by God's grace, have given you will be of lasting value. I shall pray for you.' And he was hers 'with deepest sincerity, Adrian Crossway.'

I did not believe the writer of that letter was anyone's with deepest sincerity. The exquisitely inscribed words ('written' was too ordinary a word for that elegant script) merely amounted to a brush-off – and of all brush-offs, deliver me from the pious brush-off. But this one, for Zelle, would become a relic. Well, just as beauty is in the eye of the beholder, the holiness of a relic is undoubtedly in the mind of the worshipper.

I said, 'Oh, Zelle, I'm *so* glad.' It got me by. I handed the letter back and she read it again, then said how grateful she was to me for taking care of it. After that, she put it back in its envelope and poured out tea, which we drank while talking casually about the past, sometimes saying how long ago it seemed and sometimes that it only seemed like yesterday; and both were true.

Eventually I asked if she would see Lilian. She agreed at once, saying she'd like to– 'And perhaps Lilian can put some work in my way. I was glad when I read that Mr Crossway got knighted.'

'After a good long wait. I think straightforward divorce passes for respectability these days. Yes, I'm sure Lilian can find you some kind of work.' I looked at my watch. It was only a little after eleven. 'I'd like to ring her up now.'

I expected to do so from a call box but it turned out that Zelle had a telephone; she said she needed it as she often got last-minute jobs. We went into her bedroom and she left me alone.

Lilian answered at once. It was pleasant to hear her excitement when I said I had found Zelle.

'But you sly, sly Mouse! Why did you keep it to

yourself all day?'

'Because she might have been unwilling to meet us. If I'd told you where she was you'd have hounded her down.'

'I would indeed. Ask her to lunch tomorrow.'

I called Zelle, who accepted the invitation. Lilian asked to speak to her, then changed her mind. 'No, I'll wait till tomorrow. Tell her to come alone. Oh, you kind clever Mouse! I was so miserable, sitting here in this dreary bedroom.'

I had a sudden inspiration. 'Lilian, why don't you turn it into a kind of one-room flat? Line the walls with bookcases. Have a divan with a decent bedside light instead of that eye of God or whatever it is that looks down on you now. If that room's the place you feel at home in, do *make* it a home.'

There was a long silence. Then, in the voice of a woman whose eyes are visionary, she said, 'I might have a tiny refrigerator in the bathroom. And an electric kettle – and a toaster. Oh, *what* a good idea...'

While she rattled on, I found myself looking at a framed photograph which hung on the wall beside Zelle's bed. It had presumably been cut from a magazine; printed under the photograph were the words: 'Summer in East Anglia'. I instantly recognised the church and the vicarage. By mentally turning the corner of the road that ran past them I could see – say, on the edge of the oak frame – the haystack behind which I had sat cogitating with my eighteen-year-old soul. A couple of inches further, along the nondescript wallpaper, would be the lodge gates of the Crossways' house and beyond them, Rex's barn work-room. I had a sudden memory of his face, that long ago night, youthful in the blankness of sleep; and today, youthful in the blankness of age…

Then Lilian was demanding my views on fitted cupboards. Should they be in the bathroom, with glass doors? I suggested she should discuss this with Zelle, while my gaze rested on Zelle's small stained wood wardrobe, a truly villainous bit of furniture – though I was to find, when Zelle showed me what she would wear for lunch with Lilian, that it contained a genuine Chanel model.

'My dog lady gave it to me. It's five years old but Chanel never dates, does she? It's nice that she's as fashionable now as when we were girls.'

I also found it nice that Zelle owned a more expensive dress than had ever come my way – except for that never to be forgotten *robe de style* in which 'little oddity' had so much annoyed Rex's leading lady.

Already it would be two a.m. before I got home. I said I must go. 'I've a long drive ahead of me.'

'What, all by yourself? And I can't imagine you driving. You're too little.'

'Well, it's a little car.'

We promised to keep in touch, I quite looked forward to this. She still seemed to me com-pletely changed – a stranger, in fact; but by now she was a stranger I liked. Just before I left I asked if she thought *I* had changed much. She said, 'No, you're fantastically the same.'

'Fantastically', I thought, was probably the right word.

I walked until I could get a taxi; the day had been ruinous in taxi fares. (But later I found a five pound note had been put in my bag. I might have known Lilian would more than foot my expenses.)

Getting into my car in St John's Wood I had a sense of home-coming, like a snail getting back into its shell. There wasn't much traffic as late as this and even before I was out of the suburbs I was able to think with most of my mind.

The lunch party today and the first lunch party... Zelle as she had been, Zelle as the crone in the park, Zelle in her drab basement flat... Molly wearing the hat of russet leaves so like her once russet hair... Lilian, that hussy *manquée*, in her avid girlhood, Lilian now, amidst the clutter of her bedroom, saying that if time did not exist, 'now' could be 'then', Lilian holding the bit of rubble from the gents' as if it was a holy relic (so unlike the relic Zelle had now acquired) ... and Eve, still an elegant Edwardian ... and my Manchester Terrier become a Dobermann Pinscher...

And my poor Rex– Why did I hate thinking about him, both as he was and as he had been? No doubt I felt guilty at having so little patience with him, but I was now conscious of a deeper sense of guilt towards myself. Why? And why had I tonight said to Brice that it might have been *by* the grace of God if–

Suddenly I was back on that windy day when I had known I ought not to leave the Crossway, known I was crossing my fate. I had not thought about it for years – indeed, the intensity of the moment had barely outlasted the moment. I had swiftly come to see that I could not have let myself join Eve in – what was Brice's phrase?– 'The nucleus of a small harem, patiently waiting for a night'. And even if Lilian was right in thinking Rex would have married me, I had stopped longing for that from the moment I had Brice as a lover. Me, anyone's patient little wife, no, thank you! And Lilian had only said Rex would have married me if he hadn't married her, which he had. And anyway, it was all nonsense.

And yet... I was now well into the country, the roads deserted under the moon, never a light in the scattered cottages and farms. The steady movement of the car had a hypnotic rhythm, not a rhythm that made me sleepy but one which at last drove conscious thought from my mind, creating a vacuum which was suddenly flooded with illumination. I knew why it might have been *by* the grace of God if I had stayed at the Crossway.

Brice had told me I was a schoolgirl with a crush on a matinée idol. He had been wrong. The schoolgirl in me had found Rex disillusioning. What I had come to feel for him was the first fully mature emotion of my lifetime; the first and possibly the last. Certainly I had never felt so intensely about Brice or any other man. It had been genuine love, the kind of love that needs to be lived out fully, however great the cost in suffering. I had side-stepped the suffering, skipped an infinitely important phase of development.

Was there in me a frozen immaturity? Bits and pieces were all I could look back on, bits of love, bits of talent for acting, writing, even music. (I had been taught music as a child, and very well taught, but for years I had only played by ear – how like me.) And now the boot of the car housed a collection of oil paints! A nonsense was all my life would ever add up to, the nonsense life of a nonsense woman. Eve's life of devotion amounted to something far more worth while than my ragbag of experience.

She had once said I suffered from an excess of individualism and I had always thought of this as a compliment. But if the individualism remained that of a precocious child, what then?

Did I really believe all this or was I merely trying on humility to see how it felt? Basically, I was still arrogant – were not all individualists, by definition, arrogant? Why be individual? Why not be matey and merge? Incidentally, I suddenly saw why I had never got anywhere with my mysticism, that merger to end mergers. During my two years in the country I had set aside regular periods for contemplation – and always ended by contemplating the interesting job I would tackle the minute I allowed myself to stop sitting still. Even now, my soul searchings were yielding place to plans for tomorrow. At least there was one compensation for immaturity: I could always count on enormous resilience. And, come to think of it, could I not be proud of achieving so much, rather than ashamed of achieving so little? With my background, I might so easily have settled for a life of amateur theatricals, tennis, tea parties and a very dull marriage – if I ever managed to get even a dull husband; the status symbol principle had operated in the provinces quite as much as in London and conventional men seldom chose odd little wives.

Anyway, retrospection would get me nowhere – I was as bad as Lilian, searching for explanations of the inexplicable. Turn away from the past, think of those oil paints! There *had* been elderly people who had developed a real talent for painting. And was not the book I was finishing better than anything I had written before? Oh, if only I were younger in years! I hoped I believed in re-incarnation. I hoped I had hundreds of lives ahead of me. Never would I opt for nirvana.

But even in this life there was still time. 'The last act crowns the play.' I had not quoted that to myself for many years. At eighteen I had equated the last act with marriage to Rex. What, at fifty-eight, did I equate it with? The sum total of life, no doubt, which must surely be the poet's meaning. The catch about that was that, to me, no sum total would make death acceptable. Death is too much to ask of the living.

I was only two miles from home now, driving through the sleeping village. I thought kindly of my friends there. But none of them spoke my language as the London friends of my youth did (except the young nuclear disarmer – and I did not quite speak his). Perhaps I would just *visit* Brice. It would be amusing to help Lilian with her room. And I ought to see more of Rex; it was outrageous that I should feel impatient with him. And I must keep in touch with Zelle – and was I not losing touch with Molly? Besides, there was so much in London to see, so much to study. I wanted to know more about the young ... strange that though they laughed so loud, they so seldom smiled. Perhaps laughter was involuntary whereas smiling was part of an attitude to life. Fundamentally, so many of them were more serious than I and my friends had been. Youth was now conscious of the deplorable state of the world. In the 'twenties, only our private worlds had existed for us.

Now my headlights were shining along my white fence. That was to be my first oil painting, with the lane on top of the fence, and the green field on top of the lane ... and the cycling child and the cows – I could easily make those up. No, I wouldn't go to London just yet. Granny Moses must have her head.

Exciting to be here alone, in the small hours, under a brilliant moon... No other house in sight – that was what had first attracted me to the cottage. I was always a little proud because I never felt either lonely or scared. But I often felt astonished – astonished that I should be *allowed* to live here alone, to drive my own car, and sit up all night if I wanted to. Was I the only woman in the world who, at my age – and after a lifetime of quite rampant independence – still did not quite feel grown up?

The publishers hope that this book has given you enjoyable reading. Large Print Books are especially designed to be as easy to see and hold as possible. If you wish a complete list of our books please ask at your local library or write directly to:

Magna Large Print Books
Magna House, Long Preston,
Skipton, North Yorkshire.
BD23 4ND

This Large Print Book for the partially sighted, who cannot read normal print, is published under the auspices of

THE ULVERSCROFT FOUNDATION